A God of Wrath & Lies

Pine Hollow Series
Book 1

K. M. Moronova

Also by K. M. Moronova

The Pine Hollow Series

A God of Wrath & Lies

A God of Death & Rest

A Goddess of Life & Dawn

Playlist

Kodaline - Talk

Echos - Saints

Flower Face - Another Life

Blake Rose - Rest of Us

Away x Crywolf - Ghostbox

XYLO - Pretty Sad

Ramsey & Arcane - Goodbye

Taylor Swift - Exile

Ruelle - Hurts like Hell

DreamDNVR - Amnesia

Important Notice

Some of the content in this book may be triggering for some readers. The contents of this book contain aspects of suicide, mental illness, morally grey characters, death and explicit sexual scenes.

For those who wake up and still feel like they're dreaming.
This one is for us.

1

T rauma is a haunting, twisted bitch.

It twists and churns the things you think you know. Confuses what is real and what isn't. Some traumas wear on your soul tirelessly, while others... well, those traumas we simply erase.

Blood pulses over my chest and face in steady, hot waves as soft whimpers cry close to my ear... and as I hear the pain-filled cries, I know it's her.

I know it's Margo.

The steaming crimson fills my senses with metal that stings my lungs and burns my eyes. I clutch her tightly in my arms. Her black fur is matted with blood. My chest throbs as if a thick knife is lodged deep within it. I beg for anyone to pull it out, but no one helps. I hear someone crying in the darkness of the night. Someone else is screaming.

What the fuck. What the *fuck*.

My eyes race to find anything except darkness, but I'm blinded. The only pieces of this dream I can see are myself and my dog... and all the blood she leaks.

Margo goes still in my arms and that pain in my heart grows until it shatters me.

I wake with a start, sweat beading down my back.

The comforts of my shed whirl around me as I steady my mind to the familiar basic walls and the scent of my candles that I let burn overnight again. They're *Cypress and Pine*, my favorite scent because it calms me, the constant flame easing my weary mind.

Mom agreed to let me renovate our little shed in the backyard a few years ago and said that I could do whatever I wanted with it. It probably isn't much to the normal person, but it's everything to me. It's where I spent so much time with my aunt and Margo.

I glance up to the window. The gloomy, rainy weather here on the coast of Lamnah makes it hard to tell what time it is, but I know it's well past noon already. My nightmares have been leaving me blurry. Every day when I wake, the line between reality and dream becomes increasingly smudged.

I press my arm against my eyes to dry the tears that brim from my dream. But it wasn't just a dream—my eyes linger over the spot where Margo used to warm my feet.

My toes shift under the covers, cold, because she is dead.

I can't help but wonder if whether her death hadn't been so horrific if it would be easier to let her go.

She is gone.

I know this. I remind myself constantly.

I shift off my bed, pull my sweater off the reading chair, and press start on my coffee maker. The machine purrs out bitter liquid as I gaze through the small window over my bed.

It's raining today. It's hard to distinguish the dripping sounds from the coffee and the patterns of the rain as it ticks against the roof. My eyes shift to the lower corner of the window, where there is an outline of a hand that brushed away the dust. The windows need a good cleaning. Everything in the shed has grown dusty as of late, but I sort of enjoy the dust that collects along the window panes. I trace my finger along old prints, wondering when I left them there. My mind is weary, tired—so fucking tired—and my sleep brings me no peace.

Am I to exist in this haze forever? Are my endless woes and misery never to leave me? I shut my eyes and let out a long breath.

The coffee maker dings, echoing softly in my mind, sounding farther away than just a few steps from where I stand, but nonetheless it steals my attention. My mouth waters for the bitterness to satiate its needs. I grab my favorite mug, the one that says *Congrats, Graduate!* It was a gift from my aunt. She drove all the way from Versnik on the south end of Lamnah to see me walk across the stage. I was in the Class of Four Hundred, marking four centuries after the War of Fernestia. She drove five hours just to see me officially become an adult and leave to go do *better* things with my life.

I wish she'd never come to that graduation. If she hadn't, she would still be alive.

I pour creamer into my mug, paling the dark drink. I take a deep gulp of it and exhale as the bitter hot liquid slips down my throat, not tasting as rich as I remember this particular batch of roasted beans being.

She died nearly two years ago now. No one could have known an oncoming car would swerve into her lane. I've missed her every day since. The woman practically raised me alongside my mother, and she never missed an event. Never. For my fifteenth birthday she bought me a large laundry basket and I was upset because who wants a laundry basket for their birthday? But it wasn't clothing that filled the basket under the blanket. That's when I met her, my partner in crime, my best friend.

"A puppy?"

I remember how happy I was. I immediately named her Margo. My aunt hated it because she said the name was dated, but I never understood her disdain for it. Her own name was Margo—she went by Aunt Maggie. I wanted to name the puppy after her because she was leaving that next week to live in Versnik. She wouldn't be close anymore, not as close as she should be.

So when Margo died, it was like losing my aunt all over again.

I suppress a shudder as the dream and scent of blood sting my nose. I rest my hand on the doorknob with unease as I ready myself for my daily walk. When I open this door, I will be in my forest again. Just like any other day.

When I open this door, I cross the border I've set for myself where my grief must remain. It's not allowed to follow me past the frame and into the *real* world. Because I'm still real, aren't I?

I know one thing that *was* real.

Margo.

But the funny—or sad—thing about death is that it affects each soul differently. My mother couldn't process my aunt's passing. She just pretends like she is still out there some-where, far away, living her life and smiling. On the other hand, my father wasn't as scathed by death's touch, or at least pretends not to be.

And me? Well, isn't it obvious? I'm having a hard time. A really, *really* hard time. What really fucked me up was the wake we held for Aunt Maggie in the Chapel of the Gods. My mom insisted on doing an open casket. I was expecting to see my aunt smiling like she always was . . . but her frown . . . her cold hands. It changed me. I began to question the reality of things.

I've never been quite the same since I saw her pale skin and cold, unmoving face. She was always smiling when she was alive, but she wore a long frown in death, one that made her look ten years older than she was.

I wanted to wake her. To shake her and bring her back. She couldn't just . . . not be real anymore. I decided to push off college and just run around with the boys in this small town while I worked part-time at a cafe. Margo was the only grounding aspect of my life. Dogs have a way of doing that, you know—healing the mentally ill. She kept my sickness at bay.

But then she died too.

Why did the gods take them? It's not fair. Mom always ensured me that the gods exist in tandem to our lives. That long ago, during the war, our religion awoke and revealed the true gods of our world. That they are merciful, but nothing can live forever. I decided at the tender age of five that I didn't like the gods. I detested the God of Death the most for taking the most precious things in life.

Life itself.

I hoped he was a lonely asshole. I think this often now— how horrible a god he is.

How cruel he is.

Even the forest seems to be slipping away at death's hand. Over the years it's held fewer and fewer creatures, as if they are being taken from our world. The ponderosas have blackened and their needles have tanned with dreary rest.

The forest seems as sick as I feel.

As I walk through the forest, tall with the gloomy pines, I think of Margo. Both of them. They each left their mark here. I can hear it in the wails of the trees as they sway and crack in the wind, the snaps of branches sounding so close, like a whisper in my ear but at the same time far away. The forest misses them too.

I take a deep breath in and the scent of rain mixed with

pine sap fills me. I exhale loudly into the sky and let the rain pelt my face. The drops send cold rivulets of water through my muddied soul.

I don't worry about many things these days, even though I'm twenty and still living at home. Well, that's debatable—I technically live in my shed. Maybe it's because I'm a little fucked up in the head or because my parents feel sorry for me, but either way they leave me be. Each time I muster up the energy to head into their house, I suddenly get over-whelmed with anxiety and despair. I don't want them to judge me with their eyes. I know I've been a letdown. But the days just blur and I'm not even sure how long it's been since I've visited.

I am in my own world out here. In *my* forest. And I've noticed in these last few weeks that there is an intruder in my woods.

The sun is already dipping past the mountains, making the already overcast and rainy day more dreary. I know, I have the tendency to sleep in late. Horribly, irresponsibly late, but I'm too tired and empty to give a shit. I find the most solace exploring the woods at night anyway. Maybe I'm hoping to find old ghosts out here, whispers of my past. Ones that have long since passed.

But tonight, my mission is to figure out why this male has been camping out at my neighbor's house. Maybe it's his son? Old Man Bruno has never spoken much of his family so I find it unbelievable that this man would just show up.

I slip past Old Man Bruno's makeshift gate, mesmerized

by the fireflies that hum and light the evening with their warm green glow. I didn't know we had fireflies this far from the mainland. I stop to admire them for a few minutes. The rain has stopped now and left dark puddles in dips of the forest's marshy zones. I catch a glimpse of my reflection and quickly shift my eyes away.

I hate seeing myself. I look like a train wreck since Margo. Three months of tangled dark hair and pale skin. My normal olive hue has been diminished by the time I've spent wallowing in my shed and beneath the forest canopy away from sunlight. Even my eyes don't have their usual honey-brown glow.

I just look muddied. A tired, wandering soul.

Bruno lives across the road that splits our fifty-acre woods in half. He owns the left side and my parents own the right. He made a short, flimsy fence years ago to border off his house, but his wooden gate is always left open. I like Bruno. He is an odd old man but has a lot of heart and many interesting stories. I haven't seen him for a while and I've noticed new trails on *my* side of the pine woods. That's when I found a strange male and his dog blazing them.

At first I was just annoyed, but now? I'm pissed. He keeps wandering closer to my shed and I'm not one to share my end of the woods.

I know, sharing is caring. But I'm not a sharing person. Not at all. And normally I don't have a problem walking up to people and telling them to fuck off, but this male is unreasonably attractive. Not to mention he has a beautiful dog named Murph.

It might be a little weird that I know his dog's name, but it's because I hear him calling for the furry, wolf-looking creature from time to time when he strays too close to my side of the woods.

But no more. I'm done. Tonight, I'm telling him to stay off my property—well, my parents' land, but same thing. I'm going to march right up to—

Old Man Bruno's cabin door swings open and smacks the exterior wall. I immediately hit the deck. (And by that I mean the forest floor.) I hold my breath and thank whatever gods are watching me that I'm in thick enough tall grass to hide. It also helps that it's dusk, which draws a question to my mind.

Where the hell is he going this late? I still haven't caught his name and I know it's probably a really, *really* stupid idea to follow him into the woods at night, but I'm overly curious as to where he is going at this hour. Where he's *been* going.

The male steps out and pulls his brown leather coat over his shoulders. His black hair is long and pulled in a tight bun that sits on the back of his head. Everything beneath his ears is shaved. His jaw is sharp and his lips are pulled taut with focus. He has a tattoo of a thorny choker around his throat that sits above his jugular, making his appearance all the more unapproachable. He is hot. Too hot. And oddly clear—his presence is sharper than the world around him. I get a feeling of trouble when I look at him. Like he's someone my parents would absolutely hate if I brought him home . . . wait, stop. I'm here to tell him to fuck off. I shake my head and refocus.

He looks over the treeline and underbrush, I freeze as his eyes pass over me. When he starts walking down the trail, I release my breath. Thank gods he didn't see me. After he and Murph are far enough ahead, I slowly stand, eager to follow behind.

As I straighten myself, I notice he forgot to shut the door behind him. Old Man Bruno would be upset if the "Moss Sparrows" got in. I know it sounds crazy, but the ninety-year-old man believes in the spirits of the forest so firmly that oftentimes I catch myself wondering about the creatures he babbles about.

Sure, my religion surrounds gods, but we don't have made-up creatures in our books. Bruno takes his fantasies much too far. I've known him my entire life and he's shared so many stories with me about the forest, the beings and wisps that ebb and flow through the pines. And in this particular situation, I remember him telling me the door must be shut at all times to keep the Moss Sparrows out. He always said I'd know one when I saw it because they have large moss balls on their heads. My lips kick up at the old man's creativity. Of course, I've never seen one with my own eyes, but part of me always wonders. Maybe that's why I love it here so much. The way my mind can wonder and be free out here with the trees. I could never leave it.

I hastily move up to the door and reach to shut it when I catch a glisten of something shiny in the room. I'm snoopy, so

I push the door open wider to see what it is. There's a golden dagger lying on the coffee table. It sits pretty in a black velvet box. The sharp blade is almost iridescent in the dark room. Parts of his cabin are so dark they are nearly blurry, all except the dagger. I raise a brow and suppress the goosebumps that threaten, but I've seen weirder things strung about Bruno's house. The old man collects odd trinkets.

I slip the door shut and quickly pace down the trail to follow the male wherever it is he's going. He and the dog walk further and further into the forest. I begin to get a feeling that maybe I shouldn't be following them—and not just for moral reasons. Maybe I should stop and go home . . . if I know what's good for me. But if I always listened to my reason then I'd never have adventures or find out where Murph and the beautiful, mysterious male are going.

They start to pick up the pace, making me take some loud, uncareful steps. I start to worry that he will notice me trailing them like a creeper, but I've come too far to turn back now. *Where are you going?*

Murph leaps onto a lone boulder that protrudes from the earth. We are deep in the woods, nearing the river that slices the land from the national forest. Pine needles and broken branches litter the floor around us. The scent of fresh sap floods my nostrils. I haven't noticed the forest this . . . *alive* for a long time. I don't know when things began to change, but the creatures of the forest have become few and far between and the smells, the sounds, the *life* of my forest seems to have faded over the years. Especially recently.

My arms ripple with goosebumps against the chill in the air and the hum of the evening insects. The male hops onto the rock as well and takes a breath. *Finally, gods.* His exhale curls in the air. Was it this cold earlier? Murph lets out a low whine and he turns to him. His hair, now in a low ponytail, wisps over his shoulder. He pats the dog's head gently.

"Tomorrow," he whispers into the thin air, his voice unusually clear. It rings in my ears as if it's the first word I've heard in a long while. What? What tomorrow? Why did I follow him all the way out here just to watch him pet his dog? My bones begin to feel weary as the chill sets in them. My thighs burn from crouching and being stealthy for the last hour, and although I'm only twenty, the rain and cold breeze still make my bones ache.

I should leave . . .

Just as my doubts begin to cave in on me, I notice a light emanate from his palm. What is he holding? It's a beautiful light. Wait. Now Murph has a light too and the collar around his neck illuminates. Warm yellowish-orange illumination pulses through the darkness, almost reaching me in my corner of the forest, casting away the shadows that the forest encases me in.

I'm nearly standing, about to reveal my hiding spot when I hear his voice again. "You can come out now," he says softly. So calmly. All my breath leaves my body. I was worried he would be angry with me for following him, or at least a little confused, but he leaves no hint of it. Instead, he seems quite pleased. His dark hair is even richer under the star-lit universe, his amber eyes their constellation.

I stand from behind the bush. "I . . . Uh, I'm sorry I followed you. I was just curious where you were going so late . . ." *And I was going to tell you to fuck off.* I fumble my fingers, trying to find any sort of reassurance with them.

He smiles easily at me. "Don't be. What's your name?"

I stare, baffled that he isn't weirded out. "Elodie . . . and you?"

"Wren. This is Murph."

I nod curtly. *Is this really happening?* I pinch my leg. *Yup.* It has to be real—he is radiant and glows with life.

"Would you like to come with us?" he asks.

I raise a brow.

He doesn't offer an answer. Instead, he just holds my gaze and winks. Murph lets out a low howl and a cloud of mist spills above the rock. The ebony dog walks into the heavy mist and Wren motions for me to follow as he disappears behind its shroud along with the dog.

I catch my breath as I try to decide what to do. Before I can choose, my feet are already taking me towards the mist where Wren disappeared. Am I really going to follow a stranger to a place unspoken? I bite my lip, leaving deep indents of my teeth. Honestly, I could use something crazy. Life hasn't been good and it's not like I have better things going on.

On the off chance it's not real—why not enjoy this while it lasts?

"Wren?" I whisper, standing against the mist, nose tingling with the brisk brush of the damp air. The smell of crisp smoke fills my senses. Bark that's been freshly snapped. It's clearer than anything I've ever inhaled, laced with a song my body yearns for. I don't need to be an expert to know this mist isn't of our world. But that sounds crazy, right?

A hand appears through the white cloud and offers itself to me. Wren's. I hesitantly place my palm on his. I shouldn't just go with a stranger. I really should go home, but this feels right. My soul, my bones, my heart all tell me to trust him. So I do. His hand is surprisingly warm in the cool air. He guides me smoothly, and once I pass through the shroud, I'm engulfed by darkness.

I can't see anything. My heart starts to beat loudly in my chest. His hand slips from mine and I'm left alone.

Alone. Am I real? The mist shifts around me and cools my exposed skin.

Will she come if I call her? I know I'm supposed to leave my grief in my shed, that when I cross that line I leave it behind, but here in the dark mist I feel the urge to call her. Just as much as I do in my dreams.

"Margo?"

A hand presses against mine. "Who is Margo?" Wren whispers in my ear. I tense at his touch and deep voice, but I feel relieved by his presence. Normally I would be weirded out by a male being so forward with touching me. I rather dislike it. But Wren seems . . . different. And not just because of his sharp features and scent of crisp pines. He's different in the way that my skin comes alive under his palm. The calmness and warmth he sends through his fingers makes me want to be close to him, as if we've known one another for a long time.

"Margo is my—well, *was* my dog." *She isn't real anymore.* I keep the last part to myself.

It's weird not being able to see him as he speaks. I can only keep track of him by the movement of his hand. It crests the top of my shoulder and brushes against my chin. "*Was* . . . Such a somber thing to come to pass. Here, follow me." He tugs my hand and guides me through the shroud until we reach the end of it.

The sky explodes as we break from the mist. Moonlight beams from above and illuminates the field below. Where did the forest go? Fields extend out into the gray sea of tinted blue grasses. A breeze blows dark strands of my hair across my face, and my eyes follow the wisps to the sky. The moon is high and waning. Wait, there are two moons. No, four? They nearly look like planets.

Wren smiles and inhales deeply. I unconsciously copy him and take a deep breath of the strange new air. It penetrates my lungs and leaves me dizzy. It's almost sweet, and undeniably the most *real* sensation I've experienced.

"What is this place? Is it real?" *Gods—I said that last part out loud.* I glance over at him. His tan skin is ethereal in the blue moonlight. His dark hair has an azure tint to it and his amber eyes brim with flecks of crystal gems reflected from the sky. "Are *you* real?" I add unapologetically, wincing a bit at my audacity.

He pulls the corners of his lips into a smirk. "Am *I* real?" He shifts his dark eyes at me and I find a kindness in them I wasn't expecting to see there. "I can promise you that I am real. This place is real too." He lifts his face to the moons above. "It's called Tomorrow."

"Tomorrow?" I almost scoff.

Wren nods. "Yes, Tomorrow. You can think of this as the realm beside yours."

"So this isn't real? I don't understand what you're getting at. Are you saying this is like a magical realm?"

He gives me that wry smile once more. "Sure, if that helps, think of this as a magical realm." He whistles for Murph. The grasses rustle and a large black wolf-looking creature pops out of the underbrush. My mouth gapes.

That is *not* Murph. I look to Wren for some shock on his face at the beast that responded to his call, but he only pats it on the head with affection. The creature is as immense as a horse.

"Murph? What happened to him?" I stammer. The beast's body is two—no, three times the size it was just moments ago. His features are a mass of dark shadows that wisp off of his fur. Eyes a pale yellow that scorns the moonlight. His claws dig deep into the earth, like the roots of the elder trees. White ghostly leaves flutter transparently from him, like an aura of the forest itself. "What *is* he?"

Wren approaches and nuzzles his nose against Murph's.

A warm light sparks between them and engulfs Wren. His clothes are no longer a leather jacket and worn pants. They've shifted into a lovely sage-green cloak, earthy-toned tunic, and pants. His ears twist upwards and a collar made of ancient-looking dark wood curves around the skin of his throat, replacing the tattoo. The same transparent leaves now flutter through his raven-like hair.

This has all left me breathless. What in the hell is happening right now? If he was beautiful before, now he is the king of the fucking faeries. I try to keep myself reined in. I'm twenty years old and I've had my fair share of men. But we don't have men *this* beautiful in Lamnah.

"Murph is a Pine Hollow," he finally says. I stare at him expectantly because there's no way he can expect me to know what the fuck that is, and he continues. "And I am a Cypress. We are forest guardians." He says it so plainly, as if his words are common knowledge. I continue to stare in bewilderment.

Murph takes a heavy step toward me. I take a step back, still wary of the creature. *Do they ride these beasts like horses?* I shake the absurd thought from my mind.

"We can ride him if you'd like."

"Pfffft!" I nearly send snot flying from my nose while holding back a full-blown laugh. Wren looks at me with confusion in his eyes and Murph cocks his head to the side. He must have read my mind on that one.

"Yeah, yeah, laugh all you want. I'm not joking." Wren rolls his eyes with annoyance.

I manage to contain my giggles. "I appreciate the offer,

but I really should be getting home now. Maybe I can explore more in the morning?" Wren flinches and turns to face me.

"Yeah, about that . . . You can only go through Bresian, the path between worlds, once a day," he says in a low whisper, as if to keep the words from my ears.

"What?" I snap at him. "You didn't think this would have been useful information *before* you invited me through?"

Wren covers his mouth in thought. "Yes, I suppose that would have been wise. But you're here now, and I have the feeling that you were itching for an adventure anyway. *You* were the one following me, remember?" He winks at me. If he weren't so compelling and handsome, I would have sat down and refused to budge a single step. But . . .

"Fine. You're right. I *was* sort of stalking you." I sigh. "Where will we go, though?"

He lets out a beautiful laugh, one I won't dare forget anytime soon. I watch him carefully as he enters my personal bubble. He places his hand on my cheek and shuts his eyes. My heart hammers against the walls of my ribs. A pulse of need rushes through my body. I bite my lower lip to keep it from seeking his. His face is polished in the dewy midnight glow. I shut my eyes and wait for the press of him.

Because I think he is going to kiss me. Like a fool.

Instead, my cheek warms into a glow. My eyes fling open. His eyes are dark and hollow, and his pupils are slits. Golden ones. My focus pulls towards my cheek again and I feel the tug of something around my neck, grabbing my jugular with restraint. This I know, immediately, is real. Wait, was I really expecting him to kiss me? Was I going to let him? I press my lips in a hard, thin line with disappointment. I really have let my boredom and wallowing let me make questionable choices.

The corners of Wren's mouth turn upwards. "Well, for starters, you'll need to wear this."

Margo. Is this how your collar felt against your fur? Did it tug tightly against your neck and cast doubt in your heart? I entertain the thought.

"Why?" I mutter, reaching up to feel my collar. I prick my finger on a lengthy thorn. A bead of blood forms. I furrow my brow—it's just like his collar.

"Because you need to wear the Vernovian Thorn if you want to stay in my village. The townsfolk will not accept you otherwise."

Vernov-a-what?

I am about to say that I don't intend on staying long, but it won't be of any use. He said I can't go back until a day has passed. I give a reluctant nod and let my eyes drop to my feet. I'm exhausted. Wholly and entirely exhausted. My weary bones beg for rest after walking all over the place today.

Wren seems to notice. "Here." He swoops his arms around me and places me on Murph's back. The Pine Hollow's shadow aura dances around me. It's strange. I can feel the life energy as it twirls through my fingers. The translucent leaves welcome my hand with a soft brush against my skin. Wren hops up behind me, scooting in close. "We'll be there in no time. Hold on like this." His arms wrap around me and I feel his chest press against my spine. My cheeks flush with heat.

Murph lets out a low *woof* and charges forward. The wind presses against my face and I have to squint to see. We are practically flying through the field. The waves of grass at this speed look like green wisps of a liquid forest. As Murph's paws touch the earth, the ground lightens with a million orbs of light. Are those fireflies? Funny that they have them in a magical realm too. What did I think would exist here? Not Pine Hollows and Cypresses, that's for sure. And yet, my heart thrums with the excitement I feel. The beauty is almost too enchanting for me to take in.

Wren leans in harder against my back. I try to ignore it but my face heats once more and I'm so fucking glad he can't see it. He breathes heavily and whispers in my ear, "You'll love this."

"Love what?" I find it odd that he acts so . . . familiar around me. I don't dislike it, I just can't really put a finger on what it is about him.

"You'll see." It must be my imagination that he squeezes me tighter.

As the words leave his lips, I see what he's talking about. We glide swiftly up the last of the hills and break the forest's edge. A slew of petals swirls around us, leaving me nearly numb with their fragrance of lilacs. Murph comes to a halt, surely solely for me to take everything in.

The valleys ahead dip low and rise high with lush green shrubs dappling every slope. Small white clouds—flowers, I think, but I could be wrong—stretch across every inch of the underbrush. Tall trees, and I mean *tall*, tower up to the sky. We did go up a hill to reach the edge of the forest but somehow it feels like we went down into a cave of underground ancient trees that pillar the sky above. Beams of light push through their impossibly large branches, scattering the world beneath.

Wren was right. I love this.

"It's . . . It's beautiful," I whisper.

He gives a low, short laugh. I feel the vibration against my spine. "I knew you would. Murph, let's go home."

Murph grunts and races down the valleys and through a thicket. Once on the other side, we are suddenly in a small, enchanting town. I turn my head to check behind me because I can't piece together how we just got here.

Cobblestone bricks and moss make up the paths before us. I would call them roads, but they simply are not roads. I can tell that light feet tread here—though I don't see any feet.

"Where is everyone?"

Wren gives another short laugh. "It's nearly two in the morning. No one is up at this hour." He makes it sound like this isn't an absolute change of reality for me. Of course no one would be up at this hour. How similar our two worlds are.

I sigh. "Yeah, I'm tired. Can we rest and explore tomorrow?"

"Of course." He hops off Murph and helps guide me to the ground. He nods towards a small cottage across from us. It's the closest one to the beginning of the village; the rest of the cottages sit a little further back past the main shops ahead. The roof is made entirely of straw. Green vines engulf most of what's visible on the siding. Cobblestones line the walls of the two-story home and four-pane windows peek through the lush greenery. A small, well-kept yard greets us. Blue, glowing mushrooms and little balls of moss edge the entirety of the borders.

A smile breaches my lips. This place is entirely too perfect. It reminds me of my small shed at home, or at least how I wish my shed looked. Although excitement tugs my heart, my weary bones are much heavier. They yearn for a bed to lie in.

Wren leads the way into the cottage. The door isn't a typical rectangle-shaped frame. Instead, it is curved at the top. It gives a slight creaking sound as he nudges it open. Murph settles himself on the front lawn, a few fireflies rising from the grass around him. He is much too big to enter the house. Poor thing. At least the weather seems favorable here. As I enter the cottage, my senses are flooded with an array of sweet and earthy scents. It's dark inside, but I can tell it's cozy. Wren wraps his hand around mine and guides me up the stairs to a room at the back of the second floor. The walls moan as we walk by. Now all I can smell is Wren. He has a distinct earthy air about him, like cedars, or maybe damp wood that has drifted onto shore. Whatever it is, it consumes me. I fight the urge to lean into him to breathe in more.

The room is clean and surprisingly empty. A simple bed with a thin comforter sits in the center. The blanket looks handmade, quilted with a foreign thread. There is a dresser on the west-facing wall and a mirror wrapped in a vine plant on the east. That's all there is. I don't care to dissect his decor choices—all I care for now is rest. I'm spent and can't help but wonder if Bresian saps the energy of those who pass through. I trudge over to the bed and let my body slump to its offer of rest.

"Let me know if you need anything, okay?" Wren speaks kindly. I can't quite figure him out. He is kind and I feel like he knows me somehow, though I am certain we've never met. I would remember anyone with a face like his. Still, I get a sort of nostalgic feeling about him. Something that is just familiar.

My fingers trail up to my collar of twisted branches and magic. "Can you take this off while I sleep?" Why would he need to place it there in the first place if everyone in town is asleep?

He frowns and shakes his head slowly. "I'm sorry, Elodie, I can't." My hopes drop, but I'm leaving tomorrow night—right? I nod curtly and lay down, covering my body and face with the comforter. It smells of brambles.

I flinch as I feel the bed sink on the other side. I whirl around to face him. He is sitting on the side opposite me. His dark eyes meet mine. His collar glistens in the dim light. Oh, how I want to taste it. But I push back those unspeakable thoughts.

"What are you doing?" I ask, a little more hostile than I intended.

He raises a brow. "What do you mean?"

I seethe with annoyance. I'm tired and he is trying to play games with me. "Why are you staying?"

His eyes flicker with realization. "Oh, this is my room. I don't have a spare for you. If you're uncomfortable I can sleep on the floor. I'm sorry, our customs are different here. I didn't think anything of it," he says warmly, grabbing his pillow before I can respond and plopping it on the floor.

Guilt tackles me and I'm not in the mood to wrestle with it. It's *one* night and it's not like I mind. I shake my head apologetically. "No, it's fine."

Wren cocks his head. "Are you sure?" I nod and turn back around to face the edge of the bed. He settles in, and unfortunately the space between us is nonexistent. I can feel his shoulder blades devour mine. I feel so small next to him, but oddly safe. I've felt this security before, being tucked safely in the nook of a male's back. I hate how much I've missed this feeling. After Aunt Maggie died, I started living impulsively, because life is entirely too short to not experience the things you want. I wanted to feel alive, to fill the urges and needs I gained becoming an adult. Yeah, we're talking about sex. But I missed the subtle things too. The closeness of another.

I let my bones rest, warm in this corner of the world. I intend to explore everything here tomorrow. *Ha.* Tomorrow, in *Tomorrow.* My mind feebly finds joy in the words.

2

I wake several times throughout the night. The first time is because the room is chilly, and I scrunch my knees to my chest in an effort to help retain heat. The second time I find myself burrowed in Wren's neck. His jawline rests tenderly on my forehead. My body seizes and I stop myself from flinging myself to the floor. I listen to his breathing and he seems to be sound asleep. Thank the gods. His arm is placed on my side, lazed in the nook of my hip.

How did we end up like this? I'm comfortable but need to escape his embrace. I'm much too vulnerable and will catch feelings if he holds me like this. I shiver at the thought of him waking as I untangle us. His breath hitches and he lets out a weary sigh as I slip from under his arm. I try to fall back asleep but each time I fade into dreams I feel his hand search for me or mine for him.

No use. I need to get up.

I slip from the bed and sneak out of the room and down the hall. The sun is just beginning to peek through the windows. I walk more comfortably once I'm standing at the top of the stairs. I can't help but smile at the piles of books that line the right side of the steps. It's odd to think that books and one's ability to clutter are the same here as they are in my realm. I make my way down and glide my fingers gently down the rail. At the bottom, I turn to see the rows of pages, worn and tired. I decide to grab one and brush off the cover. It's an untitled book, but I take it with me nonetheless.

Light footsteps tap against the old floorboards and catch my ear. Is there someone else here? I tuck the book under my arm and explore the cottage. It's modest, with simple old furniture and a dusty, homey feeling. It gives me warmth and a sense of coziness. I run my fingers across the wooden mantle above the fireplace and glance down to the floor. Margo loved lying at the foot of fireplaces. She would stretch out her toes and let out a long sigh at the pleasure of warmth and sleep, snuggled with her favorite toy and blanket. The important things. I hover over the hearth for a few long moments, staring deep into the smoldering coals. Is this real?

Margo. She *was* real. I think.

A scraping sound makes me flinch and I spin to find a small boy, around eight maybe, standing behind me with a puzzled look on his face. He has a spoon in his mouth. Green mounds of moss crown his head, lush with vibrant green. His large blue eyes are beaming into mine. His tan, chubby cheeks scream to be pinched. Old Man Bruno's voice echoes in my head. *Moss Sparrows have balls of moss on their heads.* It can't be—is this all in my head? I squeeze the book in my hands tighter, feeling the cover tense under my fingertips. This all feels so very real.

"Oh, hello, little one." I smile warmly. *I wonder if he knows about stranger danger.* I pause. I guess I can't really speak to that, given that I followed Wren here when my intention was to tell him off. Would have been nice if Wren had told me that someone else lived here. I clench my hand at my irritation with the Cypress.

The boy tilts his head back and forth as he considers me. "Who are you?" he mumbles with the spoon still closed between his lips.

I kneel to his level. "I'm Elodie Marrowbone and who are you?"

"Marley." He smiles wide. "Marley Winters, and I'm nine years old!" he states proudly. I'd almost forgotten how much children say random things about themselves. My Aunt Maggie never had children and I'm an only child so I don't have a ton of experience around them.

"Ah, I see. How do you know Wren?" I might as well try to get some information out of this kid. They don't look similar enough for him to be Wren's child.

"Wren? Hmm . . . Oh! You mean Mr. Bartholomew." He raises his spoon at me. I lean back to avoid the tap he intended for my nose. "He is my caretaker. I'm an orphan and his apprentice for the Nesbrim guard." The spoon goes back into his mouth.

There are orphans in places like this too? That hardly seems fair. My heart throbs for Marley. His eyes glimmer as I hear Wren's steps behind me. I turn towards the stairs and am struck by how impeccable he looks this early in the morning. His hair is let down and stops at his pecs. The translucent leaves shimmer with their mysterious charm. His black shirt and pants are on the tighter side and show off his toned muscles. Wren smiles easily at me, making my heart yearn for attention and my thighs burn.

His eyes drunk with sleep, he rubs them as he lets out a long yawn. I can't help but yawn in unison. "Morning." His voice is still raspy.

I swallow hard, Marley raising a brow at my extended pause as I gawk at the gorgeous creature that is Wren. Gods.

"Good morning." My lip kicks up and I'm beyond excited to see what this world has to offer. I'm determined to explore as much as I can today. If it goes well maybe I can see if I can get Wren's number. Oh, wait, do they have phones here? Well, in any case, I know where to find him and vice versa.

Wren stretches his lean arms into the air above him and fastens his hair back into a tight bun. I subconsciously let my eyes drift to the mirror above the mantle and am relatively surprised at my *not so bad but acceptable* appearance. My black hair is a bit messy but I've always thought I look more appealing with chaotic hair. My tan skin looks healthier than ever and my face well rested. There's a light in my honey-brown eyes that I don't remember being there yesterday. Perhaps it's been too long since I've been this excited about . . . well, anything.

"I was thinking we could go to a breakfast shop in town. Then there are a few other merchants I'd like you to see," Wren says as he clips his sage cloak broach in place between his collarbones. My stomach is already growling before he can say what he has in mind. His lips draw up into a charming grin. Our amber- and honey-toned eyes dance for a few moments before Marley coughs to break the trance.

"Am I invited too, Sir Bartholomew?" The boy pouts and his puppy eyes seal the deal. Wren nods warmly at him and rubs Marley's light brown hair, making a mess of the strands and moss on the boy's head. "Yes!" He fists his hand and sprints up the stairs to get dressed. Wren and I exchange a friendly glance before he notices the book in my hands.

"Do you read?"

"Often . . . Well, I used to. I used to love reading." I turn the book in my hands, the worn cover making me nostalgic. He walks closer to me until his pine- and cedar-steeped scent fills me and sends goosebumps down my neck.

"This one is beautiful. It's a tale of a boy of memories who must save the world." His eyes grow distant at the cover. I crack open the pages and realize it's handwritten and not a traditionally typed book. Wren smiles and takes the book gently from me. "It's more of a journal. We can dive deeper into it later. But let's go eat!" His eyes dart to the stairs as Marley flies down the steps. His buttoned shirt is off by a slot and creates an uneven but adorably fitting image. He pulls his brown leather shoes on and is running out the door before we can even mutter a word.

Wren and I share a glance and chuckle as we follow the eager boy outside.

Three bright suns leave little place for any shadows here. My eyes narrow at the beaming warm light, my skin tingling under its rays. Birds, I think, swoop through the tall, arching oaks above. They leave shimmers of gold flecks in their wake and sing a song of melancholy. The village that was dead in the early hours of the morning is now teeming with life. Mystical . . . people? Beings of all sorts trot along the stones, some short with the same moss balls that Marley has. Others are tall and have branches wrapped around their necks like Wren and I do.

My eyes are pulled toward the higher beings. Beautiful— more beautiful than I'd like to admit. Half-clothed ethereal men and women bear wings larger than their bodies, clad in shimmering ivory feathers that knock the breath from my lungs. They remind me of barn owls, the bronze ones, with feathers that stretch far into the sky. They swoon in the morning's dawn. Dancing with the dew perhaps. I've almost forgotten I'm walking when Wren's laugh pulls my focus back to him.

"This place is so beautiful . . . Do we really have the entire day to enjoy it?"

Wren takes a wrap of tobacco from his pocket. It looks just like a cigarette but has more of a brown casing holding the contents. I watch intently as he slips the joint through his lips and lights it with *my* lighter. The pink case stands out like a thorn in this world.

"Why do you have my lighter?" I raise a brow at him but his smirking lips keep my expression soft. Fuck, he is so alluring.

Wren takes a deep pull from the joint and exhales a plume of black smoke. Okay, maybe it's not tobacco? What the hell do creatures here smoke?

"I may have been to your shed a few times while you were out." He knits his dark brows together in a sly attempt for my mercy. I don't know what to say. He was in my shed . . . but is bold enough to not lie. That's what I like about Wren. He's got a bone for honesty and not many other males have that.

"Fuck you. You're lucky I like you." I nudge him with my shoulder and trot ahead through his mystical front yard, hoping his eyes are following me. The mushrooms are no longer glowing now that the sun beams down on them, but the lush ivy and shrubs that cling close to the fence are alive with radiant emerald leaves.

A swell of excitement thrums through my bones. My chest feels light, breathless, like I don't have a worry in the fucking world. Is it okay for me to feel this? Is this real? As I take a glance back at Wren and Marley, who are trying to wake up Murph, I realize I don't care right now. If this isn't real then paint me the queen of delusions and let me live this dreamy reality, one that has felt more real than any of my time on the human side of Bresian.

The four of us walk down the cobblestone street towards the village. I study the buildings and shops that we pass. They are stacked like bricks. Perfect little vines wrap around them. Blushes of pink and the coolness of blue canopies hold more emerging mystical beings as they stir with their daily activities here. Some have ears, horns, moss balls, wings. I can't keep track as we continue walking. I try not to gawk too much because Wren is trying to keep me on the down-low, hence my Vernovian Thorn that I now see so many other Cypresses wearing on their necks.

We approach a small shop entrance. Pots filled to the brim with colorful flowers and wisps of tall foliage make the doorway stand out as the happiest place I've ever seen—if locations can be happy.

"I hope you're hungry." Wren takes one last pull from his joint and puts it out on a tray in front of the shop.

I grip my stomach as it grumbles rudely. "I'm starving." He slides his arm across my shoulder and pulls me in close to his body. His chest is taut beneath his cloak and my lewd thoughts are at war with my rational mind.

"Me too," he whispers in my ear.

I tense and shoot him an astonished glance. He winks at me and nods ahead. I pout at his deflection and trail to where Marley has already gotten us a table by a large window over-looking the main street. His smile couldn't be wider. His tongue is off to the side as he studies the menu and I wonder if he can even read.

The air is warm in this cafe, sweet with the scent of hot

food and pastries. We pass a case of glass filled with sugary breads and pie slices. The berries used are a mysterious dark purple and I immediately know what I'm ordering. As we take our seats in the booth with Marley, I catch a whiff of something bitter and saliva fills my mouth with my hope that I'm smelling coffee. As an addict, I would know the scent anywhere.

The owner swings by our table and sets down water and, thank the gods, coffee as she introduces herself as Hazel. She has a beautiful white thorn collar and black leaves flutter through her golden hair. Her eyes are like granite. Hazel takes our orders and whisks away to give them to the chef. Wren leans back and takes a drink of water before smiling at me. Everything he does is so seamless. He does everything with ease. I know we are technically strangers but there's nowhere else I want to be right now.

"I'm surprised how similar this realm is to the human world," I mumble to break the heat I feel from his gaze. Wren sets his elbow on the table and leans against his palm.

"Really? We aren't as different as you'd think, I promise you that. Well, except for your beauty."

I nearly choke on my coffee. "I think you're mistaken."

He quirks his brow and reaches his hand out to the corner of my mouth, swiping away a drip of coffee from my lip. "I don't lie. You're absolutely *devastating*. Marley, have you ever seen me as enthralled with a female?"

Marley frowns as he reaches over for Wren's black coffee. "No, I haven't, sir." I blush and glance out the window to hide my heating cheeks. The Moss Sparrow takes a big gulp and instantly winces. "Yuck! Why do you drink this stuff, Sir Bartholomew?" We share a laugh at the boy's distaste for the bitter drink.

"You'll understand when you're older, Marley." Wren chuckles and takes his coffee back, downing it as Hazel comes back with plates of food. Sizzling eggs and sausages steam next to two fluffy, buttery biscuits and the slice of purple berry pie I saw in the case.

I lick my lips and wolf down the food with ease. Marley eats as savagely as I do while Wren is much more polite. He cuts into his food with his knife and takes small bites. The flavors are unlike anything I've tasted before—savory and blooming on my tongue with all the seasonings this world grants. I'm floored.

"How's your food? Are you even tasting it?" Wren mumbles through a mouthful.

"Huh?" I glance up at him, eggs toppling down my chin. "Mmhmm, it's wonderful!" He smiles at me, like he enjoys my uncouth behavior. He'd be the first. All the males in my world were embarrassed by my "I don't give shit" attitude.

We finish up at the cafe and thank the owner. Wren must be well known here because he tells her to add it to his tab and she blushes as he winks at her. A sting of jealousy tears through me. I'd thought maybe he only gave me his charm, but clearly he is a flirt.

Murph grunts at us as we emerge from the café. His black, wisping fur is almost smoke-like in the daylight. Wren greets him with a pat on the muzzle and the beast shuts his yellow eyes in greeting. Marley climbs on top of the Hollow's back and clutches his stomach.

"I'm so full!" he chirps happily and lays down along Murph's spine, a fitting place to rest for one so small. I kick up my lip. I've been smiling so much today and it feels really good—hurts a little, even.

We spend the afternoon visiting shops and picking up some groceries for supper. I gawk at every Cypress we meet and a few three-horned merchants that Wren calls Dread-iuses. I take in every vine, cobblestone brick, and creature we interact with until my eyes are full and my mind is burning for rest.

As we walk back to Wren's cottage, the suns are setting and the crest of the four moons are peeking over the tall, arching trees that we passed last night. I feel a weight pressing on my heart. I don't want to go back home, not yet. But Mom and Dad will worry if I just ghost them like this. I watch as Marley takes his claim on the couch and snuggles his gray blanket. Wren heads for the stairs but I stop at the foot of them.

"Thank you so much for today, Wren." I meet his gaze and his amber eyes flutter with warmth.

"Of course. Are you tired? We can play a game of chess until we fall asleep if you'd like. Or tell stories. I'm curious to hear of your life," he says eagerly. I can tell he enjoys spending time with me as much as I do with him. But I have to go home.

"Oh, I would love that, but I really should head home now. Maybe tomorrow or next week?" I reach up to touch his hand on the railing but he takes a step toward me and his face hardens.

"But didn't you have a nice day? You should stay here with me. Come on, we'll have fun."

What? Why is he trying to keep me here? A pit forms in my stomach, sending shivers up my back, and bells begin to ring in my head.

Fuck.

"I'm sorry, Wren." I take a step backward toward the door. "But I need to go home now." I turn calmly and try to keep my composure. Wren isn't a bad guy. He is kind, soft, alluring. He won't do anything against my will. He will let me leave.

His cold hand grasps my wrist tightly and I freeze. Every cell in my body is screaming for me to run. I hesitantly look over my shoulder at him. His entire presence is different, darker. He has an ominous air about him that wasn't there before and it makes my skin crawl.

I'm so fucking stupid. Of course he didn't lure me here to have fun. There's always a catch and I fell right into his trap. With bait as tempting as him, who wouldn't?

I decide to take my chance with the element of surprise, and in a split second I tear my arm from his grip and whirl towards the door, wrenching it open before Wren has the chance to process my decision.

"Elodie, wait!" he rasps as I sprint across the front yard.

Murph stands to follow. I clench my teeth. I don't stand a chance against either of their speeds. What should I do? My heart clatters against my ribs. My lips feel dry and my eyes are hot with fear.

I shake my head and focus ahead. Wren's shout draws the attention of the villagers. They turn to face me as I race by them. I catch a few gasps and worried glances. I ignore them and keep pushing forward. The angelic beings above flap their wings slowly as they too notice me.

Everyone can see me. They can see me. My lips start to tingle and my fingertips burn. A panic attack is nothing surprising to me, especially in this chase. I try to not think about it. I need to find a place to hide.

There are no corners I take that Wren isn't two steps behind. I try to shake him but it's useless. I pass the cafe, the shops, and some faces that I recognize from meeting today. My legs begin to tremble and I start to forget why I'm running. But I can't ignore the voice in my head that tells me to get the fuck away from Wren, to run as far as my legs will take me.

I hook another turn down a narrow alley and am met with a dead end—a wall at least three stories high with aged stones. Green vines cling to it and sprout little white flowers to greet me. I press my hands against the cold wall and don't turn to face Wren. My fingers tingle and my lips are numb. I take a few steadying breaths to counteract the anxiety and fear warring within me.

I hear him stop a few feet behind me as he takes a few

labored breaths. I turn to face him, pushing my hot back against the icy stones. They drain the heat from my body but the nervous sweat remains. I watch him carefully. His hands are placed over his knees and trembling. Good—I gave him a run for his money at least.

"What do you want?" I snap at him. "Just let me go home!"

He takes another gulp of air before bringing his eyes to mine, cold and dark. He straightens and clenches his fists in fury. "I—I . . ."

I'm not surprised he can't make up a lie on the spot. "You what? You're trying to keep me here for gods know why. I want to leave. *Now*." I make each word clear and sharp.

A shadow falls over his gaze. He wrinkles his nose, surely with disgust at my shouts. "I can't let you."

Goosebumps crawl up my arm. I feel uncomfortable in my skin under his heavy gaze.

"Why not?"

Wren breaks his glance from me. I can see the reluctance in his eyes. "I just can't." He pauses and tries to compose himself. "Now *please* come back to the cottage. I won't ask nicely again." I believe him. His air is eerie and his tightly clenched fists make me flinch.

I stare at him and don't move from the damp stones at my back. He'll have to fight me the entire way back. Wren gives a weary shrug and his dark hair slips over his ear and into his face. It's the most uncomposed I've seen him. He takes a step toward me and I tense every muscle in my calves. I can't decide whether to fight him or to comply. My eyes close as a heaviness tugs at them. I try to fight it, but it's almost like magic is willing them shut. My body sinks to the earth beneath me.

"Please don't make this difficult," Wren whispers in my ear. I try to fight, try to yell or scream out, but my mouth won't obey. I'm conscious but paralyzed. I let out a low sigh as I feel him hoist me over his back. My eyes slip open and I watch helplessly as he treks me back to the cottage. Faces of strangers cast glances at me. No one is willing to help. I feel the helpless pit sink further into my heart.

Murph waits by the cottage with what I think is a concerned expression. He whimpers as Wren angrily stomps past him. He doesn't stop in the living quarters and marches up the stairs and into his bedroom. He plops me on the bed and takes a few steps back, crossing his arms at me. The second his touch is gone I can move freely once more, and I cross my arms back at him. I refuse to meet his gaze.

"Be mad all you want. Don't try to run away again," Wren says sternly.

I lie down and keep my eyes shut, tugging the blanket over my shoulders. I won't give him a response. No matter what I say it won't matter. He huffs angrily and leaves the room, slamming the door behind him.

Looks like I'm spending another day here.

3

I sleep through the morning and well into the afternoon, and pace for the rest of day in Wren's room. He must have slept on the couch last night because I haven't seen him. Evening falls slowly as I plan out how to break for the forest. I hardly remember the way. Murph blazed through the fields like it was a mere few steps into this enchanted world, but I know it will take me hours to reach the path back. The worn floorboards creak under my feet as I continue to walk back and forth from one end of the room to the other.

I pause at the window and lean my elbows against the frame. It's dark outside but the light from the four moons leaves an ample amount of visibility. The rooftops are all made of the same straw-like material. It reminds me of a place I once visited. Waves crashed there and the rain never seemed to stop falling, leaving the grass well watered and bright. Mom brought extra blankets for that exact reason. She knew how cold and wet the air was at her father's cottage on the northern shores of Fernestia. There were normal people and animals there though of course, not these strange beings.

My eyes stop scrolling over the rooftops and land on a male's figure against the twilight. He's looking at me. I tense and straighten, taking a hesitant step back. He notices that I've finally caught a glimpse of him. How long has he been watching me?

A creeping feeling surges over me but I try to maintain my senses. The male stands and unfolds large wings from his back. They stretch further than the ones I saw this morning. Instead of ivory, his feathers are black with shimmers of gold at the tips. He has two large horns that extend from the crown of his skull and curve backwards, the sharp points aimed toward the night sky. They contrast marvelously against his white, luminescent hair, the strands of which sway over his eyes as he glides toward the window. I've never seen a male so iridescently stunning in my whole life. Handsome doesn't do him justice. He is beautiful, like a sad song sung in the twilight. The moon itself wraps him with a soft glow of sorrow.

I tap my leg with my finger and flinch at the feeling of my skin. *Real.* I take a few more steps back as he gracefully lands at the cottage and places a gentle hand against the window. His eyes are like winter fire. They blaze with an icy azure flame that chills my core. No doubt this male—or god, or angel—is as powerful as they come. I can't fathom the magic he wields, yet he is careful and soft so as not to frighten me. A somber smile forms on his face and he doesn't try to open the window.

I clasp my hand over my heart as I take a hesitant step forward. He doesn't give me that bad boy vibe that I get around Wren. Once standing in front of the window, I force myself to meet his eyes. There's curiosity in them. He looks young, around my age, maybe a little older if the beings here age the same as I do. His brows are dark, his lashes long. He has scars that trail over his neck, and more on his forearms. They are dull and blackened against his tan skin, looking like sharp branches from dead trees. If he wasn't so close, I'd mistake them for tattoos. I sip in a short breath before muttering, "Who . . . are you?"

His eyes glimmer at me, causing my heart to skip a beat. "I'm Kastian. Who are you?" His voice carries a small accent that I don't recognize. He studies me from head to toe as if he is fascinated by my mortal stature, but confusion blends in when he sees my collar.

"Elodie," I stammer. I open my mouth to say more but I can't form any thoughts with him staring at me with his ocean-painted eyes.

He cocks his head to the side. "El-o-dee," he sounds it out. The corners of my mouth prick upward at his efforts. I give him a nod, trying to ignore how odd my name must be for the creatures of this world. "Elodie." He says it again, clearer this time. Now we are both smiling at one another.

I press my hand on the glass softly and he sets his index

finger on the other side of the glass from mine. There's a moment of peace. A moment where it's just him and I, two beings from separate worlds. I'm entranced by him. There's a melody in my heart that seems to call for him.

The floorboards creak at my door.

I spin to face it as the light enters from the hallway. Wren appears and gives me a side glance filled with annoyance. I look back to the window, my hand still pressed on the glass. Kastian is gone—as if he was never there.

Wren clears his throat and draws my attention back to him. "I'm sorry . . . for being so callous earlier." He hardly chokes the words out. "Please forgive me." He dips his head. I narrow my eyes at him. I don't fucking buy it for a second. He sounds genuine, but he put *this* on me and is keeping me against my will. My fingers find the collar made of ancient oak, sliding along the veins of the brambles. He's not sorry, not even a little.

"Whatever."

He lets out a sigh and takes a few steps toward me. I flinch and take a step back. He stops and gives me a look I can only describe as wounded. "You must be hungry. Come downstairs and eat something . . . Please?" He steps back to the door and waits. My stomach curls and I can't ignore its plea for food any longer. I relent and follow him out and down the stairs. I decide to keep my interaction with Kastian to myself.

The table is set for three. Marley is already shoveling food in his mouth. I'm not sure if he is aware of the chase that went down yesterday but I don't want to make him uneasy so I choose to act normal.

I let my body ease into the handcrafted wooden chair. The table is old and carved from a lovely smelling oak. Even after the test of time, it releases strong aromatic pulses into the air around me. Is the forest itself here thrumming with magic? I wonder.

Wren quietly fills my plate and sets it in front of me. Thick-cut meat spills its juice onto the plate. It seeps into my potatoes and assortment of steamed vegetables. I raise a brow at the meat, wondering if these beings' food sources are similar to mine. It definitely smells good. Drool passes my lip and I catch it with a swipe of my tongue. I don't wait for Wren to serve himself—I'm with Marley and just dig in.

Dinner is awkwardly quiet. No one feels the need to say anything and I'm okay with that. I prefer the silence anyway. It leaves me with my thoughts, planning how to escape and wondering who that ethereal male was. He could still be out there among the rooftops, perched and waiting, but for what? Why do I hope the answer is me?

I let out a sigh as I polish off my potatoes.

I finish my meal and push my chair out to leave. My first plan is to slip through the front door. Murph might be busy eating or sleeping. I casually walk through the living area towards the door and Wren leans in his chair to peer at me from past the kitchen wall.

"Where are you going?"

I try to lie my way through it. "I want to say hi to Murph."

He gives me a stern gaze and I spin to walk up the stairs instead. I hear him grunt and continue eating. He and Marley start having a conversation now that I've left. I sneak back into the room with plan B playing out in my mind. I can still hear Wren's deep mumbling and Marley's banter so I know it's now or never.

It's time.

I tiptoe to the window and peek out its panes. There's no sight of Kastian. I flip the lock up and carefully open the glass. A soft breeze pushes against my face and beckons me to enter the darkness of night. There's a tug coming from within me. I can't fathom what magic pulls me, but I listen to it.

I set my foot on the frame of the window, hoist myself up, and wrap my body on the side of the house. I glance down. Though I'm only a story up, it will be a harrowing fall. These cottages seem much taller outside than they do inside. I close my eyes and will myself to release my grasp against the building. If I don't just do it, I never will. My fingers release the cobblestone edge and my body falls feet-first to the ground below. I keep my eyes shut. If I open them, I'll scream and give myself away. I brace for the landing but it never comes.

"What are you doing, Elodie?"

My eyes jolt open and my stomach turns. Kastian has me in his arms and we are worlds above the cottage and small, whimsical village. My breath hitches and I nearly lose my supper. I cling to his shoulders tightly. His thin black shirt isn't much of a barrier between us. The silkiness of the fabric feels slick against my skin. He grunts as my shuffling makes his balance falter.

"Elodie, it's all right. I've got you." He lets out a short laugh.

I still and peek up at his face. My arms are tightly wrapped around his neck and his azure eyes are fixed intently on mine, calm. They are so tranquil. "How did you know I was going to jump?" I rasp.

His white hair flutters against my cheek. Our hair mixes in black and white waves. His ebony horns are twisted and long, more texture on them than I can possibly fathom.

He smirks. "I've been watching you since I saw your scene in the square earlier. What does that Cypress want with you anyway?" He tilts his head at my collar. Kastian reaches to touch the ancient oak around my neck but I flinch as his hand comes close and he stops. An expression I don't recognize crosses his face. "And why do you have the Vernovian Thorn?" I'm as confused as he is on that one.

I try to form straight sentences. "I, um . . . well, I followed Wren from my home . . . into the forest. I don't know what he wants with me." My fingers reach for my collar. "I don't know why he put this on me either," I admit.

Kastian gives me a crooked glance and says nothing for a few moments. "Well, where would you like me to take you? You were running away, right?" he finally mutters.

I don't trust Wren and I definitely don't trust this bird-angel-man either.

"I just need to get to the edge of that field over there." I point down to the valleys that look like the ones Murph took us through. Kastian obliges and his massive wings flap heavily. Then he tucks them and we glide quickly to the ground, more so than I like. I let out a sharp squeal in his chest and I swear I hear him laugh.

He evens out as we near the surface of the green waves below. The four moons bless him with a light meant for only him. It's beautiful. *He* is beautiful. The arches of the great trees make my heart thrum. Stars are embedded as their leaves in the vast universe above.

He sets me down gently on my feet and I gaze into his stormy eyes as he takes a step back. My blood feels thick. I wouldn't mind if we were to meet again. "Thank you . . . for helping me back there." My hand finds the back of my head in an embarrassed rub.

Kastian folds his arms and keeps an even expression. His wings relax behind him and touch the ground. "Would you like some company back home?" he offers. I bite my lip. He's helpful and doesn't seem to be trying to keep me here. But what if he just wants to know where I live? He could try to entrap me as Wren did. I clench my fists and let out a sigh.

He tilts his head once more and smiles at me. "I get it. Be safe, Elodie." He brushes my cheek and then swoops off without another word. The wind of his wings pushes me back a step and by the time I look back up, he is gone. His ebony and golden feathered wings are nowhere in the sky.

My hand finds my cheek and I rub the spot he did, finding myself taken with him. Damn these beautiful men and their way of making me lose my wits. I quickly remind myself why I'm out here in the first place and shake my head.

I start in the direction that I think will take me home and battle with my thoughts. Maybe I should've let him guide me home. It would've been better than walking all this way alone. My eyes trail across the landscape. The forest ahead is quiet, darker than the rest of this world. This has to be the way back home. It looks unmagical and simple as it stretches further toward what I hope is Bresian, the path between. It's just like me and my life back at home—unmagical and simple. Will Mom be waiting for me? A pang of guilt tears at my skin. She must be so worried. I've been gone for a whole day and night now. I pick up the pace. The tall, moon-washed grasses wave across my ankles.

The forest is gloomy, much like mine on the other side. The sway of the grass reminds me of the trails Margo and I would venture out to during the midnight hours. We were never able to brave the forest too far in the dark—well, *I* wasn't. Margo would often keep the pace and look back at me as if trying to coax me further. Her brown eyes were calm and steady, just visible with the trickles of moonlight that dappled her fur.

These are memories I will never forget. Even now, I graze the forest's edge with my eyes in search of her waiting, but I don't see anything. There's only a stir in the breeze and a soft hum of the branches above.

A flash of red blurs my thoughts and the cold, painful feeling squeezes my chest again. Staggering whimpers fill my ears and I freeze. No—no, don't think about it. I shake my head to push away the panic rising up the back of my throat. I inhale deeply and smooth my hair in an attempt to comfort myself.

No matter how often I tell myself to let the horrors of that night go, the feelings creep up my spine if I think of her too much. It's why I made the rule. Once I cross the line, the frame of my shed, I can't think of her. Not in that way.

Never again.

I finally reach the start of the trees after what seems like hours of walking and cursing at my feet for hurting so bad. I lean against the trunk of a great ponderosa to let my legs take the rest they yearn for. I breathe in deeply, taking in the crispness of the evening air. Dew settles on the tips of grass and the scent of it fills me.

I glance back towards the four moons and the stunning arched trees that pillar this world, the sky bending to their will as if the universe is that heavy of a weight. A weak smile brims my lips. The taste of it is sweet —bittersweet. My eyes search the fields below one last time, to see the beauty once more before returning to my simple, plain, depressing realm. But I don't find beauty or shimmering fields of glory.

No.

I find something that makes gooseflesh trickle up my arms and down my spine.

Murph is bounding towards me, charging with a fierceness about him. He's no longer the sweet creature that roamed the village with us yesterday. He is a vicious Pine

Hollow of this realm. One with shadows splitting at his feet and rippling through the fields. And atop his black, bristling fur is his rider.

A wrathful and shadow-cast male.

Wren.

4

My heart pounds as I crash through the underbrush. Greens, yellows, and turquoise flash by me in blurs. My breath stings with each desperate gasp and I've lost all sense of direction. Was I headed this way? No—that way. *Shit.* My feet carry me swiftly despite my whirling mind. They aren't confused like my brain is, thank the gods.

Each second that passes—every godsdamn second— brings Murph closer. I can feel the ground beneath my feet tremble with each leap he makes, the pounding of his strong paws gaining on me. No matter how many turns I make and trees I pivot around to try and shake them, they are just moments behind.

"Elodie!" Wren's voice is deep, filled with a fiery rage.

If I never hear my name shouted with such disdain ever

again it will be too soon. What does he want with me? Why can't I just go home? It's so close. Nearly there.

I trip over a large root that sends me face-first into lush moss. My teeth graze a mouthful of it but my hands are quick to push me up. I spit out the moss and wrinkle my nose at the earthy taste that is left residing on my tongue. Grains of sand wedge into the crevices of my molars and make loud crunches as I clench my teeth at the approaching Pine Hollow. I press myself to the ground and hold my breath.

Murph glides over me. His shadows are cold as they wisp over my body. He doesn't see me. I shoot back up, but his nose tips him off that he blew past me. I can hear his claws burrow deep into the forest floor and he stops on a dime, angling toward me swiftly.

"Shit!" I hiss under my breath and throw my body back into a surging sprint. *I can make it. I can make it.*

"Elodie!" Wren snarls. He dismounts Murph with a swish of his sage cloak and pursues me on foot. His black boots clash heavily on the ground, sending waves of fear reverberating through my bones.

I tumble a few times but roll and force myself to keep moving. I'm regretting every step, wishing I had asked Kastian to stay. Wren's footsteps inch closer with each horrible breath.

Then I see it. I see the path, Bresian. It looks like a sheer curtain, as if hung in the forest for some silly prank. But I can see it against the moonlight. The waves in the silk call to me.

A smile spreads across my lips and I almost whimper with the joy of reaching the crossing.

Home . . . I want to be home.

I hear Wren leap behind me as I manage to grasp one of my hands on the tear in the sheer fabric of our worlds. My hand thrums with a strange magic that forms the mystical wall. *I'm going to make it. I'm here.* Wren's cold hands clench my ankles tightly and send me into the earth, hard enough that it knocks the breath from my body and my wrists crack with the weight of catching me. Before I can struggle back to my feet, Wren is already on top of me. He pins my legs with his and he isn't gentle. His strong arms thrust my shoulders into the ground, putting more pressure on my already throbbing wrists.

I wince and let out an agonizing cry. So close . . . I'm right here. My eyes blur with tears that threaten from the pain.

I try to shake him off but he has me completely restrained. He doesn't say anything, just keeps me against the earth until I still. My body trembles underneath him and I know he notices it. He leans forward after a few silent minutes, pressing his chest against my back heavily. I let out another painful groan as my wrists burrow further into the dirt and twist. He brings his mouth to my ear, his breath hot against my skin as he whispers, "Did you think I wouldn't catch you? Do you have any idea who you're running from?" My bones shiver under him and my muscles scream at me to get away.

But I can't. I can tell he's waiting for a response but I

won't give it to him. He already has me and there's nothing else I can do except keep my mind out of his reach. I turn to glare at him. His eyes are dark ambers under the shade of his hair. He returns a glare filled with as much fury as my own.

I let my head rest on the ground. The coolness feels nice on my cheeks. My heart gradually slows and I let my limbs relax. Wren waits a few more minutes to make sure that the fight is really out of me.

It is—I've never felt more exhausted in my life. Especially after hitting the ground endless times in the chase. Now that I've stopped running, my adrenaline has passed and I can feel the damage I've done to my feeble body. My legs ache and pulse with raw pain. My throat burns and the trembling won't stop. Finally, he gives a low sigh, as if *I'm* the one that threatens *his* freedom.

"Please . . . no more, Elodie. I'm tired. You're tired." He eases his weight off my back. "Give me your wrists."

I don't. I'm not going to make this easy for him in any way, shape, or form. I just continue to lie staring off into the forest. I swear I see a shadow shift behind a tree, but after a few moments of stillness I think maybe it's just my mind playing tricks on me.

"I said give me your wrists," he growls into my neck.

I don't move.

He growls again and rises enough on his knees to flip me over on my back to face him. His clothes are covered in debris. Pine needles, moss, and dirt are smeared across his clothes and his beautiful, innocent sage cloak is ripped and

54

tattered. I bite back a smile at how disheveled he looks. He deserves it. I'm sure I don't look much better. His eyes narrow at me but he doesn't bother talking. He clenches my wrists tightly and I squeak as pain shoots through my arms and deep into my marrow.

"Sit still and it will hurt less," he mutters, his eyes holding less fury than before. I slacken my arms, detesting the thought of being *submissive,* but what the fuck am I supposed to do? He caught me. Again. In all my stupidity.

Why didn't I ask Kastian to help me? I could have been home already, tucked in after apologizing to my parents. They must be so, so worried. My heart sinks at the thought of how many hours they must have combed through the forest looking for me. As if losing Aunt Maggie wasn't hard enough, now they've lost me too.

My breath hitches as he ties a rope made of golden vines across my bruised wrists. They ache and I pray that they aren't broken. I can't understand his cruelty. He seemed so kind when I met him, so filled with whimsy. I loved our day in the village. I should've known he lured me here. He was too . . . *perfect.* And I was too hopeful.

"Stop looking at me like that."

I continue to glare at him anyway, boring hate that I hope he feels into his soul. "Why . . . Tell me why," I mutter quietly. I bite my cheek as punishment for even speaking to him.

He sighs and moves off of me, tying my feet together now. "I'm the Commander of the High Court and Intake. I don't want to hurt you, Elodie, you can trust me . . . but you have to stop trying to escape."

I blurt a disgusted laugh at him. "You expect me to trust *you*? I don't care who you are! You can be the King of this godsforsaken realm and I still won't care. Just . . . let me go home," I snap at him, and then say softer, "Please." I decide to swallow my pride. It sucks and I feel like a fool, but if pleading will work then I'll try anything. He pauses as if the words reach him, but after a few moments I feel him shake sense back into his head.

He finishes tying my ankles and whistles for Murph. He doesn't respond. I'm not worth the wasted breath. My mind races at the thought of what's to become of me. A feast for all the mystical beings? Or maybe a hunt? They seem awfully good at hunting people and luring them in as I was.

Wren hoists me on Murph's back. I refuse to meet the beast's eyes. He has betrayed me too, Pine Hollow or not. Wren mounts and nudges himself behind me. My legs are off to the side and he wraps his arms around my midsection to keep me secure. Then we are on our way.

My tendons ache. My feet ache. My soul aches.

I'm weary from the night, from the rage and injustice that burns in my heart. I let myself lean against him as we ride back. I don't bother looking at the beautiful sights on the way back to that cottage. This place won't sparkle the same now that it's my prison—possibly my grave. So I let my head rest heavily against Wren's shoulder. He smells of moss and pine, deep woodlands and musk.

I glance up at him. His dark eyes are focused ahead. He must notice, because he looks down to check on me. I don't flinch. I refuse to look away. I want him to feel the guilt of keeping me from returning home. His eyes trail over my wrists that still sting and then back to meet my gaze. "I'm sorry," he mumbles.

I close my eyes as a response and let him soak in his conscience as I dip into a dizzying sleep.

5

T he next morning I wake up in his bed. To my surprise, he's in it too. It's still dark outside but I can make out his figure in the dim light. I clench my teeth and seethe as I rub my wrists. They pulse with pain at my touch, making me wince. Hopefully, the bruises will heal quickly. It's looking more like I'll have to fight my way out.

I lay my head back on the pillow and gaze at the ceiling. In my void of thoughts, I feel a tug at my neck. I glance over to Wren and his eyes are on me. I narrow my gaze and let my eyes find his hands. He is holding a *leash*. One of golden thread and white slips of leaves and thorns. I sit up a bit, and lo and behold, the leash leads to my collar.

Disgusting. Vile. Monster.

"Are you seriously treating me like a dog?" I snarl at him,

making no motions to move as my body screams at me in agony.

His expression remains empty. "Stop running away like one," he retorts. My jaw tightens and I lie back down. I am completely and utterly stuck here.

"Are you going to kill me?" I might as well ask. I'm at the leash level of a prisoner now.

A small snort. "What? Of course not."

"Then why?"

"I told you, you have to trust me. I have orders that I need to follow," he murmurs sleepily. "We will head to Nesbrim at dawn. For now, get some rest." I exhale a simmering breath. *Do I have to trust him?* I don't have to do anything and he'd be smart not to forget it.

I must have been more tired than I thought because when I wake up again Wren is standing at my bedside ready to go. Leash in hand. I give him a long, hard glare and he just tugs at the golden rope. My neck jerks forward and I am out of bed.

Once dressed and fed we are already on Murph's back bounding through the small village. Marley bid Wren a touching farewell and gave me a kiss on the cheek too. I made sure he didn't see how much pain I was in, or my fear. He shouldn't remember me that way, and I do hope we'll meet again someday. It's obvious how much he adores Wren. It makes me almost forget how much disdain I hold for the Cypress.

Almost.

The vines and oak trees sway in the breeze. On the far

side of the village, each cottage is unique with different colored bricks—reds, browns, beige. Birds and butterflies fight for space on the leaves and flowers that cling to the walls. Lilac and honey fill the air, making my senses fill with their warmth. It's difficult to stay brooding with such wonder and bliss surrounding us. It makes it less shameful to smile too, knowing that Wren can't see my face with me sitting in front of him. Then it hits me—I still don't know the name of this endearing place.

It takes nearly everything in me to make myself ask, but I somehow find the words. "What's the name of this village?"

Wren's chest is tight against my back, arms wrapped in front of me and clenched around Murph's scruff to hold me in place. I'm lucky I didn't get the ankle ties today. Not even the Pine Hollow requires a collar and leash, yet here I am. He doesn't respond for a few moments and I think he'd rather not tell me. Then he mutters, "Caziel."

Caziel, I repeat in my head, reminiscing on the cafe and the sweet purple berry pie we shared just days ago.

Merchants and villagers sweep their porches and balconies, dusting the air with glitter. It's the most beautiful dust I've ever seen, though I'm curious as to what it's made out of. The angelic sky creatures swoop well above us and beyond the cloud lines. A part of me yearns for that freedom. Not just from this place—*Tomorrow*—but also from my earthly bonds. To escape everything. Surely at those heights . . . surely I wouldn't feel this emptiness that the loss of Aunt Maggie and Margo left me with.

Murph moves nimbly through the cobbled streets and we come out on the other end of Caziel. I turn my head to get one last glimpse of it. Who knows when, or if, I'll ever see it again. The morning beams hit the buildings perfectly. Each vine that clings to the cottages waves at me as we continue to charge ahead. I can't help but frown. I wish I had more time to explore the streets and meet more villagers.

I wish for a lot of silly things, it seems.

We ride for hours.

I try to keep myself busy by looking at the landscapes and thinking of ways to escape, but one can only look at amazing trees and whimsical creatures in the distance for so long with so many questions piling in their head before they go mad. The worst part is I can't even think of a way to escape. This collar is made of some sort of magical bind and Wren is too fast and witty. Not to mention the traitor, Murph.

"What's in . . . Nes-whatever?" I'd rather have some idle chit-chat than this endless awkwardness. Wren ignores me. I let out a long sigh and lean back heavily to make it harder for him to grip Murph's scruff.

"Hey—stop that," he growls.

"Oh. So you *can* talk?" I snort at him. "I need a break. It's hot. I'm uncomfortable. I have to pee. I—"

"Okay, okay. Just, please . . . stop talking." He tugs Murph and we come to a stop near a bundle of twisted oaks taller than anything in the real world, but I've already been *awed* out of them at this point. You can only see a unicorn so many times before it's just a horse with a fucking horn on its head.

Wren dismounts and reaches a hand to help me. I scoff at his offer and he scowls at me. "Are you always this unbearable?" He rubs his temples.

I jump down and stalk a few feet away into the shade of the ancient oaks. "Only after being leashed like an animal," I snap. Wren rolls his eyes and walks over to a large boulder to rest against.

I glance at him and Murph as I make my way around the trees. They are both looking out towards the direction where I'm guessing *Nes-something* is. The trees are magnificent up close. Smaller emerald vines wrap them thoroughly and sprout small white flowers that practically glow. I brush my hand across the vines, feeling their age and the wealth of the land flow through them. As I turn the corner, I give a final glance at my captors. They're still aloof.

It can't hurt to try. My bare feet are already carrying me towards the thick woods just a few hundred feet away. Did I forget to mention I lost my shoe privileges? But Wren isn't as smart as he thinks. I've trekked worse barefoot. My mom forgot to pack my shoes on our family camping trip last summer and I wasn't about to let my entire weekend be ruined just because my feet weren't wrapped in the safety of a shoe. No. I let my feet develop blisters and cuts on that trip, and since then I've gone barefoot often in the forest.

Who did he think he was dealing with? I'm not a city-dwelling mortal.

Maybe if I can make it to the brush, I'll have a better

chance at escaping. I'm tickled with my deceit and tiptoe swiftly.

"Elodie." Wren sounds annoyed as usual.

I plaster a wry smile on my face as I turn to meet him. "I can't go to the bathroom so close to you." I tip my head towards the woods. "I'll just be a minute." I dance on one foot to make my case more believable. He just furrows his brows further.

"Do you think I'm stupid? Hurry up or you'll have to just hold it."

"No."

"No, what?" He clenches his teeth and runs a hand through his black hair with frustration.

"*No*, I won't go in front of you and no I will *not* hold it." I raise my chin. Honestly, what's he going to do about it? I'll have my way.

Wren stomps over to me and I flinch as he grasps my wrist. "I'm not playing your games, Elodie."

I meet his glare and tear my wrist from his hand. He takes a step back and raises his brow. "Don't touch me, you *vile* snake," I shout at him, making him flinch.

He considers me for a long moment as we size each other up.

"Fine. You have two minutes. Make it quick." He looks me up and down and walks back to the boulder. He snaps his fingers and the leash vanishes into thin air. I can hardly believe he backed down. I weigh my options—try to run now and probably get caught, or make him trust me little by little, and then when he isn't anticipating it, then I'll make my escape.

I relieve myself and return as promised, hands behind my back and chin high. He seems stunned that I returned like a good girl. His eyes are wide with disbelief.

"I have to admit, I was getting ready to chase you down again." He brushes a dark strand of hair, too short to be pulled back in his bun, from his face.

I narrow my gaze at him. "I told you." He stares at me with that untrusting gaze, but I can tell that my plan is working. The shadows in his eyes aren't as dark as they were moments ago.

We ride for the remainder of the day. The sun, surprisingly, doesn't burn skin here as it does in my world. The rays are warm, but it's different. Perhaps the UV rays don't reach this place. My skin is radiant and almost glimmers with energy, like the time my aunt spilled gold glitter on my skin and it took a week and a half to fully wash off. She made fun of me for months. For half a second I think of what it would be like if I were to stay here, but that thought fades quickly. I have to get back home. The idea of my parents worrying themselves ill over me makes my heart ache.

At sunset, we finally reach Nes-something. It's an entire city, or *court* as Wren referred it as. The outer walls extend high into the sky, but the buildings within reach higher. We enter through a large golden gate. A few guards are lazed along the walls drinking what I assume is mead and sharing a laugh. The houses inside are just as cottage-like as the ones in

Caziel. Vines climb the sides of them and even run along the fences. Not many people are on the streets. They must be inside since it's already sundown. The warm glow from their windows makes me curious what their lives are like here.

Murph must know the way because he turns and takes paths that wind us deep into the court. The streets are mazes and I'm already lost before we are three turns in.

"I expect you to behave while we are here in Nesbrim." Wren leans in against my back and says it loud enough to make me understand that he won't tolerate misbehaving. I bite my tongue to keep my mouth in check. I haven't been treated like a child in a long-ass time. *Ah, Nesbrim—that's what it's called.* My long dark hair wisps over my shoulder as the wind picks up at our backs. "Do you understand?" he growls.

I roll my eyes, not that he can see. "Yes. And how should I behave, Sir *Bartholomew*?"

"First, none of your sass. I recommend not talking at all unless you must. Let me do the talking, okay?" He sounds vulnerable, more so than he has all day.

"Fine."

He's satisfied with that answer and leans back. We remain silent until we enter the inner gates.

Marbled pillars that reach at least a few hundred feet up stand on each side of the path. We are on a hill, the only hill within Nesbrim. I can see nearly everything below and beyond the walls. I hate to admit it, but this court truly is beautiful.

Murph lays down to let us off this time. He must be tired after traveling all day. I can't help but feel sorry for him for working so hard for his master, but I'm still peeved because, at the end of the day, he still betrayed me too.

I follow Wren as he leads me toward the large palace. The roof is clad in gold and the outer walls have a glimmering bronze sheen. The path leading to it is made of beige pavers surrounded by teeming greenery between each brick. Lamp-posts on each side of the path light as we walk past them. Dusk is at its peak and the stars above are staring down. I can't be happy about my situation, but at least it's something different. It's something new and distracting. I realize I haven't thought of Margo as much today, and while it is a good thing to actually be following my *one* rule for once, I can't help but feel sad about it. I wouldn't want to be forgotten. Not even for a second.

Wren stops abruptly and I walk right into him. "Hey—don't just stop like that," I grumble as I rub my stumped nose. He doesn't turn around but I can tell that the air has become tense between us.

"Elodie." He takes a deep breath, almost like he feels guilty about bringing me here after all. "I don't know what *she* wants with you." He faces me. His Vernovian Thorn bobs as he takes a gulp. Is that concern in his gaze? "I will try to speak well of you, but just know that *she* will not accept any poor behavior. I guess . . . what I'm trying to say is that she *will* kill you if you aren't careful. So please follow my advice and don't speak unless you have to. You're the first she's requested to see in a long, long time."

"Since?" I dare ask.

"Since . . . well, before I even walked in this realm." Wren's amber eyes meet mine. I suppress a shudder and give a curt nod. I will be on my best behavior then, and not say anything unless necessary. It will only aid in my efforts towards getting Wren to trust me anyway.

"Why does she want to see *me*?"

He studies me with weary eyes. "She wants to determine if you are a descendent of the god she's been in search of."

I furrow my brows with this information. A descendent? Of what god? Why is this lady looking for me?

Wren lifts his hand and barely presses on the enormous door in front of him. A circle appears on the door where he touches it, and it begins to open on its own.

I stare in awe.

The magnificent doors are crusted with golden thorns and ivory statues. The figures on each door are carved beautifully. The ripples in their clothing and expressions are smooth and cathartic. They are reaching desperately for one another. The left side imprisons a male god. He has horns like Kastian's and large wings. He stares longingly at the woman carved on the other side. She is a god as well, clad in a gorgeous fighting robe. Gold flakes have been pressed against the areas of the somber stone where her real clothing must have been shrouded with luxury. She has ears that sit flat like a lamb's and small nub horns that peek through her hair. She wears a crown of claws on her head.

My eyes trail back to the male god. The female's crown is made of claws of his species. Are they fighting? Why do they reach so desperately for one another if they are enemies? They couldn't be more opposed. He appears to be dark and malicious while she is the image of kindness, light itself. I frown as I catch the grief that seems to seep from them. They are always reaching for one another. The artist must have been horribly melancholic. The wounds of the heart are immortal after all.

I steal a few last glances at the doors as we enter the palace before I return my gaze to the back of Wren's head. He lets his dark hair down and translucent leaves shimmer as he walks.

The grand hall is empty. Ceilings arc at the top, traced with paints of gold, green, and sky blue forming swirls and dots, leaves and birds. Such simplistic and beautiful art. It looks like it was painted eons ago, like the slightest breeze could crumble the strokes. I glance ahead of Wren and find that we still have a long walk until we reach the doors at the end of the glimmering corridor.

"Hey, who are the statues on the doors?" I poke his back. His sage cloak is soft against my fingertip but I can feel his hard muscles beneath.

"The two on the front entrance?"

"Have we passed any other statues?"

He glances back at me and narrows his eyes. "The sass

again? Really?" I give him my best snide grin. He rolls his eyes and lets out a sigh. "They are the Rhythm gods of this realm—well, the most important ones, at least. Talia is the God of Rebirth and Life itself. Borvon is the God of Death and Ruin. They were the ancient gods that reigned for centuries—maybe even eons." My eyes widen. I was raised to know of the gods, but I didn't know they really existed, not like this, and looked so human for that matter. "This is the High Court where they ruled and spent most of their time. It's no surprise that their images have been preserved in the very walls."

"Is that who we are going to see?" I nearly choke on my words. Meet the gods? I've just gotten on board with magic and flying people. Sure, my religion believes in them, but actually meeting them? Even creatures with moss balls on their heads and leaves and . . .

Sweat beads down my forehead. I'm going to meet the gods I've prayed to all my life? I instantly feel conscious of all the shade I threw at the God of Death for so many years. *Please tell me Borvon never received my prayers.*

"What? Of course not—Talia died many years ago, and Borvon the year before her." Wren's voice trails off a bit. I wonder if he knew them. But why are we here if not to see them?

"Oh. Well, who are we meeting then?" I have a bad feeling.

He takes a deep inhale. "Her Highness Lady Violet of the High Court."

I poke him in the back again and he flinches this time. "Sounds like you don't like her. Maybe I'll tell on you," I tease him with a purr. Humor is my go-to when I'm scared shitless. Wren sees right through me. His eyes soften.

"You will do no such thing."

We slow as the doors are now before us. I stop behind him, debating if I really should just try to run away again or not. But my leash becomes visible again and Wren has it clutched tightly in his fist. His dark eyes meet mine once more. "Ready?"

"Like I have a fucking choice." I clench my trembling fists.

6

T he doors open and for a moment I lose sense of
where I am. A throne room larger than any I could
ever fathom lies before us, filled with creatures I
find both beautiful and terrifying at the same time. Horns of
every earthbound creature I've ever known—and ones I don't
—swirl and project from many of the heads that now face us. I
see hair of gold, browns, yellows, and white. Wings of the
same colors reside behind many of their backs. Robes of
lavish silks and threads loosely cover the attendants' shoulders. *Gods*, they are all such ethereal beings.

I become all too aware of my appearance, hoping it is
even remotely acceptable. I feel entirely misplaced.

"Wren, they're all looking." I take a hesitant gulp. He
glances at me and straightens his posture. I take the hint and
do the same. He starts walking steadily ahead at a slow and

elegant pace. I try to keep my feet as proper as I can but I'm fucking barefoot and covered in dirt. So I guess I'm just going to be the little mortal in her knit sweater and bare feet. Fucking hell.

Golden ribbons arc down from the ceilings and drape around pillars that flank the grandiose room. White plaster lines the walls and brightens the already illuminated chamber. Ahead are a handful of stairs and an extravagant throne with a beautiful woman sitting, bored, atop it.

We continue to walk forward at the pace Wren has set. Eyes from all creatures follow us heavily. I can feel my breath catching from their stares, but the woman on the throne makes me feel much, much worse with her gaze alone.

I steal a glance at the crowd to my left. I meet a set of lovely amethyst eyes. I don't know why I look specifically at this man. He is staring at me just like the rest of the creatures so it's not like he's special or anything, aside from the fact that he's devilishly attractive.

His body is formed by the gods' themselves. Veins run down his neck and forearms, while his collarbone calls me from beneath his loose-fit robe of ebony silk. His hair is ashy gray brushed with tips of gold. Not blonde, literally gold. I stare much longer than I should and time graciously seems to slow as I pass him. His lips turn upward and I get a glimpse of his teeth, sharp canines and pearly whites. I focus to make sure my lips aren't parted. His wings are gold and feathered thickly like an owl of quality breeding. My father always feels compelled to point them out on our excursions in the woods.

He loves anything that has wings and a beak. It makes sense. He's a zoologist, after all.

The male has thick golden brackets shielding his spine and throat that are shaped like the respective bones beneath. A large ribcage of gold, I'm guessing armor, wraps around his torso.

It takes everything I have to pull my gaze from him, from the stranger in the crowd. He completely made me forget why I'm even here. I shake my head to give myself clarity once more.

"Trust me, you don't want Arulius's attention," Wren mumbles under his breath and I flinch. How long did he watch me admire the handsome male? I flush a bit and try to keep my head down. *Arulius*. Even his name is flawless. I wonder if he is a warrior. He wears armor that I've not seen in this world yet. An image of Kastian emerges from my memory. Arulius has the same build and wings, but they are so different.

So opposite.

Kastian is of night and darkness, ravenlike and lonely like a crow, while Arulius is of the light, iridescent with gold. They share one thing in common. I suppress a lewd thought. They're both beautiful males that don't compare with any back in my realm.

We finally reach the steps beneath the ruling high lady. I practically shudder under her heavy gaze. Wren kneels and I follow his lead. The floor is cool beneath my skin. I didn't realize how weary I've become from traveling all day. Surely even horseback would be easier than Pine Hollow riding. There's no grace with them.

Wren places his right arm over his chest and glances up. "Lady Violet." He draws a sharp breath as she descends gracefully. I fight the urge to look up. I can only hear the taps of her light steps and the pressure of her intense presence. Is this her aura? I've never experienced anything so physically daunting from another's energy. Hers weighs down on my shoulders. "This is the human you've been searching for, my lady. Her name is Elodie." Wren turns his head to me and I meet his dark gaze. His eyes narrow and I pick up that it's time for me to look at her.

Violet's black heels stop inches from my hand that's pressed against the marble floors. The shoes are made of bones, wrapped around the arch of her foot like a rib cage, and the heel itself is a sharp bone. I can only imagine the purpose of such a heel. The hairs on my arms raise with goosebumps. I slowly tilt my head up to meet her.

For all that is holy, she is a goddess as much as the one on the heavenly doors out front. She's the definition of beautiful. Her hair is the universe, black with silvers and purples and blues dusted throughout. Her eyes are red, much like the blood that Margo bled. The nausea of that night floods over me, causing a shudder to run through me, and I feel myself tilting. Wren steadies me while I swallow hard. My lips tingle with numbness and my fingertips too. All my panic attacks seem to start this way. Violet crouches down and I hold my breath. Wren does too. His grip on me tightens, which only makes me more anxious.

"Pleasure to meet you . . . Elodie." Violet's voice is soft and warm, unlike her presence. Her face is a wall of expressionless features. She truly is a ruler—cold, distant, unnecessarily fearsome. I manage a curt nod and don't dare open my mouth. She stands and her crimson dress sends a second wave of nausea through me. I push out the thoughts of Margo. Blood . . . so much blood pulses into my mind. *Don't think about it. Don't think about it.*

Wren stands and pulls me up next to him. I'd much rather he left me on the ground because I can't force myself to look her in the eyes again. I focus on her pale shoulder. That's the best I can do.

Wren clears his throat. "Lady Violet, this human is quite—"

"Wren, I appreciate your efforts, but you needn't plead on her behalf. I've already made up my mind." She regards me and reaches out to grab my arm. It takes everything and more to stop myself from running. I catch my tongue between my teeth and the taste of metal fills my mouth. Her cold fingers slide down my wrist and she digs her nails into my skin. A small cry escapes me. "She will be put to Inxtrelium tomorrow." Her lips curl sinisterly and she releases my arm. I instinctively withdraw and rub the skin where she touched me as if I've been cursed.

"What—Inxtrelium? We never discussed this." Wren's eyes widen with betrayal, his voice cracking. "You said—"

"I know what I said. The dreams have spoken and the court has decided. Now clean her up and make sure she is dressed properly for tomorrow." Violet turns and her galaxy strands glimmer in the space between us. I shiver because I know what she intends for me isn't good. I feel sick. I sense Wren's anxiety peaking beside me and the walls themselves seem to be caving in. Why is he trying so hard to help me? He's the one that brought me here in the first place.

He tries once more. "Please, Violet, reconsider. You can't kill—" He dips his head desperately and gives me a look filled with remorse. I only hear one word, and one word only.

Kill? My flesh chills and the metal tang on my tongue makes me nearly gag.

Violet stops and turns to face him. She takes a cruel step forward and Wren takes a staggered one back. "Don't you *dare* speak against me, Wren." Her sharp voice echoes in the tall room and the audience shuffles uncomfortably. Wren doesn't speak again and dips his head toward her. "Now go." She waves her hand at him and he quickly spins towards the doors we walked in through.

His steps aren't nearly as elegant and careful as when we arrived and I can see beads of sweat rolling down his neck. I tail him out and make eye contact with Arulius once more. He has the same concern in his gaze as Wren.

What is Inxtrelium? What does it have to do with me and why did Wren say *kill?* Maybe I'm being too rash . . . He won't let me die, right? I try to keep my mind clear until I can

A God of Wrath & Lies

ask Wren about it more. I shouldn't just jump to conclusions, but gods, it doesn't sound good.

He remains mute until we are outside. Not just outside, but until we are nearing Murph at the gates to the High Court. He wraps his black strands of hair in a ponytail and leans against Murph's side. The Pine Hollow licks his cheek as though he can sense his stress. I cross my arms and furrow my brow at him.

He lets a deep breath out. "I . . . I didn't want this. She told me you were potentially her successor and that was the reason for her desperation to retrieve you. I never . . . I never imagined this. She fucking lied to me." He glances at me with sunken eyes and runs a heavy hand over his neck.

"What does *Inxtrelium* mean?"

He studies me with warring eyes. "To death."

A pit drops in my gut and my bones shiver. "Well, you're not going to let them kill me, are you? Take me home!"

He doesn't say a fucking thing. I stare at him with bewilderment. The betrayal he feels from Violet is tenfold what I feel from him right now.

He won't even look at me.

I need to escape right fucking *now*! My heart thrashes abrasively against my bones. I glance toward the fields we entered from. He'll catch me in a heartbeat, but I have to try, don't I? I don't want to die. I've seen what it looks like—my aunt's long frown and Margo . . .

I bite my lip and the taste of iron is bitter on my tongue once more.

He clenches his fists and still can't bring himself to look at me. "I'm sorry, Elodie. I . . . I—"

I don't wait for him to finish his sentence. I'm already running, sprinting as fast and hard as I can because I don't want to die. I don't want to go away and not exist. I'm still not even certain whether I'm real, but if I die, I'm really gone. I guess I'll find out if I truly was ever real . . . if Margo was ever real. Tears stream from my eyes and fly off my cheeks as I run down the path and streets below.

Wren lets out a short gasp behind me. He can't possibly be surprised that I'm fleeing to save my own life. *Idiot. Stupid idiot.* I have to get back home. Back to Mom and Dad and . . . and back for myself too. I deserve to live for myself, don't I? Who else will remember Margo in my stead? I crash in the cobblestone streets below and roll a few times before using the momentum to continue my sprint down the nearest alley that looks familiar. It takes a few wrong turns, but I manage to find the gates we entered.

Wren is already closing in on me. I can hear his heavy breaths nearing with each leap I take, so I push my legs harder.

Please, please, please. Carry me faster.

I dare a glance back and his sage cloak has flown off his body. All that remains are his earth-toned clothes underneath. They reveal his muscles and efforts. All his training has proved to be worth it. His eyes tell me he doesn't want this fate for me, but he continues ruthlessly anyway. I let out a small cry of fear and keep running. My mind whirls and my breaths get tighter and sharper. I can't keep this up much longer and I can't outrun him.

What should I do? Should I turn and fight? That seems to be my only option at this point. I search the field frantically for anything I can use as a weapon. Rocks, sticks, weeds. Ah! A bone lies half-buried in the dry dirt ahead. I surge towards it, bowing and spinning as I rip the bone from the earth, facing Wren as the dust I kicked up swirls around us. He comes to an abrupt stop and studies the weapon I now wield.

A scowl forms against his sharp features. "Elodie. Please don't do this." The words get caught in his throat. Good. I hope it hurts—but I hope it hurts more when I stab him.

I bare my teeth at him.

"I won't willingly *die*." I clutch the bone tightly. It's old and jagged at the end that I tore from the ground. Splinters of ivory and brown are pointed at him.

He grinds his teeth and takes a defensive stance, eyeing my bone. "I don't want to hurt you, Elodie."

"Ah, but you already fucking have, Wren." I laugh cynically back.

He circles me and I follow him with the bone. I have zero training and I'm tired, but I think I can fight him off. He is horrible at hiding his emotions. I can tell he is upset and doesn't want to follow his orders. So why does he? Does Violet have that much power here? "Just let me go home, Wren. Let me go home."

He lets a small smile slip. "You can't hurt me, Elodie."

And just like that, all the pity I have for him is gone. I won't hesitate to save myself.

Wren takes a swift step forward and swipes at the bone to try to take it from me. I pull my arm back in time and leap to my right. He pivots on his foot and lunges after me. I manage to raise my knee in time and it meets his chest with a *thud*. I swing hard and bone meets his side. He lets out the breath that I force out of him as I push with all my might to send him backward. I hold tightly to the bone as it tears out of his side, releasing a spew of crimson. He groans in pain as his blood soaks my shirt. I can feel the prickles of my trauma try to rise, but I push down the shiver. I can't lose focus. He topples to his side and coughs a few times. I don't waste a single second. I'm already striding down the hill once more.

I stabbed him. I try to keep my conscience clean but I fight against the voices. *You killed him. He's dying.* No—I steady my mind. I made sure to aim low, away from anything vital.

Murph bounds up beside me and his black fur bristles as he tries to nip at my feet, nearly tripping me. "Murph, no! I don't want to hurt you too. Go back!" I shout and wave my bone at the beast. His ghost leaves lie flat against his fur and he raises his lips in a snarl. I don't blame him for being wrathful towards me. I've possibly mortally wounded his only person.

Am I really going to hurt Murph just for trying to help his owner? He can't possibly understand how wicked the politics are or what Wren is going to let them do to me. Hot tears roll down my face again and Wren is already on my heels once more. I can hear his labored breaths and wince at the pain he must be enduring.

The universe has come for me and there is nothing, *nothing* I can do.

My legs betray me and my knees buckle, sending me to the ground with no mercy. Murph skids through the weeds to a stop and Wren is on top of me before I can even roll over. He presses a firm hand against my spine and my face presses against twigs and dirt. I let out a guttural scream, one an animal releases when they know they're going to die. Wet liquid falls from his side and heats my back. I feel sick.

Haven't we already done this? Except with less at stake?

I let the last of the tears seep into the earth. I tried my best and it wasn't enough. I gave it all I had. At some point, don't we all have to accept defeat? I gaze into the distance. It's dark. Night has long since fallen. The stars are different here and the four moons are all crescents tonight. I let out a heavy breath. I refuse to look at Wren as the hot tears stream from my eyes.

We have no words to say. We've known each other for days but I already know where his allegiance lies. He is the perfect disciple of his Lady of the High Court.

Wren binds my wrists and finally gets off of my back. I have no intention to move. They can kill me right here and I can die lying here gazing at the stars.

"Stand," he commands.

I don't.

He bends down and lifts me by my arms. I wince but refuse to let out a cry of pain. He hoists me over his shoulder and places me on Murph. He groans. The wound in his side pulses and blood trickles onto my leg. Heat spreads as crimson coats my pants, familiar. Why is that sensation so familiar? I try to not focus on it so I face the sky. I glance at him, my face no doubt covered with scrapes and bruises. He meets my gaze and a wave of grief washes over his eyes. I hope the life looks like it's been ripped from me and that he remembers my feeble body for the rest of however long he lives. That *he* signed my death warrant and wrapped me like a gift for the reaper.

He opens his mouth like he's about to say something when a sharp, wet snap slices the silence between us.

Wren croaks as his body cripples before me. Behind him, Kastian tilts his head to the side. His white hair glistens against the rising moon and his deep azure gaze pierces through me.

My heart skips a beat at the sight of him. Did he come to save me? Like I'm some damsel who keeps falling into trouble? At this moment I don't care. I don't care about anything except getting away from Wren. Kastian must see the flicker of desperation in my eyes because he pulls his blade from Wren's back and shoves him off to the side. I watch as Wren's raven hair waves through the air on his way down. He lets out a pain-filled cough as he slams against the earth.

Before he or I can mutter a word, Murph is already whirling on us. His snarl holds a pang of worry for his felled master. Kastian closes the gap between us quickly and wraps his arms around my midsection, lifting me into the sky with him. His ebony wings send a rush of wind beneath us and we are well above the skyline within mere moments.

I gaze down at the Pine Hollow as it circles Wren's body with worry. I can't help but feel bad. I know what they were trying to do and what they would have let Violet do to me, but still, I'm human. I feel empathy for them. I furrow my brows and shut my eyes. When I open them again, I'm met with Kastian's blue gaze and my heart nearly stops.

For a few seconds we just stare at one another. He isn't as serious or arrogant like Wren is, which is refreshing, especially after today. Kastian holds me close and fills me with the scent of sage and ashes. It's such a peculiar smell, but then again, we are in another world from mine. This scent could rightfully be very normal here.

"I could have gotten away, you know," I finally mutter under my breath. I find it harder than I thought it would be to look away from him, but my shame gets the best of me.

He considers me. I can practically see his wheels turning in his head. Am I really that hard to speak to? What's making him so withheld? So . . . careful? "I'm sorry. I just couldn't let him take you again." Kastian lowers his head and bites his lower lip. Just watching him makes my thighs burn. Why are all the males here so handsome? I've had plenty of experience with mortals, but something tells me they all pale in comparison to Kastian, to Arulius, and I hate to even think it, but even Wren.

"Again?" I whisper with suspicion. "You saw him take me the first time?" I hold in the scowl that I want to make. Now that I think of it, I did see a shadow in the forest moments after Wren caught me. I thought it was my imagination, but Kastian just proved that I was right.

He nods curtly and glances at me with remorse. "I didn't want to be a bother, but I couldn't stop thinking about you. So, I followed you today and watched from afar." He furrows his brows and clutches me a little tighter. "I heard what Violet said tonight in the High Court. I'm not going to let *Wren the Wretched* let her *highness* slaughter you like a grobblestot." My bones prickle with ice at his words.

Slaughter. Wren the Wretched? Grobblestot? I'm assuming the latter is equivalent to a *pig* in my world. What have I blindly walked into . . . Why do I still want to trust there's a small amount of good left in Wren? Maybe it's the pain I see in his eyes. I swallow the lump that's been sitting in my throat.

"Why did you help me?" I stammer. "Not that I'm not grateful, but you hardly know me. So . . . why?" I hold his gaze and can see the struggle he tangles with as he tries to form the words.

"I don't know," he whispers breathlessly, and then louder, "I had this feeling when we met. A connection. I'm just . . . so drawn to you." He manages a weak smile.

I give him one back. "Oh. Is it because I am human?" It makes sense. I'm sure they don't get many humans in this world, right? Of course he would be interested in me. It's not like I'm unfathomably beautiful or anything, not even close when compared to all the gorgeous sky women I've seen flying about.

So why do I feel a little disappointed? I let a small sigh out. "What now? I'm assuming if I try to head back to Bresian, Wren will just catch me."

Kastian looks towards the west sky. "I can bring you to my court if you'd like. It is safe there from Violet and her minions. At least until we come up with a plan." He glances down at Murph and Wren. I follow his gaze. Hopefully Wren is okay, but the motherfucker had it coming. Whatever earned him the name *Wren the Wretched* has to have been something truly awful.

I nod. "I think that would be best for now. Thank you again, you know, for helping me." Heat forms in my cheeks as he begins gliding west and wraps his arms around my lower back and behind my neck. His ebony wings tipped in gold flutter against the breeze softly. Cool air brushes my skin as we pass through the night sky. His hands are strong but touch me so gently. I lean into his chest and inhale. Lovely, lonely Kastian. He smells of sage. I only have twenty-three candles and a box of the dry plants to fumigate my shed—not an obsession at all.

I can hear the smile in his voice. "Of course . . . You know, I detest the cruelty of these lands." He hesitates. "They have shown me no kindness either." His words are heavy, making my heart sink a bit. He shows signs of someone who's been injured deeply. Wounds that cannot be seen on the outside but only reveal themselves in the weight of words and in the shadows cast across a gaze. I wonder what heartless creature could have inflicted them on such an innocent soul as his.

We fly for hours. I doze off a bit at first, but when I wake I have a million questions that reawaken with my rested mind.

I press him for information on Nesbrim and Violet. If I'm to survive and return home, then I need to know fully what I'm dealing with. He fills me in on the order of the courts and the rule of Violet.

She has ruled for over eight hundred years. Naturally, I gasp at that—I wasn't aware of the lifespans of the creatures here. When Wren mentioned the gods Talia and Borvon, I figured only *they* lived such long lives. I was foolish to think that.

I learn that Violet has a deep hatred for all of Tomorrow, the natural rules of the realm, and the order of the Rhythm. Her reign has been solely focused on breaking the very foundations of this world, ruining old scripts and stopping the academics of the ancient gods and deities. Whatever her reasoning be, Kastian says that her passion has been unrelenting and bloody. Any descendants of the gods or suspected descendants are quickly thwarted and cast away.

Is that how the gods of death and life met their demise?

Wren said that Violet believes me to be one of these descendants. His story reminds me of the ones my mother would tell me about gods and their senseless battles, though I never expected them to be this intricate. I stop at the thought. No. No—I followed Wren of my own free will. He lured me, sure. But I stepped over late that night and now I'm paying the price of curiosity.

Dawn breaks the sky as a dark land stretching as far as the eye can see comes into view. The trees are charred, with blackened bark, and what used to be a forest floor is plagued with ash. The ash is as deep as a fresh blanket of snow. Not a single footstep of some unfortunate creature even stirs the ground here. No animals breathe below and only a vast expanse of bones and dust lay beneath us. A shiver runs up my arm and I know Kastian notices, as he's already sighing.

"There's a reason they don't dare follow me to my court," he mutters. "Everything here is dead."

7

K astian's court may be gloomy from the lack of life, but I find myself to rather enjoy it. At first it's a little daunting, but the silence of this place brings me peace. Maybe it's because I feel connected to Margo here, so close to death and the lands that harbor it.

His estate is an ivory howlite castle that rises from the earth itself. It nearly glows from the light cast from the moons above. I catch myself holding my breath as we descend onto the marvelous white steps in front of enormous black doors at the entrance.

All I can do is stare. At the jagged stone walls, the black bark of dead trees that line the estate, and Kastian's beautiful dark wings against the night sky. He smiles with a bit of hope in his eyes.

"You don't hate it?" The vulnerability in his deep voice

makes my heart ache.

I shake my head. "No, it's quite lovely." I run my finger-tips up along the stair railing. The curves and twists in the stone remind me of the roots of the dead oak tree Margo led me to last year. We visited that ancient spot more times than I could count that summer. She had an odd affinity for the tree. Oftentimes my mom would tag along and we'd all three spend evenings reading under the looming branches. I smile at the fond memories.

"You are the first person to say that." Kastian rubs the back of his neck, cheeks reddening as his azure eyes gaze at my skin. My heart lurches for him, but I try to stay composed while I wait for him at the top of the stairs. He smirks and lifts his hand to his lips. He gusts a small breath of wind into his palm and sends black glittering dust against the doors. They open without his touch, wringing out a small gasp from me. He takes a steady step forward and reaches a hand back for me, his olive skin radiant in the light. I clench a hand over my chest in hesitation but something in my heart urges me forward. His hand gleams in the moonlight and when I slide my palm into his it fits perfectly. Kastian gives it a light squeeze and I hold my breath as I follow him into the foyer.

The step over the threshold turns the worn jagged walls from old and tattered looking to new and lavish. I blink twice to make sure I am seeing things right. Kastian lets out a low laugh, one that immediately draws my lips up in response to the delightful sound. He leans against the far wall close to the hallway ahead.

"You are seeing right. My court is warded so it appears all dreary like the rest of these dying lands. Did you think I would live in such a worn-down estate?" His voice is cheery and he thankfully finds amusement in my awe.

"This . . . this is amazing. Really." I spin slowly as I allow my eyes to take in everything. An enormous dining hall lies to the left. Curtains of black hang from at least twenty feet up. The table extends from wall to wall and could easily seat fifty people. To the right is an alluring sunroom, so alluring that I have to pinch my leg to make sure this is real. I gape at the greenery in the windows and vines that scale the three-story conservatory. "I—I . . ." I have to pause and take a gulp, lest I continue to stutter like an idiot. "I love it."

He just smiles and nods towards the conservatory. "It's been my project for the last few years."

Something I've been wondering is how long the creatures here live. Kastian doesn't mind when I ask things. He wouldn't shut it down as Wren would. I walk over to him and look up to meet his eyes.

"Can I ask how old you are?"

He studies my face and mutters, "I'm only twenty-two years old." He sees the curiosity behind my gaze and contin- ues, "Though in Tomorrow we do live rather long lives. Much longer than those of humans. We are immortal, even, if we are never extinguished." I lift a hand to my lips. The gods on the doors of the high court must have been very old. Violet and Wren too. What about Pine Hollows? Do all creatures in this realm live extensively long lives?

"I was hoping you were like, a thousand years old or something," I finally blurt out. He covers his mouth as he hides a laugh.

"You'd rather I be old and grumpy?"

I wink at him. "No, definitely not. But you'd be *so* wise." We share a quiet laugh. It seems it's just the two of us in this enormous manor. Our voices carry high into the second story rafters with vast emptiness. *Does he live here alone?* I ponder, and then a worse thought comes to mind.

Has he always lived here alone?

Kastian shows me the remainder of his castle. The white floors and black drapes flow throughout the home except for the third story. The floors transition into black tiles that are shaped like circles and stars. It's almost as if they are trying to lead me somewhere with their beauty. But when I ask Kastian, he just says I won't want to see the entirety of the third floor, and he seems distant about it so I let it go. I'll have to ask later. There is a time and place for everything, after all.

My room and his chamber reside on the second floor. There are plenty of additional rooms but they are all empty. There's no sign of any living creature in this barren castle except the two of us. My heart lurches again as I think of him being here in solitude for gods know how long.

As we reach my door, I build up the courage to ask. "Kastian, does anyone else live here with you?" He shakes his head and gazes into the long hall, distant with memories. I reach out my hand and touch his shoulder. He flinches under my fingertips. "Why?" It must be a touchy subject, of course.

Why wouldn't it be? I would be vulnerable too if I lived alone in this castle of dread.

He takes a long, somber breath. "Anything or anyone who stays here too long dies. Well . . . anything except me." He shrugs and says it quickly, rip-the-Band-Aid-off type of way.

I can't find words. I should say something comforting, or *I'm sorry,* but instead I say nothing, and I hate myself for it. Anything—why can't I mutter anything? I settle for lowering my head so as not to throw too much pity his way.

His white hair flicks as he combs his fingers through his bangs, making them bristle gently over his black horns. "I'll see you in the morning. If you need anything, I'll just be down the hall." He doesn't look back as he makes his way toward his chamber.

"Kastian?"

He stops, his raven-like wings trailing on the tiles. "Yeah?"

"What happens when creatures die in Tomorrow?"

Kastian doesn't move for a few long seconds. When he finally glances at me from over his shoulder, I'm met with cold glaciers. His eyes are filled with so much pain and weariness.

"Tomorrow," he mutters, walking towards his chamber.

"Tomorrow . . ." I whisper to myself, knowing I'll have a restless day.

I feel a pit sink into my heart, one of fear and sorrow. What kills the people who stay here too long? I'm reminded of the blackened forest and bones littered throughout the land. Kastian's court must be cursed, but I don't let myself think about it too long. I try to settle into my new temporary room but a horrible thought keeps me up for the remainder of the day as I try to find rest.

Wren is searching for me. I can feel it in my marrow.

He survived his wound and I have a feeling Violet will kill him if he doesn't return with me. I can't help but feel a small shred of pity for him, but I will not be sacrificing myself for him, or *anyone* here, for that matter.

I roll in the soft sheets and take a deep breath in. The fabric smells of sage and ash, much like Kastian's scent. I nuzzle myself into them until my senses are completely filled with him. I eventually find enough peace to fall asleep, and when I finally wake up the sun is up and beams of sunlight warm my cheeks. I blink sleep-filled tears from my eyes as I let out a yawn and roll to my back. The fluffy comforter is plush and holds me securely as I gaze at the ceiling. Images of flying gods are painted on the arcs of the rafters above me. I push myself up to my elbow to get a closer look. They are all beautiful and clad in gold and ivory, all except one—and it looks too similar to Kastian to not be him. Even the horns are similar, each tipped with two points at the end, and they contrast against the white locks of hair. He is a dark owl amongst the light. His feathers have no place with them.

I reach my hand to the ceiling. I can feel his loneliness. I know what it's like to be an outcast, alone and surrounded by death and sorrow. My aunt's long frown and Margo's unmoving body fill the spaces of my mind. I wipe a tear that makes its way down my cheek. Today I'll learn more about the creatures of this world. If I'm to return home, I'll need Kastian and his knowledge of this world. I bite down on my lip and I try to distance the feelings that are building within the walls of my heart. I want to be close with Kastian. I can't explain it, but something is pulling me towards him. Maybe it's our similarities in being outcasts, or perhaps it's my odd attraction to his beastly features.

I shake my head. *Don't even think about it, Elodie.*

I manage to find my way to the dining room off the foyer's left side and find Kastian already seated with a plate filled with bread and fruits in front of him. There's another plate set off to his right side for me. I walk casually over to the chair and pull it out. He lifts his head from the book he has in his hands and smiles warmly at me. My breath catches in my throat as I try to say good morning. He is more stunning in the early hours of the morning before he is dressed and washed. Kastian's white hair is messy and ruffled against the roots of his black horns. His blue eyes are still drunk with dreams and he sits rather elegantly in his ash-colored robe. I tense as my eyes trail down below the table and find that he isn't wearing pants beneath his cover.

"Good morning, Elodie," he chirps and takes a sip of tea. He motions for me to sit, as I have absentmindedly forgotten that I was about to sit down for breakfast. I take a sip of air and sit down. *Foolish, foolish woman,* I scold myself.

"Good morning." I beam at him. Words can't explain how grateful I am for this, for him bringing me somewhere safe and treating me with such . . . normality. I know he will help me return home because he's already more than proved himself. I feel at ease here, though I should probably return home before my parents call the police—if they haven't already.

"What are you reading?" I mutter as I skip tearing the bread and just take a huge bite that I instantly regret. He watches me with a pleasant grin.

"It's a book written long ago by the God of Memories. He often writes stories of his time on the human side. They are somber stories, though. I don't think you'd like them." He passes a tray of butter and sets it between our plates. I nod thoughtfully. There is a god for everything here. My brain flips to something he said last night, that he felt a connection between us and he was curious about me. I wonder if he means it, because I feel it too.

"There's so much that I never knew existed." I slather my next bite of bread with butter before shoving it in my mouth. The savory flavors bloom on my taste buds. Everything is better here—the men, the food, the sky. He sets his elbow against the table and lets a small laugh slip out. We eat and have a casual chit-chat about ourselves, nothing too deep, but I do learn that he likes flying at night and doesn't mind his solitude. We chat until I have nothing left but tea to sip on. I bring my knees up to my chest in the large chair and face him as I cozy in. "So, I'm curious—what is this place? What are you?"

Kastian takes a swig from his mug. "Well, let's start with

this place. You already know it's called Tomorrow." I nod. "But I doubt you know what this world is exactly. It's a bit difficult to explain, but basically it is the realm of gods and deities—creatures of the afterlife and their souls, but probably not to your normal understanding of them."

I furrow my brow and clutch my mug tightly, feeling foolish for every time I thought Old Man Bruno was a mad man. I reminisce about his tellings of the creatures he believed danced at dusk. I realize how close our worlds truly are. "Can you explain more?"

"Well, we have gods, spirits, and creatures of many things. We work together in a collective to keep the realms moving and thriving. The Rhythm." His tone turns dark. "However, Violet has been trying, and succeeding, to destroy our order. She began with the libraries centuries ago that held the ancient texts, and for the last few hundred years without the knowledge to pass along to the new gods, there has been utter chaos. Gods are born with no known purpose. The rituals that were once taught and guided are now unknown. Forests and entire sea societies have fallen and continue to collapse." I think of my forest back at home, the ponderosas and their blackening bark, the dwindling forest animals. Is it all connected?

He takes a deep breath, looking at me with heaviness in his gaze. "I was born with no purpose. Sent to live here in lands that no one dares step foot in. I've tried to find my meaning—I even begged Violet to guide me, to give me just one small hint as to who I am, but to no avail. She refuses to have the order restored. Even she has no idea which gods are who anymore."

How horrible. Kastian was sent here to live in exile for his entire existence? I clench my teeth and force my rage down. "Why is she so upset with the order? Why did she send you here to live by yourself?"

"She didn't send me to live by myself." I raise a brow. "All my other companions that were banished here with me . . . perished long ago. The land rejected their bodies and their bones rest where I buried them. It seems like just yesterday." He trails off, staring into his mug and frowning with nostalgia brimming his gaze.

I frown. That's way worse than being sent to live here alone. Much, much worse.

"You asked me last night what happens when creatures die here. Second death is permanent. There's no coming back, at least not anymore. The God of Dawn, or you probably know her as Life, departed a long time ago."

I gasp and think of how we nearly ended Wren. Fucking hell, I didn't want to permanently kill him! A little warning would have been nice. "Thanks for not offing Wren, then."

"I can tell you find the good in him. I see it too. That is the only reason I granted him mercy." I let out a sigh and smile wearily. Kastian is too kind for his own good. I really adore that about him.

He considers what to say next for a long moment. "As for Violet, there are a few different stories of her rage. I'll tell you the one I believe to be the closest to the truth." He sets his mug down and leans back in his chair, lifting a leg to rest it on his knee. I focus as hard as I can to not look below his chest.

"Violet was once a beautiful and happy god. The God of Ruling. She was born with the power to compel and was burdened with the immense responsibility to lead and sustain the order. Back when she was just a few hundred years old, she met the love of her life, Lucius. Some believe that he wasn't a god, some say he was just a sea spirit of the ocean's shores. A few counts claim that he was a god of great darkness. A god of blood." I shiver as he speaks of Lucius. " They were infatuated, inseparable, and for a long time our realm lived and thrived under her rule." His eyes grow distant as if he can picture it.

My stomach turns. "But?"

He stares into his cup for a few more seconds.

"But then the Goddess of Rebirth entered Nesbrim one day and claimed it was Lucius's time to be reincarnated. She granted him new life and he was reborn on the human side of Bresian. Violet begged to be returned with him, to live a mortal life alongside Lucius." Kastian furrows his brow. "But the goddess Talia refused her. *It wasn't her time*, she would say. Violet was inconsolable and became enraged with the rhythm of the gods. She had no power to punish Talia as she was one of the few gods who could not be compelled, so she did what she could to dismantle the realm of Tomorrow. If she was to suffer for eternity, all else would too."

He gazes off into the windows behind me. "I don't believe Violet was always evil. I think that she has suffered a loss so great, so unfair, that she lost the part of her that cared for anything else."

I didn't have a lover torn from my arms. But I've had my aunt and Margo stolen from me . . .

"Though she is evil for her actions, if this continues there will be no more Tomorrow or human realm."

I set my cup down and wrap my arms around my knees. "What a sad story," I whisper. "I . . . I can't say I blame her. I know what it's like to lose someone. If I knew someone intentionally did it and wouldn't let me be with them, I don't know what I would do."

I think for a moment. If someone had taken Margo on purpose and let me suffer intentionally, I would be wrathful. I mull it over. "But I definitely wouldn't take it out on both realms. That's pretty horrible."

Kastian flicks a surprised glance at me. Maybe that was too dark for him, too heavy. "Who did you lose?" His voice is comforting. The azure waves in his eyes fill with a warmth that makes me melt.

I hesitate. Does he want me to unpack all the weight I carry? I study him. He is serious—his eyes are firm and he leans in, intent to hear. That small act is comfort enough for me to open up. I take a short breath. "My aunt and my best friend. My dog . . . Margo." I can hardly get her name out of my mouth. Tears are already welling in my eyes just speaking about both of them. I think of our happy days working on the shed and enjoying the sunshine. But as my thoughts linger, blood and whimpers threaten to cave in my mind again.

Kastian reaches his hand out and sets it on top of mine. His palm is two times mine. I blink the tears from my eyes and try not to meet his gaze, but end up staring deep into his ocean eyes anyway. They are filled with grief and sorrow, so kind and understanding. His warmth radiates from him. Then something else fills his gaze, making my brows knit together with curiosity. An idea?

"Elodie." He stands and his ebony wings slouch to the floor, the gold-tipped feathers grazing against the tiles. I look up at him and quirk a brow, waiting. "You've no doubt met Wren's Pine Hollow?"

I nod. Where is he going with this? His face animates and he lifts me easily from my chair. I'm left breathless as his strong arms wrap around me and he carries me out of the dining room and up the stairs in a hurry.

"Kastian!" My face flushes red and heat fills my cheeks. All that lies between us are my pajamas and his robe. His muscles are taut beneath the thin material and I haven't forgotten about the lack of pants. "What are you doing?" I'm already beginning to smile just from his contagious grin.

"We are going to go to the Hollow Keeper. Elodie, dogs who have died in your realm come to ours as Pine Hollows." His words blur as goosebumps shiver up my arms and an eerie sound screeches. It's so piercing that it reverberates in my temples and through my core.

"What?" My heart skips. Please let this be real. I pinch my arm, still not wanting to believe.

Kastian grips me tighter and his smile bares his sharp canines. "We're going to get Margo back."

I hesitate. "You're not lying, are you?" I feel bad to even ask that, but honestly, I can't believe what he's just said. He gives me a sympathetic look. I almost see hurt behind his gaze, but he hides it well. He sets me on the stairs.

Kastian brushes his palm against my cheek. "I would never lie to you."

I meet his gaze, his bright blue eyes steady. "I just . . . I can't have hope." I take a step back. "I can't hope that she is real again and then have her not be. And why would you help me with this? On a whim—it just seems too good to be true." I break away and look at my intertwined hands, feeling the wall I built so long ago beginning to waver.

He lets out a sigh. "I can tell you've been hurt before, not just with the loss of Margo but with your aunt as well. I'm sure in the department of men too, given Wren . . ." He takes a step toward me, closing the gap between us like it was never there to begin with. He wraps his arms around me and I freeze at his affection and comfort.

No one has tried to comfort me like this before, when my shields are up and I'm borderline insulting him by continuously assuming the worst of him. My heart warms against my ribs. He holds me tightly and my face is pressed to his chest. I can hear his heart flutter as mine does.

"I promise you, Margo is there." He pulls away and sets his hands on my shoulders, which are now trembling. "And I have no plans for the day, so what could be better than setting out to find a dear Pine Hollow?" He grins at me and nudges me to head up the stairs. "Now go get ready. Unless you like traveling in pajamas?" He raises a brow at my attire.

A thought close to my heart tears a hole into my soul. "What about my Aunt Maggie? Do all souls come to Tomorrow?" Goosebumps ripple down my arms just saying the words aloud.

"Yes, Elodie, all souls come here. But people are harder to find in Tomorrow. They arrive with altered appearances sometimes, and the world is vast. Pine Hollows all converge with their respective Keeper."

"But you're saying one day . . ."

He smiles warmly at me, wrenching every last drop of blood from my heart. "One day you may see her again here too."

I smile entirely too warmly, not just with my lips but my heart. My eyes brim with tears and all I can manage is a nod. I hope my smile is enough to tell him how much this means to me, because I can't form the words. If I try, the tears will be let loose. He returns my smile and I know he received my silent message.

Tears stream freely once I shut my door and I bawl for the better part of the ten minutes that I spend getting dressed and ready. Is it okay that I have this chance? This small hope that I can be reunited with Margo? I think of the story of Violet and Lucius. I hurt for her, so deeply and entirely. Could she not have moved on in all this time? My soul trembles at the idea of holding on to such heavy pain for centuries and an undying vengeance for eternity. It's only been three years since my aunt died, and only three months since Margo passed. I can't imagine holding a pain as heavy as this for so long.

Kastian is waiting at the bottom of the steps when I finally contain my tears and dress properly. I found a lavish pair of dark green pants and an auburn overcoat. I didn't expect to find colors here in a place like this, but I was pleasantly surprised. His large wings are stretched out and ready. He turns to me and reaches out a hand for me. I set my hand in his with confidence and let him pick me up once more.

"You look . . . colorful." Kastian smirks.

I narrow my eyes on him. "Well it's better than your all-black attire. As if this place wasn't already depressing enough."

He lets out a chuckle. My gods, this ethereal male is perfect. "I didn't answer all your questions earlier," he mutters. I look at him and raise a brow. I asked so many questions earlier and the news of Margo swamped my brain. "You asked what I am. I'm a Glade Eostrix." My eyes widen. He's the only one I've seen with black wings and horns. The rest have ivory wings and are relatively human looking. Well, besides Arulius. I remember the golden-winged Eostrix from Violet's court. His cold amethyst eyes are not ones I will soon forget.

"So you're not a god?"

"Not that I know of, but none of us know our true places anymore." He steps out the double doors and we are in the air in a matter of seconds. His feathers are soundless against the sky. "Are you not a goddess?" he teases.

The corners of my lips turn up. "Who said I wasn't? I'm dramatic and melancholic, you know. Seems to fit the requirements."

"Is that a stab at my kind? Well, I guess Violet is pretty dramatic." He laughs, and I can't help but join in as well.

I stare at his features as he focuses on flying. His jawline is sharp and has just enough stubble to show, dark like his eyebrows. Glacier eyes that make me feel the heat in my core while my skin burns with his touch. He's taking me to find Margo, this creature of Tomorrow who owes me nothing. He wants to be close to me and connect with me, but I can't imagine why. I bury my face in his neck and take in the scent of sage that fills me. There's a voice in me that says I want more. I try to silence it, but we can't hide from our hearts, can we.

I smile at the thought—my dark-winged Eostrix . . . my only companion here in Tomorrow.

Is this real?

I'm beginning to think that I am real again. For the first time in months, my eyes feel like they are brimming with life that I once felt long ago. The sunken pit of nothingness is less intense now.

8

We fly for hours. I flood Kastian with questions, and to my delight, he's more than happy to answer. I'm oddly . . . content? I would even go as far as to say happy. In any case, I am very comfortable talking to him. Maybe it's because he's never once made me feel like a nuisance. No one back home would directly tell me that I'm annoying them or odd to be around, but I always feel self-conscious about it. My anxiety would readily win the battle of better judgment. It stirs a question in me—I wonder if he has many people to talk to. He lives utterly alone and hasn't mentioned any living creatures here besides Violet and Wren. I wonder if there is a story there. He obviously knows them, but he seems to spend a great deal of time alone in his Glade. I wonder what he was doing in Caziel that night when I spotted him on the rooftop.

Kastian lands on a hillside for a break as the sun peaks in the center of the sky. It's a bare hill with no trees or shrubs in sight, only tall grasses and weeds. I'm uneasy landing here as I can only worry about Wren hunting us. I glance nervously from side to side before stretching and letting my guard down. Not surprisingly, Kastian notices my unease, and he smiles at me reassuringly.

"There's no need to be worried. I'll protect you if Wren catches up to us." He lets his ebony wings slump to his feet and lies down in the emerald grasses to rest.

I furrow my brows at him. "I don't need to be protected. I can fight him, I just need a weapon." Kastian raises a brow and makes a slight frown.

"I'm sorry, I didn't mean to make you feel like you *need* to be protected. I don't doubt that you're as strong as you are willful. I saw what you did with that serrated bone." He smirks apologetically. I bite my lower lip down to hold it in place. His eyes flick to my lips. I can't keep smiling at him so easily—he might get the wrong idea. *I* might get the wrong idea, because I'm already hoping he wants me too.

"What makes you think he will catch up to us?" I ask more quietly. "How would he even know where we're going?"

Kastian lies on his side and rests his chin on his palm, gazing at me with his azure eyes. "Well, for one, there is the Vernovian Thorn." As he says the words, my fingers lift to my throat. How could I forget that this was here? In the thick of things, it just slipped my mind.

Shit. My collar. My prison that Wren forced upon me.

"The Cypress that presents the Vernovian Thorn will be able to track you anywhere you go. Wren is no doubt on his way here as we speak." He pauses as he probably notices the fear that consumes my eyes. "But I'm a lot stronger than him, and faster." He lets his eyes gaze past me into the fields beyond. That's more than likely the reason he landed us here in the open. So he can be aware of all of our surroundings.

I purse my lips in thought. "Why does Violet think I'm some descendent of a god she's mad at?" We stare at one another. His eyes are a storm of thunder and lightning. Darker blues encase an explosion of brightly lit winter fire, a sky of blues and turquoise. I suddenly become aware of how intently I'm gazing into his eyes and of how he studies me in return. His eyes trail down my figure and snap back to me with a blink. My cheeks are hot. What was I doing again?

"I'm not sure why Violet is so sure about you . . . Have you noticed anything since arriving? Anything that might spark a memory, or perhaps sleeping power?" he mumbles and runs a hand over the side of my arm. I hold my breath. He's too beautiful and touches me too softly. A warmth stirs in my chest and trails down to my lower abdomen.

"A—a memory?" I take a slow breath to steady myself. "No, nothing . . . I'm just a normal person." He smiles easily at me. Does he know how he's making me feel right now with the slow circles he draws on my skin?

"Well, there is something we can try to figure out what

you really are." His hand stops on my arm and he rests his palm against my shoulder.

"What?"

"There is an archive of ancient scripts hidden within a small underground city. Liasium. The God of Memories keeps all the scripts. Not even Violet knows of the place." His gaze is on me but it seems so distant, as if he's looking into someone else's eyes. "Hmm. I don't know why I know that." His brows knit together. "How odd." He brushes his ivory hair from his face and glances carefully up at me. I give him a confused smile. I don't know why he knew that either, but then again, we've just met and I'm already thinking of keeping him.

"Should we stop there first? I'm eager to find Margo, but could there be a way to get this thorn collar off too?" I touch the Vernovian Thorn again. Maybe I can try to pull it off. My finger pricks against one of the barbs, drawing blood on the tip of my finger. I flinch at the sting and stare at the crimson dot that forms.

Kastian softens his gaze. "The only way is by the Cypress himself."

Shit. Well, there goes that idea.

Kastian tenderly wraps his hand around mine. My breath leaves my body and is replaced with an unbearable heat. His hand is so much larger than mine, calloused and scarred from battles unknown to me. Unable to say anything, I watch as he brings his face closer and places my finger into his mouth.

His mouth.

An ache swirls between my thighs and my cheeks burn. His eyes are closed, and his black lashes are delicate against his sun-kissed face. He's so close to me that there's no way he doesn't hear my heart pounding against my chest, throbbing and aching for him.

I clear my throat as his tongue gently caresses my finger. "I—I . . . um, Kastian?" I stammer. His blue eyes open and the way he looks at me . . . Gods, the way he looks at me with my finger between his teeth makes my breath catch. His ebony horns tilt up as he pulls me from his mouth. I'm a little disappointed with myself for saying anything at all. The air wraps a chill against my wet skin.

"Yes?" he rasps and gazes into my soul. This time I can tell he's only seeing me. I bring my hand close to my chest. He smirks as if it wasn't unusual for a beast to do what he just did. "I was healing you. I promise my intentions were not tainted." He swipes his mouth slowly and licks his lips as if I tasted delicious. Fuck. I wish his intentions were tainted like mine.

Now I wish I hadn't said anything. I betrayed myself. Why would I think that he would try to pull anything lewd like that on me? I suck my lips in and bite down on them. But the way he looks at me, I can't be imagining it. I inspect my finger and he's right, it's healed.

"Heh. Sorry Kastian." I dip my head, praying he doesn't see the heat in my face.

He lets out an airy laugh. "I'm the one who should apologize. I should have asked. I just . . . It looked painful and I wanted to take that from you." He sits up and stretches his arms. His wings flex with them and I'm tempted to prick my finger again on "accident".

"Thank you," I manage. He beams at me and nods.

We decide to stop at the village first. It would be beneficial to us if Wren doesn't know our whereabouts, and a small voice rings in my head that he would catch us if we went straight to the Hollow Keeper. I don't tell Kastian that I'm worried because I'd told Wren about Margo too, that he might already know that we will be heading there. I don't want him to get annoyed or try to back out of going to the Hollow Keeper. If anything, us traveling a different direction would throw him off. Right?

Since we've already lost hours of the day flying in a different direction, we have to stop for the evening in the mountains between the glades and Liasium. The trees here are godly sized. Everything here seems to be so. We are at least two hundred feet in the air, and while I understand it's safer up here than on the ground, I still tremble at the idea of sleeping up this high. Not to mention the awful gusts of wind that rattle the branches at this height.

"Do we have to stay up here tonight?" I complain anyway, trembling as I dare to glance down.

Kastian chooses a large branch that we can easily rest on. He presses his back against the trunk and stretches out his legs. His ocean eyes are luminous against the evening sun. "Unfortunately." He waves at me to come closer. I scoot toward him, trying my best to not look down again. "It's safer up here, and if I hear anything we can quickly depart. Pine Hollows cannot climb and it would take Wren a long time to reach us here," he mumbles as he opens his arms and black wings as I approach.

Does he want me to sit next to him? I try to push down the excitement that swells inside me. I've enjoyed men in every way back home. It *has* been a while, maybe I can—*Stop. He's just trying to comfort me and it's cold up here. That's all.* I tame my lewd thoughts and inch closer to him, propping my back against his wing and under his right arm. His ebony feathers drape over me and I'm instantly consumed by warmth. I smile and try my best to remain properly leaned against him.

"Thank you," I murmur.

Kastian nuzzles his head against the top of mine.

My heart starts to pound against my ribs as his hand slides over my stomach and wraps me closer to him. I can't see his face, but the way he delicately touches my skin and the way his wing holds me—I can tell he's smiling too. Why do I feel so drawn to him? It's almost unbearable, like we were created from the same pool of water.

"Elodie?" he whispers, his breath warm against my forehead.

"Yes?" I wrap my hand over his.

He's silent for a few moments and I'm beginning to think he may have fallen asleep. He did fly all day after all. I envy the winged creatures here. To fly so freely and gracefully—

what it must feel like to have the wind between your feathers and the sky at your mercy.

"Even though you're a human . . ." He takes a hesitant breath. "You're quite beautiful." I sip in a breath and hold it as he continues. "You are so unique . . . and sad. Damaged like I am. I can't help but want to be close to you," he murmurs. My heart aches at those words. I want to be close too, because I *am* sad . . . So fucking damaged, as he says. We're so similar in that way. I wonder what his pain is. I summon enough courage to ask.

"I . . . I feel it too." He takes a short breath and I swear I can feel his heart thump through his chest. "You said you're damaged? If it's not too forward, can you tell me that story? Your story?" I press myself into him more, letting my cheek rest on his broad shoulder, taking in his scent and taut chest. He seizes at the question. I instantly regret asking. Guilt tugs within me. "You don't have to—"

"No, it's okay," he breathes. He grips me a little tighter and his thumb starts to rub circles softly against my stomach. "I'm not sure where to begin, so I guess I'll just start from the beginning." He takes a deep breath and—

Chunks of wood splinter into us with a force that knocks the wind out of me.

I let out a shriek from the shock. My body hasn't been impaled, but Kastian—he shielded me from the impact. His hot, slick blood covers my face and all bare parts of my skin. My eyes meet his as we begin to slide off the side of the branch into a free fall toward the world below.

Flurries of impending doom gust through me. Kastian grips me tightly and I manage to see the gruesome wounds that ruined his poor wings. It's horrible. They are embedded with large splinters of wood, some the width of a fence post. The blood gushes from them and floats above us as we continue to fall to our deaths. His eyes are wide. He must sense how bad our situation is, but to my surprise, he smiles weakly at me, eyes promising *it will be okay.*

What just happened? How could Wren have possibly attacked us from so high? My mind whirls, but Kastian's gaze grounds me.

My tears glide up the sides of my face. It's my fault. It's all my fault. I shouldn't have distracted him. Stupid—so fucking stupid. I wrap my arms around him tightly. His heart races just as mine does.

"I'm sorry, Elodie." His voice is barely audible above the rushing wind that whips at us. "I should've been paying more attention."

I shake my head. "No, I'm sorry," I cry. At least we will go together. At least I will be with Margo—*wait.* I won't be. Margo is *here.*

She is here!

I bite my lip. I can't die. I have to figure something out. I quickly turn my head up. Someone attacked us, but who? I narrow my eyes against the darkness. Bright golden wings chase after us from above. As the creature grows closer, I can hear the wind defying its speed, whistling loudly and stinging my ears.

My eyes widen as I recognize the flying beast. His gold armor shimmers against the shadows.

Arulius.

Purple eyes connect to mine as he grabs my sides. I scream, not because I'm afraid, but because I don't want him to take me and leave Kastian to fall to his death. Alone. He's always been alone.

Please.

I cling tightly to Kastian's body. His blue eyes hold the fury of a thousand gods as he recognizes the golden-winged god too.

"You fucking bastard!" Kastian roars. The immensity of his shout sends shivers down my spine. Arulius chuckles and wraps his arms further around me. His gauntlets chill my bare skin across my collarbone. He has me. But why? Why did *he* come? Did Violet send him to help Wren?

"You know what happens if you don't let go, Kastian," he purrs, his lips so close to my ear that I can hear the sincerity in his voice. The malice.

My eyes widen. We are getting closer to the ground and I know what Arulius implies. Kastian's blue gaze softens as he looks at me once more.

No.

"Elodie. It's okay."

Lies—it's *not* okay. We aren't going to be okay. His grip loosens so I clutch him tighter.

"It's okay."

No. No. No.

"Elodie." His eyes plead—he wants me to let go. How could he—I won't—not for anything. Not even for *Margo*. My heart shatters at that thought. Why did I think that? My tears stream freely. He leans forward and nuzzles my nose with his. "It's okay," he says one more time. I shake my head with despair.

No. No, it's not fucking okay.

He smiles weakly and presses against me with his hands. I try to hold on. I really do. I try to hold on as if I can, but against him pushing me away and Arulius pulling, I can't.

My fingers slip from his, and I lose him.

I whirl to Arulius. His purple eyes burn with amusement. I thrash my body. "Let me go! Let me go!" I scream and kick and claw at him.

He opens his wings and the air catches, jerking my head and causing pain to shoot up my neck. He leaves us suspended in the sky as Kastian continues to fall like a gravely wounded bird. I shriek again and flail violently. Arulius growls as he struggles to keep me contained.

It's working. I tilt my head back and meet his gaze. His amethyst eyes widen as it dawns on him what I'm about to do. His neck is covered with gold brackets, but my mouth finds a gap between his Adam's apple and jugular.

I bite down with a force that would shatter my teeth if I had accidentally bit one of those golden plates, but thank the gods I find flesh instead. His shriek erodes the sky. His vibrations tremble within my teeth and I pull back viciously, taking a part of him with me. He releases me with a hiss and I feel the air whistle through me as I fall once more.

I spit out the piece of Arulius's flesh and am overwhelmed with the metallic sting that it leaves in my mouth. I don't have time to focus on that now though. We are nearly to the ground.

"Kastian!" I shriek. He looks up, horror breaking over his features.

"Elodie, what did you do?" he cries. He attempts to open his wings, but when he does blood and wood shoot from them. He groans painfully but keeps them open. I fall quicker than him now, and our hands almost meet as the grass details below become all too clear.

This is it.

I smile deeply as our fingertips connect. A spark of warmth and calmness wash over me.

We are going to die.

I shut my eyes and accept my fate. I accept everything— this moment and everything that ever led up to it. Margo and I, we were never meant to meet again. I try to picture her before . . . before . . . How did she die? My eyes shoot open. *Why can't I remember?*

Blood and crimson, pain in my heart, hushed whimpers echoing around me and someone crying. But what *actually* happened . . .

A rough tug upwards against my ribs cracks the bones within me and I spit blood over my hands. I wrench in pain and feel arms against my center. An awful crunching sound beneath me hollows my heart.

Kastian?

What just happened?

My body is on fire but I manage to look up just enough to see. Arulius has me again. He shoots me a displeased look and casts me off to the side. My body slams against the earth and my breath leaves my body upon impact, even though we were but feet from the ground.

Where's Kastian? I lift my head and agony shreds through me. My arms tremble unforgivingly but I force myself up anyway. It's darker on the ground than it was in the sky, but I make out my dark-winged Eostrix's form. It's mangled and twisted, twitching as the muscles try to desperately figure out what went wrong.

My insides churn. I'm looking, but I don't want to believe what I'm seeing. Arulius stands above him with a sinister smile that crawls up my spine. My shock slowly leaks into rage.

Why should I live and Kastian die? He was only trying to help me find Margo . . .

Footsteps grind the earth and the lash of a cape flaps in the breeze. I hear his familiar voice as he approaches Arulius from behind the tree. No, it can't be. My heart slips off its narrow ledge.

Wren.

It's my fault. They were after me. Fury builds in my heart and I clench my blood-stained teeth. I can't tell what's my blood and what is Arulius's. My insides twitch and scream as I force myself to crawl toward Kastian.

"Kas . . . Kastian," I rasp. Everything throbs like hellfire within me. Every movement sends nausea and dizziness through every fiber of my being. "Kas . . ."

Wren kneels next to me and strokes my wet hair from my face. "I thought I told you not to hurt her," he snaps at Arulius.

The golden male glances at me and shrugs. "She'll be fine once you heal her. Look at what she fucking did to me." He turns his neck so Wren can see the missing flesh. The Cypress lets out a sigh and ignores him.

Wren worries his lower lip and sets his hand on my shoulder. "I have to heal you, Elodie. You have to stop moving." I shake my head feebly and continue to push forward. His hand presses firmly on my shoulder, preventing me from making any progress. The pressure stings my ribs so potently that my vision blurs. Something hot and wet wells in my throat. An excruciating cough sends blood over my arms. I shudder but push forward through the pain. "Elodie!" Wren roars at me.

I clench my teeth, tasting metal. I won't give up. I won't stop. I won't lose another friend. My eyes still focus on Kastian's crumpled body. He's still moving . . . or trembling.

"Elodie, if you keep moving, you *will* die. I have to heal you." Wren sets both of his hands against my shoulders now.

"I won't . . . let you," I rasp. I let out a short cough with more blood and continue. "Not unless . . . unless you heal . . . Kastian." A gurgle of crimson rolls in my throat. I feel like I'm drowning in myself.

Wren grips me tightly and his amber eyes shift to Kastian. "He tried to *kill* me, Elodie." I shake my head and continue to push with my legs. My arms are all but worthless now. The pain in my upper body makes me sure that the wounds are fatal.

"Kastian," I whisper now.

His broken body is silent.

Wren huffs and stalks over to my friend's body. It takes everything I have and more to keep my head up to watch as Wren places his hands on Kastian. A light as beautiful as a soundless song dances through the shadows of night. A gut-curling snapping fills the air and those perfect ebony wings return to their elegant form.

I hear him. Kastian lets out a soft gasp.

"There," Wren grunts and stalks back to me, his feet stomping in a rhythm that I'm sure matches his irritation with me. But I don't care. We're alive and honestly . . . I won't fight Wren anymore, not if it means keeping Kastian safe. I will try everything in my power to escape alone if I have to. But no more endangering him. We are drawn to one another for a reason and I'm not willing to put him in danger.

I let my arms give out and I'm granted a face full of wet grass. Then the pain comes—oh, gods, does it come. My breaths are sharp and shallow. An odd sound reverberates from each inhale that wasn't there before. Wren's cold hands roll me to my back and I feel what I'm sure is a bone puncture through soft tissue inside my chest.

"Shit," Wren curses and places his hands on me. My eyes are set on the world above, the many moons and stars twinkling as if they welcome me to join them. My vision begins to blur again once Wren's light washes out the night sky.

Then there is darkness.

9

My dreams are deep and hard to wake from. I regain consciousness a few times throughout what I believe is a few days, based on the number of daylight and darkness intervals that pass.

The first time I fully wake up, my head spins and I am incredibly disoriented. Dark, lush strands of hair and translucent leaves curl near my face. Wren is here, always making sure I'm close. Violet really must have him under her thumb. Then the sleep washes over me again.

The next time I wake, the room is dark. My head feels better and my chest doesn't throb as terribly. I push myself up to one arm and examine my surroundings. It's a small room, might even be a closet. The bed I'm in has two pillows. I place a hand against the other and it's warm. Someone else was here. Wren? Where's Kastian? I try to get up but I'm so tired, weariness tears through me and I lie back down, falling asleep before I can find out who's guarding me.

On what I think is the third day, I wake up feeling pleasant. It's daytime. The light trickles in from curtains that flow with a soft breeze pushing through the windows. I sit up slowly and wince as my ribs ache. The sheets tug on my side and I become acutely aware that I'm not alone. I glance over to my right and find Wren lying next to me.

He's awake and watching me carefully, his amber eyes boring holes into me. *Gods.* He holds an expressionless gaze as I sit like a drugged and groggy fool, gaping at him because . . . well, what the fuck am I supposed to say? Everything in me screams to run, to fight. But then I remember Kastian's broken and twisted body, his rasping breaths and ruined wings . . . and what Wren did for him. He saved him. My ribs throb again and I clench my teeth, raising my hand to my chest to make sure I'm still intact, still real.

"Careful." He speaks softly. I glance at him warily. Why is he being so nice? I resent him for the softness because it makes me hate him less, if that's even possible. Though, he *did* save Kastian . . . What's his motive? I watch him with unease as he sits up and sets a warm hand against my back. I become all too aware at that moment of my lack of a shirt. All that stands between his hand and my skin is a thin wrap of bandage. My face flushes and heat stings my throat. I wrinkle my nose at him.

Gods, why him?

He guides me down to my back and I sip in a short

breath, readying myself for pain. But to my surprise, it doesn't hurt. I let out a long sigh of relief. Wren lies back down at my side and smooths his hand over my rib cage. I flinch at his touch but don't say anything. His warmth feels nice against my healing bones and some morally grey part of me craves his attention.

I turn my face toward him, sensing he wants something. His dark eyes are already waiting for me. He gives me his easy smile, the one that can stop a heart on a dime.

I don't return it. "Wren."

"Hmm?" He keeps smiling anyway.

"What are you doing?" I mutter—not with hostility, to my surprise.

He raises a brow. "What do you mean?" His thumb rubs lazy circles over my ribs and it takes everything I have to not close my eyes and accept his small gesture of comfort.

I narrow my eyes on him. "Why are you here? Why did you save me just to give me back to Violet, who *is* going to kill me?" I mutter, looking away before rage can itch its way back into me. His face is too beautiful for someone so wicked.

He lifts his hand and disappointment floods through me as the area quickly cools in his absence. Why does his touch always feel so nice against my skin? Wren places his hand on my cheek and rolls my face back to meet his. He's closer now. My heart thumps with rage. Why is he acting like this? I shut my eyes to try to control my urge to headbutt his stupid, gorgeous face.

"Violet won't kill you. She promised me. That's the only

reason I agreed to pursue retrieving you." My eyes blink open and I try my best not to let my jaw fall. He made sure that I would not be harmed? His lips turn upward. "You are safe here . . . and I wanted to tell you something."

Safe? That's reaching.

"What?" is all I can summon.

His brows furrow. "That I'm sorry." He presses his hand against my face gently, making me flinch. "Truly, I'm sorry. I never meant any harm to fall upon you." I bite my lip. I want to trust him. I want to believe him so, so badly because there isn't darkness in his gaze. I can tell he's being truthful, but he's been violent with me. I suppress a shudder at our last encounter. How can he mean me no harm? And sending Arulius after us like that? What the hell was he thinking? That Eostrix was way more reckless and sinister than Wren has ever been. I tremble at the thought of Arulius, his piercing amethyst eyes still heavy on my mind.

"Why did you have Arulius attack us?" I whisper, gazing down his neck because I refuse to stare into his deep eyes any longer. I realize he isn't wearing a shirt as his muscles gleam in the morning light. Cheeks heating, I dart back to his eyes.

He frowns and lets his hand run down my neck to my lower arm. "He wasn't supposed to attack you two. He was only meant to snatch you and bring *you* back to the ground." His eyes are filled with anguish. Maybe he is being truthful. "As I said, I really didn't intend for any of that to happen."

I purse my lips and he doesn't miss the motion. His eyes rest on them briefly before flicking back up. "What about

Kastian?" The mention of his name makes Wren curl his fingers.

"He is well."

"Where is he?"

Wren raises a brow. "You don't believe me?" I shake my head easily. "Ouch." He winces.

"Do you *blame* me? You nearly *killed* us both." I raise my hand to my ribs. They are still painful. He follows the movement with his gaze and his fingers glide over my side. I push his hand back to his own body and glare. I don't want any part of Wren's games or schemes and I sure as hell don't want his hands touching me anymore.

"I'm sorry," he whispers. "I was really worried about you, even after I healed you."

I study him, and he seems sincere. "Is that why you've been sleeping in the same bed? Half naked?" I can feel my cheeks flush just by mentioning it. "And *who* changed my bandages?"

His cheeks blush at my accusation. "I'm only here to guard you and ensure you do not escape again . . . and it isn't uncommon for our kind to sleep this way, next to others who are not our mates." He rubs his neck. The word *mates* sends a shiver up my spine. "I changed your bandages, but I promise I didn't look or do anything that was outside of medical practice." He shuts his eyes and I have to stifle a laugh at how delicate he looks right now. His skin appears as fragile as mine. His emotions are painted over his face, unlike before. He seems like a person for the first time since our time at the cafe.

Is he that loyal to his duty to Lady Violet? He's like a different person when serving her.

"Thank you for saving him." I shut my eyes. The weariness etches back into my bones. "I know you didn't have to, so thank you." His hand brushes over my cheek once more and then my dreams sweep back over me like a lullaby.

The next evening, I wake up feeling an insatiable hunger. When was the last time I ate? My mouth is dry and my body throbs, feeling increasingly weak. Wren isn't next to me this time. I have no choice but to find food and possibly even find Kastian. This might be the only chance I get.

I peek outside my doorway and into the hall. It's a simple corridor, much like the cottage back in Caziel. The walls are tan and the floors a simple wood. It makes me miss the elegance of Kastian's court, the bright walls and ebony drapes. Most of all the conservatory with every shade of green plants that scaled the glass panes.

Two doors are across from mine. I look both ways before tiptoeing to the door on the left. I decide to search for Kastian first. As hungry as I am, I have to know that he is okay.

I slowly turn the knob and the door creaks open. I poke my head in just enough so that I can see the contents of the room. It's some sort of study for whoever owns the home we reside in. I quietly shut the door and move to the next one. I begin to open the door slowly, but footsteps lightly tap up the stairwell down the hall. I slip into the room and press my back up against the door, letting a small sigh slip through my lips.

"Who's there?" a male's deep voice rasps.

I perk up. "Kastian!" I murmur and eagerly walk into the dark room. The drapes are pulled and make it difficult to see. I pass a bookshelf before a bed comes into view, much larger than the bed I was provided. It makes sense as my eyes trail over the creature lying in it.

Kastian's wings are spread widely and drape over the edges of the mattress. The gold-tipped feathers gently brush the floor. His white hair is no longer covered in crimson and his azure gaze meets mine as I step into his view. He lets out a gasp and leaps from the bed to meet me. I beam at him as he reaches out. I desperately want him to hug me. I yearn for his touch to engulf me. His calloused hands and broad body are in my dreams more than I'd like to admit. I open my arms as he approaches and . . . he lets out a low growl, one that instantly sends shivers up my spine.

"Kasti—"

He presses a heavy hand against my mouth and pushes me against the wall with brute strength, wrenching a breath from me. I can't even scream as his hand roughly covers my lips. I try to push him away, but he grasps my wrist and slams it against the wall so hard a framed photo falls free from the plaster. My eyes widen as I stare into his eyes.

He isn't Kastian.

Well, he is—but isn't. Not the one I know. His eyes are different—cold and . . . hungry.

Kastian presses his face into my neck and inhales deeply. I shudder and try to flail but he has hold of me entirely. His taut body pins me against the wall tightly, leaving nothing for the imagination. I sip in a frightened breath and close my eyes, tears stinging as I try to hold them back.

"Elodie," he growls. Even his voice is different, beastly and dark, withered with the sounds of nightmares. I try to squirm away again but to no avail. He runs his tongue up my neck, sending heat through me, and pushes his lips to where I assume my artery lies.

My heart beats rapidly. "Mmm!" is the only thing I can say. *Please don't hurt me. Please. No!*

His kiss is hot on my skin and I know—I know he's going to bite me. Why is he doing this to me? My chest burns with fire and my head whirls with confusion and lust. The worst part is that a sick part of me enjoys him being so close to me, being pressed so tightly together against a wall. I like his rough side. I've heard many stories of creatures that drain their victims of their blood, though I always thought those stories to be lore, only something my mother would tell me during the night to keep me in my bed as a child. But maybe those stories came from this side of Bresian.

He lifts his head and removes his hand from my mouth. I let my head drop to his shoulder. He smells of sage. It cleanses my mind as I take him in. I brace myself for his teeth against my skin, but it never comes.

"Elodie." He whispers my name with such a somber voice.

"Yes?" I murmur into his neck, my mouth pressed into the cotton of his shirt.

He backs up and the air seeps into me fully again. He

wraps his arms around me tightly. "I—I'm so sorry." He backs up until his legs meet the edge of his bed and sits down, bringing me with him. My knees gently land on the bed between his thighs and he slides a hand to the back of my head, brushing underneath my hair. He pulls his head back and his blue eyes are his once more. "I didn't mean to." His ocean eyes brim with tears and he buries his face in my chest. "I'm so sorry if I hurt you."

I'm weary, not from our encounter . . . but I'm so hungry. I rest my forehead down on his shoulder. "It's okay. I'm just glad you're safe," I whisper. My breaths are short and staggered. Am I panting? Why am I so dizzy?

"Are you okay? Elo—"

I bury my teeth deep into his neck.

I don't know what comes over me but I can't resist it anymore. Instinct guides me to the spot where I know his blood pumps thickly. I pierce his skin and warm fluid flows into me. His blood. Kastian flinches, tightening his grip on my lower back and behind my head, but just as quickly loosens it. He caresses my body as I slump over his broad and hard one. Why am I doing this? *How* am I doing this? I don't want to hurt him. But . . . but . . .

I'm so fucking hungry.

We stay this way for a few minutes as I devour him. His blood is hot, sweet nectar on my tongue. He tastes of roses and pomegranates and it fills me so entirely. Ambrosial drops of him fall from my lips and trickle down my thighs. I moan at the warmth of it. The heat between my legs grows with each luscious sip.

Once my urge is sated and I no longer feel weary, I release him and drag my tongue over the wound I leave behind. I sit back, trembling as my self-awareness comes crashing into me. He's between my thighs and I have his blood on my lips. I just stare at him, unable to even mutter a word of what I've just done. What I *thought* he was going to do to me.

Why did I do that? A million questions rush through me. Something is wrong with me—I can feel it in my core. My fingers crawl up my jaw to my teeth and prick on the sharp canines that protrude. A drop of my blood rolls across my fingertip.

Hot tears stream down my cheeks while Kastian gazes at me, not with anger or fear, but with understanding and I think the onset of a smile. He reaches his hand up to my cheek and wipes a tear with his thumb. "It's okay. Gods—Elodie, don't cry." I shake my head. He's the nice one, too kind to say how disgusted he is with me.

What have I become? What did Wren do to me?

"It's okay, Elodie," he murmurs again and wipes my lower lip with his thumb, brushing off his blood, and presses his finger in his mouth.

"What's wrong with me?" I choke, running one of my trembling hands through my hair in a feeble attempt to comfort myself. I'm a fucking mess right now. My body is in overdrive and I can't keep my tears from flowing.

He pulls me closer and embraces me. "There's nothing wrong with you. You are of this world now."

Of this world? Oh, fuck.

"What do you mean?" I wrap my trembling hands around his back, feeling the girth of his elegant wings. They are perfect again. Wren healed him completely.

Kastian stands up with me in his arms and walks over to the dresser I passed earlier. "See for yourself." He sets me down and spins me toward the dresser. I didn't realize that there was a mirror above it. I catch sight of myself and my breath gets stuck in the back of my throat.

My black hair waves softly around two small cream-colored horns that protrude from my head. I slowly reach my hand up and touch where they are in the mirror. Dammit—I have horns. But . . . in an odd way, I feel like I'm seeing myself for the first time. Truly seeing myself. The color of my skin radiates with a shimmering, sun-kissed glow, my eyes a sunset of yellow hues and honey. I'm not conceited, but right now I'm awestruck by my own beauty.

But more than anything, I feel clear minded, as if all my flaws and faults, anxiety and worries have paled in comparison to what they were. I feel like myself for the first time since seeing my aunt's horrid long frown and Margo's last breath.

I feel a thrum of warmth and strength within me and I devour it.

I face Kastian. "How is this possible?" I'm not sure I'm

ready for the answer, but I just drained him of his blood, so if not now, then when?

He lifts his hand, brushing my horns between his fingers, his eyes glimmering at the sight of them. "It means you died." He says the words softly, as if to not break me.

"Oh." Never mind, I take it back—it would have been better not to know. A crushing weight lands on my heart.

Dead, like them. I am forever sleeping. So why have I never felt so awake?

The idea scares the shit out of me, but at the same time surprises me. I never thought that I wouldn't even know it happened. Is this what it was like for Aunt Maggie and Margo? I gaze down at my hands. Real.

I am here. I am real.

They are somewhere here in Tomorrow too. A smile crosses my lips. Death was such a sad and traumatizing concept for me for such a long time, but here in Tomorrow, it's something beautiful. We can meet again and tell our stories and soak in the warmth of the suns. I can take that. I can accept that I am dead if all my new friends here are too, but I will mourn my lost time with my parents and the life that was cut short.

"So that means I drink blood now? That makes no sense."

He furrows his brow. "Well, all that means is that you are an Eostrix, like me." He nervously looks away as if he is ashamed to be one. Me? An Eostrix? "Everyone who passes returns as some sort of creature that's been a part of their endless chain of reincarnation. Maybe—maybe that's why we were drawn to one another." He adds the last part cautiously. He seems so afraid to show affection or emotions. He dances around telling me how he feels. It must be hard for him to receive love. I guess we all have our toxic pasts, ones that have ruined us in ways we can't face.

"That makes more sense. I didn't know you drank blood, though." I look over my shoulder for wings, but to my dismay there are none.

"Because I hadn't needed to until . . ."

I raise a brow at him. "Until you nearly drank from me just now?"

He turns away shamefully. "When Eostrix's are weakened we need to feed. Even if we are healed." He walks back to his bed and lies down. His ebony wings are off the side and his black horns tilt as he rests his head on his palm lazily, elbow to the mattress. "I'm sure you felt starved and outrageously tired, right?" I nod and crawl into the bed next to him, feeling like I need to be close.

"Did my feeding make your hunger grow?" I ask so quietly I'm not sure he heard me. My heart beats rapidly. I have a strange urge to let him feed on me too. I curse myself internally. What would my mother think of me?

He smiles at me. "No. Not at all. It doesn't work the way it would on a human—they die rather quickly if you take too much. *We* on the other hand don't have that effect on one another. Eostrix blood is the essence of our lives, so much so that we cannot live long without it."

"Oh," I whisper. "Do you want to feed on me? I feel

bad . . . and I know now how painful the weariness of that hunger is." I watch him closely behind my lashes and heat fills my cheeks as a ravenous grin shapes his lips.

"Are you sure?" he asks in a deep, painfully hungry voice.

His tone makes me ache from my core and I nod. He slowly sits up and beckons for me to come closer to him. His horns glisten in the dark and his wings drape beautifully behind him. His shirt is tight against his skin, leaving hardly a scrap for the imagination. I tighten my lips and crawl toward him. He twirls me and comes up behind me, pressing his hard body against my back. A deep sensation ravages my body. I *want* him—and not just to bite me. I want so much more.

He leans his head over my shoulder from behind and nudges my head to the side carefully. "It will hurt at first. Are you sure you're okay with this?" His breath curls hot against my skin and my body slumps back further into his with need. I nod. "I need to hear you say it, Elodie." He pants, hardly able to control himself, and fucking gods, is it hot.

"Yes," I rasp. He lets out a low growl, one filled with pleasure.

Desire.

On my knees, his thighs are on each side of me and I know what lies between. He sets his left arm on my inner thigh and with his other hand he reaches to my chin and grasps it gently. His lips touch my neck again and I ache for his teeth to sink into me. Why? I can't fathom the answer but I want it desperately. This new urge within me sings louder than anything I can imagine, like a song I've always known but have forgotten and I'll be damned if I deny it. I deserve to have moments like this with males like him.

Kastian presses into me. His teeth are hot and I jolt at the sting they bring. His arms clench me harder and I let out a moan I've never heard myself make before. I feel . . . I feel *everything*. The ecstasy of him. The pain is brief and followed by an insatiable fire that fills me, trailing from my neck to every vein in my body. He waits a moment and then begins drinking. I jerk my hips into him and he lets out a soft moan in my neck. Then he continues to feed. I can feel my blood as he draws it from my vein. I wasn't expecting such sexual tension to come from feeding. Is this what he felt earlier? How did he manage to sit so still and not even mutter a word? I lean into him more. I'm not sure if my body is my own anymore. It's reacting without my say . . . but I'm not opposed to it. Not at all.

"Kastian." I murmur his name against his ear. I'm pulsing with pleasure. He feels so right, like I'm meant to be here with him and him with me. My skin has come alive and I need more. I *burn* for more. I want to be touched everywhere, but will he give me that pleasure? He releases me as I say his name.

"Yeah?" His voice quivers and he strokes my neck with his tongue while waiting for my response.

"I feel . . . I feel." I don't know how to say it. My insides twist.

"Turned on?" he purrs and I let out a soft laugh.

"Yeah," I say with a breathless gasp. "Unbearably so."

He moans at my words and burrows his teeth back into my neck, taking a deep gulp, and I damn near scream. Releasing me again, he pulls my face towards his and dips my head back, kissing me.

I'm stunned for only a second, then I'm kissing him back deeply, entirely. My blood on his lips blossoms sweet flavors on my tongue. I turn my body to face him and press my hands against his chest, pushing him into the bed. His wings lie flat as I topple over him. A few feathers tickle my knees and make my lips turn up. His weariness fades. I can see it in his eyes—they're filled with desire for me, only me.

A sly grin crosses his lips. "Elodie, you are a naughty Eostrix." He rolls me to my back and presses his hardness against my stomach. I arch my back as he slides a hand between my thighs and quickly finds my heat that throbs so terribly.

He kisses me again, rougher this time, and his finger rubs over my clit. A wave of pleasure washes over me and he lets out a low growl as he watches my expressions. My hand glides down his throat and sweaty stomach. I dip into his pants and find his cock, hard and ready. He flinches as I wrap him confidently—gods I can't even get my entire hand around him.

"Elodie." He breathes heavily. "Please, don't stop," he pants and his plea makes me ache uncontrollably. *Gods, help me.*

"Kastian, I want you to—"

"What the hell are you two doing?" Wren's voice cuts through our moans and heavy breathing.

Oh, fucking gods.

We both jerk our heads to Wren. He stands in the doorway with his arms crossed. His dark eyes narrow and fill with disapproval as he glances from me to my companion. Kastian slowly lifts himself off of me and I let out a small whine of protest. I don't want to be done, and his glance tells me the feeling is mutual.

"You Eostrixes are all the same. Bloodthirsty bastards." Wren stomps up to the bed and once he can see clearer, he gasps. "You *fed* on her? Kastian!" Wren shuts up once he catches sight of my horns. His skin turns pale as if he's seen a ghost. I flinch under his dreadful gaze. His eyes shift to Kastian's neck and he no doubt sees the bite wound on his neck as well.

I take a gulp. The *last* thing I need is the Cypress to be angry with me. "Wren, I was really hungry and I—"

"Elodie, stop." He shakes his head and shoots Kastian a glare before taking me by my wrist. "Kastian, we will have words later," he grumbles as he tugs me out of the room and back toward mine. Kastian lets out a low growl filled with disdain, but Wren slams the door behind him and locks it, proving to me that we are indeed prisoners.

My skin is still hot, now from embarrassment more than anything. I feel like a stranger just caught me having sex. Except Wren isn't a stranger and we weren't having sex. Well, not yet, anyway.

I let out a sigh. Why do I feel like I'm in trouble? I thought it was normal for Eostrixes to drink blood. Wren lets go of my arm once we're back in my room and I plop on the edge of the bed with my glare already burning holes into him. He just stares at me for a long time. If he's trying to make me feel ashamed, it's working. I'm losing the battle of wills already.

"What were you thinking?" he finally scolds me.

I cross my arms over my nearly bare chest. The bandages are hardly holding on after my encounter with Kastian. "I was *hungry*. I went looking for food and Kastian."

"Did you know that you'd be eating *him?*"

"Wren!" I snap, eyes flashing with horror.

He shrugs. "Well, that's what you did. Why didn't you wait for me to come back? Do you even know what you've done?"

My eyes grow wide. "No, what?"

"Now you're going to have to feed frequently." He brushes a hand through his dark hair and his mouth becomes a thin line. "I didn't know you'd turn into an *Eostrix*." He almost sounds disappointed. He lets his eyes trail over my body, surely seeing all the enhancements.

"Well, I didn't know I'd turn *at all*," I retort. "You didn't tell me that I *died*." He stills at the word.

Wren takes a seat next to me. His brown eyes storm over with emotion. "You were so much harder to heal than I thought you would be. I've never healed a human before and you were so . . . so . . . ." He takes a deep breath. "So broken." I remember the feeling of all my shattered bones and punctured organs. A shudder runs through me.

"Wren. What's really going on?" I ask with vulnerability in my cracking voice, hoping he will just give me a straight answer for once.

He looks at me and takes my hand gently. "Okay, no more lies."

10

"Why does Violet want me? Who is it she thinks I am?"

Wren lies back on his side of the bed and props his arms behind his head. "Lady Violet was having dreams," he begins.

"That doesn't—"

He gives me an annoyed glance. "Just listen, Elodie." I roll my eyes but relent and lie down next to him. "Lady Violet was having dreams. Strange dreams—screaming meemies. As I'm the Commander of Intake, she drilled me on what I've noticed in the forest as of late. I wasn't sure what she was hell-bent on finding but she was relentless. These dreams of hers, they reawakened her rage." He pauses and stares at the ceiling. "So I told her what I'd noticed on the borders of Bresian, the path between, and that there'd been a significant decrease in creatures being reborn, and the death of the forest was increasing at an alarming rate."

Rebirth? Death of the forest . . . my forest? I don't want to interrupt him, but my mind whirls with questions already. Old Man Bruno constantly speaks about how the forest cries to him in the evenings—at dusk, when the line between the gods and humans is thin, and they're near to one another. I just thought the man was crazy, but he may have been right about literally everything.

"Lady Violet went quiet for months after that. She'd only told me to keep an eye on the situation, but she became obsessed with her research on the matter. A few weeks ago, I crossed Bresian to do my normal patrol, and that's when I noticed you." He brings his dark eyes to mine and a somber expression crosses his face. I furrow my brow at him. "I was mesmerized by you, completely and entirely. You explored the forest with such devotion and you stayed for such a long time. I . . . I watched you for days before you ever knew I was there."

"Days?" My jaw drops open and my chest churns. Gods —please tell me I didn't do anything embarrassing. My face heats under his dark gaze.

He nods and a weak smile forms on his lips. "You looked so sad—lost, even. I thought at times that you didn't know your way home, but sure enough you always returned to your shed." Wren's Adam's apple bobs as he swallows nervously. "That's when I began to notice . . . other things."

"Like what?" I lean in closer. The suspense in the air saps the breath from my lungs.

He rolls to face me and grasps my hands gently in his, making me feel so small. Fragile. He's going to tell me something hard to hear. Wren has a comforting soul. I can see from the flicker in his eyes that his heart is soft. My dad says to always look for the softness in a male's soul—that's how you know which ones are genuine.

"I noticed that you never truly went home in those weeks. That you always wandered the same paths and the same pattern. I realized that you *were* lost." I open my mouth to argue but he continues. "I realized that you weren't human anymore. You were already in-between."

Goosebumps cover my flesh and a cold—no, a freezing, icy sensation envelopes my bones. My lips part. "In-between?" The whisper hardly has the volume to leave my lips.

Wren brushes his fingers across my trembling lips and nods. "You were dying in your world." I just stare at him with wide eyes. That can't be true . . . I was just there, making my rounds in the forest. I just saw Mom and Dad . . . Wait. How long ago was that?

Why can't I remember?

Fear tugs from a deep, forbidden place within me.

"Murph sensed it first. After I gained the same knowledge, I sought your body with what little amounts of aura remained and a small tether formed. I followed the tether,

Elodie. I followed it to your body in a dreary building with many floors and many other ill humans."

I was in a hospital? *No.*

"When I saw your feeble body in the bed . . . it was horrible. I knew you wouldn't wander the forest for much longer." His eyes soften. Mine fill with tears. "So I decided to bring you back with me. It wouldn't be long and I wanted the crossing to be easy for you. Yes, I lured you in . . . I lied to you. I took you to Violet. I wasn't as kind as I could've been, but I didn't know how fucked up things would get. I didn't know how to tell you." His lower lip quivers as he chokes out, "I *couldn't* tell you the truth."

No. No. Please, no. Don't say it. Don't.

"Tell me what?" I whisper, despite the cries in my head. I have to hear him say it. If he doesn't say it, it will never be real. But if he does say it . . . if he does, then . . .

Wren bites his lip. "That you'll never be going home. That I brought you here because you were going to die. You won't get to say goodbye and will never see your family again."

My heart drops.

Sinking. I'm sinking and there's no surface.

It was one thing when I thought I died from the fall. It was easier to accept. But being in the in-between for weeks and possibly longer . . . My mind can't wrap around it.

I'm not real anymore. All at once, the clarity of my new senses dissipates and I fall deep into dark waters. My pain, anxiety, my mental illness . . . Was I *ever* real? My chest tightens as I think of my mother and father. My mom's soft, summer-brown hair and her loving smile, father's tight hugs and boring stories of wildlife and work. I want to be *home*. I want to sit at the dinner table with them and eat Mom's gross pasta and laugh about it when she pretends to like it herself. I want to be home.

I want to be real.

I think of them visiting my bedside and how they found me . . . or do they even know I'm dead? How long have I been in the in-between? I tense my jaw to hold back the wail that's building in my throat.

What happened that night with Margo? Did we . . . did we die together? Memories of hot, wet blood soaking my clothing and my hands flood me again. I wince. Margo's face is clearer this time. Her softening, shortened breaths curl in the night air and blood is splattered on her beautiful dark fur, pressing it to make her look smaller than she is. Is it my blood? Hers? The pain in my chest twists and I feel something sharp graze my heart, piercing, shattering, ruining.

Wren tightens his grip on my wrist, bringing my attention back to the present. "You didn't die from your injuries from the fall, Elodie. You died in your realm and you became entirely of this one. The times just happened to line up, perhaps due to your weakened spiritual state after Arulius . . ."

I don't have words. What am I supposed to say to any of this? My mind is hollow. I want to cry and scream, but what I *really* feel is *nothing*.

A long and empty sensation of hopelessness. Blank tears filled with despair and hollowed space. How can I be dead?

Margo. My mind whispers her name. A hush falls over the two of us. He lets me process.

"I—I can't remember h-how . . . how I died."

Wren furrows his brow. "I don't have the answer to that."

"Margo," I whisper. This has to be connected. She's the last clear memory I can remember. Were my last moments with her? I find a small amount of comfort in the thought.

He sits up and brings the blanket up to my shoulders, tucking me in softly. "I know you and Kastian were headed to the Pine Hollow Keeper. We can go get Margo tomorrow. You need to rest for now. I'll speak with Violet about the arrangements."

I don't want to rest. I'm filled with too many thoughts and this horrible vast emptiness. Is this what shock feels like? After a few moments of silence, I mumble, "You never told me what Violet has to do with all this. Why does she want me and why would she let you help me?"

Wren flinches as if he'd forgotten where he was going with his story. "Violet received word the night I brought you back with me. She demanded you be brought to her for inspection immediately. She was searching for someone—desperately. I didn't want it to be you, but she was convinced." He pauses. "It was never my intention, and I would never let her harm you, Elodie." I doubt that. "I'm still trying to learn her true intentions myself, but I promise you are safe."

I let out a weary sigh. His answer will have to do. As much as I still resent him, I believe him. A part of me trusts him more than I should. It's a gut feeling.

"Rest. I will be back shortly," Wren whispers as he leans down and pecks my cheek with a kiss. Before I can say anything, a wave of sleep rushes me. Bastard—he must have used his sleep ability on me again.

My head is heavy and my eyes close quickly. To my relief, my thoughts are filled with pleasant memories of Margo instead of the emptiness that took hold of me. *Thanks, Wren.* Her deep brown eyes and soft fur tug at my heart, splitting me into a million different pieces, cast across a universe of sorrow and a sea of stars. I try to pet her, to hold her, but she slips away. I chase after her but she's too fast. It's the image of her running off into a field, farther than I can see, that truly breaks me. No matter how loud I call for her, she never looks back at me.

She never looked back.

I'm not sure how long I sleep, but when I wake up, I'm *starving.* Is it because I'm still transitioning? My stomach clenches so terribly. I open my eyes. The room is dark. The warm scent of pines and sap fills my senses. I'd know this scent anywhere at this point. It's Wren's. As my eyes adjust, I realize he is beside me, his translucent leaves glowing white, dim and ghostly against the darkness.

His neck is exposed.

My eyes fixate on his bare skin. It looks so soft, so smooth and untouched. I wrap my arms around myself. *Stop—stop it. Don't.* I tremble. The hunger is much worse than before. Pain curls in my stomach and my throat heats with an unbearable thirst. My mouth fills with saliva. His blood, is that what I'm smelling? The pines and sap? He smells so . . . unbearably sweet. I let out a soft groan. I'm losing the battle with myself.

Will he hate me if I bite him? I'm so, so hungry.

I give in. I will literally die if I don't. Dramatic or not, it's how I feel.

I inch closer to his back. Warmth floods me as my bare skin becomes flush with his. I slip my arm over him and rest my palm against his chest. I nuzzle my lips onto his bare neck, between his chin and shoulder, and pause. My breaths are short and ragged. I try to stop myself but I really can't—my instincts are in control now.

I run my tongue over his flesh and he flinches. I freeze, knowing he's conscious. Is he going to push me off and yell at me? I brace myself, but he doesn't do that. His hand finds mine on his chest and he clutches it tightly. My breaths are still heavy and stagger against his neck with heat.

"It's okay, Elodie," he murmurs softly.

I shut my eyes, giving in.

I press my lips on his artery, thanking him with a kiss for being so understanding. Then my teeth enter his neck. He flinches again and squeezes my hand. I let a muffled moan escape my lips as I pull my first gulp of his sweet, pinesap blood. It explodes within me. *So this is the taste of a Cypress.* I take a deeper second pull. He fills me with such a tangible feeling, not as sensual as Kastian's. His blood is more . . . filling. Somber and ambrosial.

Wren lets out a low gasp as I indulge a third long pull. I wonder if he feels the way I did when Kastian drank from me, the fire of lust. I don't understand how the males keep their composure. The feeling is unbearable.

I release him after a few more filling sips. My teeth are hot as I slowly pull them from his neck. I glide my tongue over his wound and leave him clean, giving him one last kiss on the wound as thanks.

I'm overflowing with delight. No more painful hunger that stings and makes me feel . . . not myself. It's an odd feeling, one I hope will pass over time. It's like someone else is controlling my emotions and needs.

I pull my arm out from under his and rest back on my pillow to watch him. I'm already dreading his scolding that I know is coming. He will want to talk about what just happened. But to my surprise, he just lies there, as if he is trying to fall back asleep. Why do I feel disappointed by that?

"I'm sorry," I whisper.

Wren is silent for a few moments. "You need to feed. It's okay, I understand," he mumbles back. I'm hit with a pang of guilt. He isn't just some blood bag, and just because he's done awful things doesn't mean that I need to be the same way. I reach my hand to his hair and brush my fingers through his dark strands. I'd been curious what the ghost-like leaves feel like against skin. They are cool and leave my fingers feeling numb in their aftermath.

"You taste like pinesap," I mutter, not entirely sure what to say, but continue anyway because it feels right. "Somber even."

He rolls to face me and his dreary expression weighs heavily on my chest. "Somber?" His mouth turns upward on one side. "I don't think that's a taste."

I smile. "I didn't think so either, and yet there it is." We share a quiet laugh.

His figure is perfect against the moonlight, his muscles smooth and relaxed. I'm content, but I yearn for more of his blood. I won't let myself indulge again though. I've sated the hunger and I can't make this a habit. A thought brushes against my conscience. *Will Kastian be upset?* I still don't know the rules of this realm and it's not like we are labeled or anything, but we have a connection, and I can say confidently that feeding feels a lot like foreplay.

Wren watches me with sleepy eyes. "What are you thinking right now?"

"Would Kastian be upset that I fed on you?" I blurt. He lets a short laugh slip. I raise a brow. "I'm being serious."

"Yes, Kastian *would* be very upset. You probably shouldn't tell him about this." Wren touches his neck and the bite heals under his fingers. His healing is incredible. Cypresses must be the only beings in this realm that can do so with just a touch of their hands, but I'll need to ask later to verify. I mull over what healing Eostrixes can perform other than just with their mouths and whether or not I have those abilities too.

Guilt waves over me. *Shit. I knew I shouldn't have done that.* "Why? I don't understand the rules."

He considers me for a moment. "I wouldn't say it's a rule as much as it's a rite . . . Eostrixes take blood-sharing very seriously. It's a connection that many don't share with just anyone."

I purse my lips in thought. "But *you* aren't an Eostrix."

His gaze fills with amusement. "No, you're right. I'm not, and that makes it even worse." My confusion resonates with him and he goes on. "Eostrixes are above Cypresses. Their blood is closest to that of the original gods, and you indulging in mine would be seen as a disgrace to your kind. A violation of the rite."

My mouth parts. "But you were so delicious," I murmur and he laughs again. I can't ignore how beautiful the sound of it is. That makes no sense . . . though it was different drinking his blood compared to Kastian's. It was filling and not as sensual. I also think it's odd that the beings here have social differences based on their species. Not so different, are we?

"I'm glad I don't taste horrible." He chuckles, his grin alluring. "But I would keep what you did between us."

I nod but keep the concern in my expression. "Does that mean I can only feed on Kastian?"

He mulls it over. "No. You need to feed regularly while

you transition and we can't have him trying to . . . you know . . . every time you feed." He looks away as he says the latter.

My face heats. "Oh, yeah," is the only thing I can muster. I gaze at his neck again, the longing still tugging at my insides, but I suppress it down.

Wren catches my gawking this time. "Are you still hungry?" He pushes up to his elbow and gazes down at me.

I shake my head shyly. Gods, how can he just ask so freely? I shut my eyes. Maybe if I stop looking at him, I will stop having the urge.

He lets out a low laugh. "Then why do you keep looking at me like that?"

Heat rushes me. "It's . . . It's like an urge. I'm burning . . . for more." His expression washes to surprise.

Did I just say burning? Gods.

His surprise fades and he lies back down. The awkward silence makes me want to bury my face in my pillow and scream.

"Let's get some sleep." He turns to face the wall once more. I roll the other direction as well. Though questions still ebb at me, sleep finds me much more swiftly than I thought it would. One thought stays with me even as I sleep though— that tomorrow, I'll be on my way to find Margo.

Margo, we will meet again.

11

Morning can't come soon enough. The second the sun breaks the distant hills, I stretch and get dressed in a hurry. The news of finding out I'm dead still chars my heart, but I'm determined to not let this day be ruined by my reality. My excitement to find Margo has me giddy from the moment my eyes open. Wren is slower to wake than I am, but he quickly gets dressed once he realizes I'll head out without him if he isn't ready in time.

I've been given new clothes. My old ones were, not surprisingly, torn to shreds. I'm pleased with the black tight pants and undershirt. The soft fabric is a nice replacement for my tattered and dirty clothes from home. From the human realm . . . Nope—not dwelling, not today. I shake my head.

A gold armored vest wraps around my chest, and while I'm not sure I want to wear it as it reminds me of Arulius,

Wren insists. *Safety reasons,* he says. I have to admit though, once on, it does look pretty good on me. The ribs are golden bone brackets placed over my underlying ones while the neck, spine, knees, and elbows are enriched with gold hovering brackets. I adore the golden gloves provided to me most of all. Long claws extend from the tips of them for fighting. My hands are exposed on the palms.

"You look like a warrior," Wren says. "I wouldn't dare pick a fight with you."

I laugh. "Yeah?" I turn to look into the mirror behind the door, and I gasp. Not because I look as frightful as Wren claims I do, but because my horns are at least an inch longer than they were last night and my ears are . . . cute. Cream-colored lamb ears, if I had to describe them. They've just sprung from nowhere.

"Oh yeah, I was going to say something about those but I wasn't sure how to put it . . . They are odd for Eostrix." I can see his smirk in the reflection and it ticks me off.

Holding my fluffy ears in my hands, I turn to face him. "They don't all get cute ears?" I grin.

He narrows his eyes and tucks his shirt into his pants. "No, they don't. Which means something weird is going on. I might need to ask Violet." I squirm at her name.

"*Or* . . . we can go to Liasium," I carefully suggest as I spin to look at my back. Still no wings.

"Liasium?"

He doesn't know about it? I narrow my eyes. "Kastian said there are old archives there with information . . . Oh!" I suddenly notice my Vernovian Thorn is no longer around my neck. I've grown used to the tight wrap of it around my skin. Being without it makes me feel a bit exposed. "What happened to my collar?"

Wren latches his belt and pulls his ebony vest over his head. "I removed it when we arrived. You're just now noticing?" I nod, then realize he doesn't have his on either.

"Where's yours?" I step toward him, noticing how tall he is. My lips only come to his upper chest. He knows what I'm after. He sits back on the bed and unzips his vest enough so that his neck is revealed. I purse my lips and bend over, placing my mouth on his neck.

"I took it off once I found out you were an Eostrix." He runs his hand down the back of my head, strands of my dark hair intertwining with his fingers. "As your keeper, it's my duty to see that you are well cared for. Violet would have my head should something go wrong."

I still. "So you are only letting me feed because it's your duty?" I whisper into his skin. I rest my chin on his shoulder, not wanting to just use him. It feels wrong. I care for him and I can't let myself feed on him as if he's a pig for the slaughter.

Wren lets his other hand rest on my back. "Well, that's one of the reasons."

"What's the other?"

His laugh stirs in his chest. "You have so many questions – you know that?" I let out a low whine and he chuckles again. "At first it was purely for duty. I've never had an Eostrix feed on me before, so I wasn't entirely sure how I felt about it. But—" He presses his face into my shoulder. "You're someone I want to be close with. Even after our bad beginning, I want to make amends. So please don't be reluctant. We are both just doing what we have to."

I can't help feeling like he's holding something back, but I'm pleased enough with his answer. If he truly means it then I shouldn't feel bad—right?

I feed from him for a few minutes, and after I'm done I feel much better, ready for the day ahead as I know we will be traveling a far distance. He heals his neck and zips his black vest back up. It's odd seeing him in anything other than his sage-colored cloak. If anything, it makes me aware of how serious a mission this is. He's stoic, like he's ready to assassinate someone. Even his long black hair is pulled back tightly in a bun. His tattoo of the thorn collar is brazen against his skin now that the Vernovian Thorn has been removed.

Kastian's waiting outside and I'm shocked to see Arulius next to him. His dark gray hair tipped with gold shimmers in the morning beams. I loathe the sight of him. I especially hate that we are wearing the same uniform. Even after the attack that nearly killed Kastian, they aren't at one another's throats, which is beyond me. I'd have already strung him up and left him somewhere to rot. The males both turn to me as Wren and I emerge from the cottage. I have to tighten my lips to keep from smiling at their gawking faces.

"Ears?" Kastian blurts.

Arulius approaches with curious eyes. I glare at him and

take an aggressive step forward. Wren sets his hand gently on my shoulder, letting me know to behave. *Asshole.*

The golden Eostrix winces as I glare at him with untrusting eyes. "I'm sorry for causing you harm, lovely." His amethyst eyes rove hungrily over my features and blink back up to my eyes.

Lovely? I keep my face stern. *Fucking asshole.*

"I truly did not intend to hurt you. Your friend, on the other hand, I *was* trying to kill." He tosses his hand back and points lazily at Kastian, who in turn glares heavily back at him.

"I *don't* like you," I say plainly.

Wren lets out a swift cough behind me and I know there's a smile plastered on his face. Arulius furrows his brow. "Fair," he mutters. "I don't particularly like you either. Who the fuck bites someone's neck like that?" *Shit.* I was really hoping he forgot about that, though who could? Wishful thinking.

He raises a hand and squishes my left ear.

"Hey!" I flinch and slap his hand away. My palm stings but he doesn't so much as blink at my strike.

"So soft." He laughs. Kastian walks up and gazes down at me too. He gives my ear a soft brush and a smile overcomes his face as well.

"Where did these come from?" he asks smoothly.

I shrug.

His eyes trail up to Wren and the two of them harden their gazes at one another. I let out an annoyed sigh, praying that Kastian won't put together that I fed on the Cypress.

"So." I clear my throat. "Margo." The three of them look at me, and Kastian's eyes brighten.

"I can carry you—"

Wren steps forward, passing him. "No. Elodie will be riding with me on Murph. You and Arulius can fly." He whistles and Murph comes bounding up with his shadows wisping around his feet. The Pine Hollow's black fur and translucent leaves bristle against the cool breeze that sweeps through the valley. I still feel betrayed by him, but can understand his actions a bit more now that Wren explained their true intentions. The Hollow eyes me with equal suspicions. Kastian and I *did* gravely wound his master.

I guess that makes us even.

"Hi, Murph." I set my hand on his snout and he lets out a low hum from deep within his throat. "Nice to see you too," I mutter. Wren watches me as I greet his friend. Will Margo be like this? My heart slows. Will I even recognize her? I worry my lower lip and face Wren.

"Ready?" he mutters and offers to help me up. I nod.

I couldn't be more ready. How long has it been since I last saw Margo? I hold onto that thought as Wren's story last night thrums within me. *You were dying.* Why can't I remember that? *Dying* seems like something that one wouldn't easily forget. Come to think of it, I can't remember how Margo passed either . . . only the recurring dream of our blood mixing, and pain. So much pain. Our staggered breaths against the silence of night. I rake every part of my mind but only find the shores of the forest. He said I returned to my shed frequently. I remember that . . . but what about my parents? I can't place the last time I saw them. That realization leaves a sickening feeling in me. The thought of my mom and dad being dead as well . . . I can't stomach the image of that, their brown eyes clouded against an angry sky. Were mine clouded and cold, fuzzy with the dreams of Tomorrow? Did I hold a tight, sewn-in-frown like my aunt did?

Murph launches off the ground and blazes toward the northern mountains, the force of which pulls me into the present. I almost forget how strong and fast of a creature he is. Wren holds onto me tightly, and although I'm no longer wearing the Vernovian Thorn, I still feel its invisible presence. Will I ever escape Wren? At least we aren't fighting to the death now and are maybe on the path to becoming true companions. I know we could be great together, but I still don't trust him. I'm still his prisoner no matter his reasoning— or rather Violet's prisoner.

Kastian and Arulius fly high above us. They could easily fly ahead, but I know they are both sticking around to keep an eye on me and Wren. It seems we each have a warrior in our pocket.

Now that I'm entirely of this realm, the colors and the scents are enhanced in a way. Brighter, stronger, closer. My skin tingles under the air itself as if I've belonged here all along. The day is overcast. I don't think I'll ever get used to the weather here, much less the sights. While it's cloudy and gloomy, the wind is sweet with pollen and the four moons, or planets, linger at the tips of the mountains. They cast a bewitching light, one of soft blues and purples, even during the day. They never seem to set. It's both breathtaking and a constant reminder that I am far from home.

Never to return . . . now that I know I'm dead.

But that doesn't mean I can't still follow my rule. I shake my head and try to see the brighter side of things. I can still leave my grief in that small shed. That grief is aged and weary. Why should my rule be different with the new tender sadness that pulls at my heart? I form a line in my mind, placing it a few hundred leagues ahead in the direction Murph is charging.

Once I cross that line, I'll leave it all behind. I won't carry it with me. I desperately think of my mom's soft smile and my father's wise eyes. And as we cross the imaginary line, I look back. I can almost see them waving goodbye. Mom's crying and Dad holds a long, grieving expression.

A goodbye I thought would never come.

One that I need.

Goodbye.

We ride for hours until my stomach cries out, demanding food. The two Eostrixes fly down and share space in the shade with us under a grouping of trees. Their wings couldn't be more different. Arulius's are crafted in the sun's image while Kastian's are of night. My dark-winged male seems uneasy around his own kind. A string tugs at my heart. I never got to hear the story behind his scars and . . . and why he is broken. I suppose I need to talk to him about my own scars too. Well, if I ever figure out how I died, that is.

"Here you are." Wren passes me a chunk of bread. "I hope it's to your liking." He tosses a loaf to Kastian and then another to Arulius. They both stare down at the bread with scowls. I muse that perhaps Eostrixes are pampered creatures, too good for the likes of bread. Not me, though.

I take a bite and wheaty, buttery goodness fills my mouth. My eyes widen. This is the best bread I've ever had. But it's the same bread from a few days ago—why does it taste so much better now? I take a second bite and observe as Kastian sets his piece down, untouched. "You don't like bread?" I mutter with my mouth full. Crumbs sprinkle into my lap.

Kastian crosses his arms. "Not in particular." He glances at me as if he can't believe I'm enjoying the bread. I wonder if it has to do with the food being provided by Wren.

Arulius smirks. "Our kind normally only feeds on blood." His eyes rove over me from head to toe and I shudder. "Like the outfit, lovely. Reminds me much of my own." He winks at me and it's the sexiest thing I've ever seen. He doesn't deserve to be so fucking beautiful.

I nearly choke. I take a deep drink of the water that Wren passes me with a sly grin. I turn on him. "Did *you* give me *his* clothes?"

Wren rubs his neck. *Guilty as charged, motherfucker.* "We don't have a ton of clothes just lying around. Those were his from years ago when he was much younger, so you don't need to worry about them being freshly used." As if that makes it better.

I take another big mouthful of my bread and roll my eyes. Wren and Arulius laugh, but Kastian seems as uncomfortable as I am. It takes everything in me to not respond. I should just be happy that we are on our way to find Margo. Yeah—focus on that.

Kastian stretches his wings and leans against a tree a few feet away from the rest of us. After I finish wolfing down my meal, I meander off to talk with him. Wren makes a low whistle and I glance back. He narrows his eyes at me and I know it's a warning to not try to escape. I nod at him with acknowledgement and smile. He returns to his boring conversation with Arulius about Nesbrim politics, the current affairs of their high lady, and the villagers. Maybe I should care more since I'm a part of this world now, but I can't be bothered about it at the moment.

Kastian lifts his head as I approach and kindness sweeps over his features. "He let you come talk to me by yourself?" he teases.

I tighten my lips. "I think Wren is trying to help me." I hesitate to say it, and his instant look of betrayal confirms why. It's true though, I believe that Wren is trying to help me. We are . . . friends, or at least I hope we can become friends, and escaping him just means more chasing and hurting. No thanks.

"Elodie, you can't be serious," he growls in a low tone. His blue eyes pierce through me like daggers. I glance down at my boots and shuffle a rock around to try to keep calm.

"He said he spoke with Violet and that she doesn't plan on hurting me. He's going to help us get Margo back too." I keep my eyes on the rock I fumble between my feet.

He sets his hand on my shoulder. When I don't look at him, he growls again. "Look at me." I reluctantly lift my eyes to his. He looks furious and maybe even a little hurt. "*I* was helping you find Margo, and I didn't take you as a prisoner to do it." His eyes crawl over my golden brackets. "He even dressed you like *them*." He raises his lip in disgust.

"I thought it looked nice on me," I mutter and furrow my brow. I was hoping he'd notice me or comment on my appearance. He takes a large step toward me and I take a small one back. His eyes blaze with fury. I feel so small. Afraid.

"It doesn't look nice, Elodie. It makes you look like another one of Violet's fucking puppets." He reaches his hand up and tilts my chin up. I flinch at his touch. "Look at these things, they are so gaudy and—" He freezes, eyes placed squarely on my lips. His fingers curl a bit more around my neck, making me wince.

"What?" I ask breathlessly, eyes widening.

He lets go of me and stalks over to Wren without saying a word. The Cypress stands as he recognizes a disgruntled male when he sees one.

"Kastian?" Wren props a hand on the dagger he's been keeping sheathed on his side.

"Answer me truthfully." The Eostrix's dark wings bristle with anger. "Did you make her feed on you?" My heart drops. I didn't say anything that would allude to him that. How could he know? I reach up to my lips and they are a bit swollen.

Wren smirks and narrows his eyes with mischief. "I wouldn't say that I *made* her. She woke me up in the middle of the night nipping at my neck." He shrugs. Arulius coughs violently as it takes him off guard, but Kastian clenches his fists with rage.

What happened to not saying anything? I fume and catch the flick of Wren's eyes at me.

"You fucking bastard. How dare you taint an Eostrix with your Cypress blood," Kastian lashes out angrily. He flexes his muscles and I catch the sheen of them in the dim overcast light. Can't we go *one* day without a fight? Gods. I should intervene before things get out of control.

"Kastian, it was my fault," I admit. They all turn to me. I instantly feel their stares bore into me and heat creeps into my cheeks, but I go on. "I woke up so hungry it hurt . . . I couldn't stop myself and I didn't know it was forbidden." I meet his gaze now. He's genuinely upset. His ocean eyes falter in a way that breaks my heart. I can't understand why though. It's not like we are bonded or whatever Wren was going on about earlier. Why should it matter what *I* do? "I don't want you to be upset. I'm sorry . . . Be mad at me though, not Wren."

He slicks his white hair back. "Don't defend him, Elodie. He knows better, while you . . . you don't." I furrow my brows. I know he isn't trying to insult me, but it still stings.

"We don't feed on Cypresses, especially the High Court's Commander, lovely," Arulius feels the need to chip in. I let my head fall with embarrassment. Why do I feel so stupid? There's no way I could have known that.

Kastian lets out a long sigh and approaches me. His soft hand brushes the black strands of hair from my face and pushes them behind my fluffy ear. "You didn't know. It's okay." I tense my jaw. *This* is a side of Kastian I don't like. Is it because we had a moment of intimacy together? It's not like I agreed to be *his*.

Wren clears his throat, and I could just kill him. He's *trying* to pick a fight, I swear. "Well, it's going to continue." Arulius and Kastian both snap their heads with widened eyes. "Violet has decreed that I take care of her and I don't mind." He kicks up his lip and grins at me.

"Wren!" I blurt. "Please don't—"

Kastian is a blur of black feathers and horns. He lashes out at Wren and Murph is up and between them in seconds, teeth bare and fur bristling. The Eostrix lands a heavy blow on Murph and his large shadow body is sent with impossible strength against the trees, two of which snap at the trunk and begin to tilt towards us. Leaves and branches rustle, and wood shattering around us sends shivers up my spine. *Murph.* His body lies beneath the trunk and in the line of falling debris.

Clashing and ripping sounds erupt behind me from what I assume are Wren and Kastian trying to draw one another's blood. No one sees Murph, but I do.

I charge forward, entirely mindful of the hundred-foot trees that begin to cast downward. I clench my teeth and push my body as hard as I can. *Faster. Faster.* My feet can't carry me quick enough as the sharp, splintered trunk completes its break and crashes down.

"Murph!" I scream and shut my eyes as I leap for him. I can't watch as another dog dies before me. Thick sticky blood encases me. My chest throbs with pain . . . The whimpering. Shadows blur my vision, dancing around me cruelly until I'm screaming.

My surroundings white out and all I know is that I'm still running forward, blindly, filled with horror. *Not Murph. You can't have Murph,* I pray to the God of Death. If that fucker ever listens, please let it be now.

"Elodie," A voice calls from far away. Everything is fuzzy. I can't make out who is calling me. There it is again—what are they saying?

"Elodie." It's closer now. I open my eyes and the clouds are above me. Leaves from the ancient trees still swirling violently above. I lift my head and try to get my bearings. What happened? Arulius is above me, tearing at his arm viciously. His amethyst eyes meet mine as he pulls his sharp teeth from his crimson flesh.

"Wha—what are you doing?" I whisper, trying to clear my vision, but the stars continue to swirl in my mind.

"Good, you're conscious," he hisses, shoving his arm in my mouth. "Drink."

My mouth fills with pools of his blood and it tastes of . . . honey and something bitter. I glance up as I gulp down. He watches me intently. Is that worry in his gaze? I swear he looks worried. My heart races as I become more aware. *Murph.* I try to move my mouth but he holds me still. Is Murph okay? Why do I need blood right now?

"You need a little more, love," he rasps. His purple gaze is heavy. I try to wriggle free but a horrible pain gnaws at my stomach and everything below, so I give in and do as he says. After a few minutes, he pulls his arm from my mouth and helps me up. My eyes immediately search my lower half for the damage.

"Oh. My. Gods." My body was entirely smashed by the fallen tree. My clothes from the waist down are drenched in blood as the force of the tree surely smashed me into near nothingness.

"Yeah, you're foolish to have leapt in like that . . . but you did save the Pine Hollow," he mutters as he looks to where Murph's body lies safely out of the way.

My heart leaps at the sight of the Hollow, still unconscious, but alive. I breathe a sigh of relief.

I turn my attention over to where fighting is still sending

slashing sounds of metal against claws through the air—wait a fucking second. Did they not care about *Murph*? What about *me*? Fury fills me.

"They didn't stop fighting?" I ask in a low, steady voice.

Arulius lets out a small scoff. "Are you kidding? Didn't even bat an eye, love."

That hurts. It really fucking hurts. I thought Kastian cared about me, and Wren . . . I thought he and I were finally friends. Or duty-bound at the least. And what about his Pine Hollow? Where was the concern for him? I let out a long, weary sigh. "Thanks, Arulius." It takes more than I'm willing to admit to get the words out. I still don't trust Arulius, beautiful or not.

"Don't mention it." He crosses his arms.

We share a long, drawn-out, uncomfortable silence as we wait for them to tire. We are wasting our time. Today we are supposed to go get Margo. I grow restless and the anger brews stronger with each slash they make at one another without even so much as looking at me.

I've had enough.

I start walking.

Arulius watches me for a few minutes, and then I hear his wings flap as he lands gracefully next to me.

"Don't try to stop me," I growl at him, keeping my eyes on the mountains ahead. I have zero idea of where I'm going but I know that it's north.

He sets his hands behind his head, gray hairs tipped with gold fluttering against the sky, and walks next to me.

"Wouldn't dream of it, love." I roll my eyes but continue to stalk off angrily.

It has been at least an hour. My rage grows as the day becomes hotter and my feet grow wearier. My breath is short and my new ears are making my head feel stupidly heavy—or maybe it's the horns. Possibly both.

We stop and I lie in the shade of a large oak tree. The shadows of the leaves ripple across my face as the sunlight dapples through.

"I can just fly you there, you know?" Arulius stands above me and gives me a sly grin. I shut my eyes and ignore him because if I have to answer I will fucking scream at him. He could have offered an hour ago, but he likes to play these types of games.

He lets out a chuckle at my stubbornness and lies down in the grass next to me. "Are you feeling okay, love?" he asks after a few minutes of peace.

I let out a long exaggerated sigh and stare up at the leaves. "I'm just tired. I'm still healing from when *you* broke my ribs and gods know what else, and what just happened . . . that didn't help." That's the simple version. The truth is that my entire body burns. I'm in pain everywhere. My ribs, my legs—and gods, the hunger is back again too. But even more than that is the weariness my mind brings me. I just need to rest.

"I can fly you there," he says again. There's less amusement in his voice this time. Now he sounds genuinely concerned.

"Maybe we should wait for the others?" I mumble.

Arulius shifts to his side. "I doubt they are coming *here*." I glance at him and raise a brow. "*If* they are even done fighting, they will most likely head straight to the Hollow Keeper."

My breaths are short. "Are you saying that you've been letting me . . . letting me walk in the wrong direction this whole time?" Sweat beads down my forehead and every bone in my body is on fire.

Arulius scans my body with his purple gaze. "Well, you were on a warpath, love. You would have killed me if I tried to stop you. Are you sure you're feeling okay? You look like shit."

"You're such an asshole," I mutter, sipping in short breaths and clenching my teeth in pain.

He chuckles dryly. "You sure are a mean one, you know that?" His amusement pisses me off. I couldn't be stuck with a worse person.

"Why am I having such a hard time adjusting?" I groan.

Arulius considers me. "If I have to guess, it'd be that you're not a full Eostrix and every transition is a bit different."

Not a full Eostrix. Wren mentioned that too. "How can I even be a mix if I am not of this world? I'm a human."

He snickers. "We are *all* of this world, lovely. It's a cycle, though I guess you wouldn't know that, and neither would Kastian as he is quite young."

"How old are you?"

"Me? Oh gosh." He bites the corner of his mouth in thought and I stare much longer than I should. "Three hundred . . . ish."

I roll my eyes again. "Oh, that's all?"

"You're *so* grumpy, love." He pokes my face. "I'll make a deal with you." He leans in closer. I take in a short breath, becoming conscious of how gorgeous he is up close. His sun-kissed skin glitters in the sunlight. His lips are plush and entice me to feel them. I get lost in his eyes, and only when he kicks up the corner of his mouth in a smile and a small dimple shows do I realize he is taking in my features as well. I dart my eyes away from him.

Any deal with Arulius is one I don't want. I've known him for all of a day and even *I* know that. I shake my head and shut my eyes. If I don't look at him, I can keep my wits about me. He's entirely too close and breathing in my personal bubble.

"Oh, come on. Don't you even want to hear it?" He pokes my face a second time and my brows couldn't knit together harder if I tried.

"Fine. What?"

He smiles, and for the first time I can see his sharp canines brimming his lips. "I'll let you feed on me if you let me feed on you."

I glare at him. "Why would you want to feed on me? So that Kastian gets pissed off at you too?"

His amethyst eyes trail the skin around my neck. "So I can figure out what other creature lies in your veins." His face hardens. "Then we can figure out how to speed up your transition, love."

"Stop calling me *love*," I hiss. "How is that a deal? Sounds like it just benefits me." I give him a wary glance.

"That's true, you would be benefiting much more than I—but I would get a nice snack." He practically hums. *A snack.* That's all I amount to. I can tell he's pleased with himself because his smile couldn't be any wider. But I don't want Kastian to get mad again. Then again, he did let a *fucking tree* fall on me and didn't even bat an eye while *Arulius*, of all the creatures and gods, saved me. And I'm my own person—he doesn't get to control what I do. Maybe it isn't such a bad idea. The pain throbs deep inside me again. I pant and arch my back at the dull spikes that shoot through my spine. "See? You're in so much pain." A flicker of worry dances across his beautiful face.

I'm going to regret this.

"Fine," I whisper. I'm *so* uncomfortable about this and can think of a billion reasons why it isn't a good idea. But I feel like I'm dying—actually dying.

Arulius sits up and leans against the oak tree. I push myself up and my head pulses with such an awful headache. I tip forward as the world spins around me. My knees knock on the ground and my hands press into the soft grass. A shudder runs through me. I'm really dying . . . after I already died? I still don't understand how any of this works. But at the worry I catch in Arulius's eyes, I recall Kastian's words that the second death is *it*.

"Here, let me help you." Arulius dips down and scoops me in his arms. I squirm and thrash against his hard muscles.

"Put me down, Arulius." I push feebly against his face. He leans back against the tree and slides down until he meets the ground with me still in his arms.

"Come on. You don't have to act tough all the time, love." He grins at me.

Gods, I hate this man. I glare at him and he just lets out a soft laugh, exposing his neck. If he thinks any of this is funny, I'll indulge and show him my humor.

I thrust myself into his skin, my teeth penetrating his neck roughly, embedding into his soft flesh. He lets out a surprised shriek and jerks his body violently. I grasp his beautiful, gold-tipped hair and yank his head back, hard, realigning my bite for a stronger pull. He bellows and it's filled with part laugh, part pleasure as I draw in his blood violently. Crimson leaks from my lips and he shudders under my mouth. He tastes like honey. Sweet and natural flavors overrun my body—and heat, so much heat floods my core and the pain starts subduing.

"You *are* mean, lovely." He moans. "Just remember I'll return the favor," he growls into my ear. I whimper as arousal flows over me. I hate that feeding makes me crazed. I hate Arulius for hurting me and Kastian. Most of all I hate how his blood lights my body with a hellfire that I'm not sure I will be able to put out.

He fills me with similar sensual urges that Kastian's blood did, but something is more pulling about Arulius. Maybe it's because of my anger towards him and how he pisses me off. Maybe it's how rough he lets me bite into his flesh while laughing and enjoying the pain. *Masochistic asshole.* I fucking love it.

I tear my teeth from his neck and meet his amethyst eyes. We stare at one another like we just entered a dangerous agreement. "Your turn," I rasp as I break our endless gaze and lick his neck clean.

"Did my blood make you feel better?" he purrs, pushing me back into the grass and pressing his body flush against mine. Oh gods . . . his erection is hard against my throbbing pussy. *Fuck.* I suck my lip in. I don't want to feel this burn—not for *Arulius* of all creatures. My traitorous body will be the end of me.

"Yes," I whisper. He grinds his hips against me and I whimper.

"Elodie, love, you're sending mixed signals here." He chuckles and leans forward and—

I scream.

His teeth are on my throat with fangs fiercely piercing into me. Blood flows into his mouth. He's an angry god demanding retribution from a sacrifice, and I'm his personal one.

Ecstasy thrills through my bones and I grip him tightly. His hair is so soft. He smells like morning rain, fresh crisp air among damp leaves. I inhale and let myself fall into his arms entirely. His lips are plush against my neck and the way he caresses my skin . . . gods. His teeth burn in my veins.

He sets his arms behind my neck and lower back as he sits up, taking me with him. He wrenches his head back, expelling a spew of blood as our eyes meet. His amethyst eyes glow with power and thrum to an unknown beat within him. They're wide as they pulse with that luminous magic of his. The way he is staring at me . . . What does he know?

"What?" I wince as I recover from his pull, still very much aware of where I sit squarely on his cock.

"Elodie, love," he pants, eyes still wide.

"Stop . . . calling me that." I breathe out heavily.

Arulius cups his hand around my nape and tugs me in for an embrace. He hugs me—delicately—and it is . . . dare I say nice?

"What is it?" I ask again, breathless this time. Confusion is pulling at me now from every path in my head.

He clutches me as if I'm going to fall apart. "Elodie," he whispers, his breath hot against my shoulder. Annoyance fills me. He's teasing me, isn't he?

I'll happily return the favor. "Arulius." I say his name with softness, pressing my lips to his neck. He stills beneath me. I become entirely aware of his muscles that splay down his back and arms. The sheer power within them heats my cheeks.

He pulls away and our eyes connect once more. He's stunning, and as he gazes into me, a universe of speckled longing dances in his eyes. I let my focus drift down to his lips, still painted with my blood. I lean forward and brush my tongue across the lower edge of his lip. *What am I doing?* I hate myself for pushing the boundary between us. But I can't hold back. For the first time in a few days I feel undeniably real again. I lick his lip. He whimpers and shuts his eyes. I feel real, like I'm actually here. Living for the first time since my aunt and Margo . . . since *I* died. Does that make me not real? I don't want to focus on that right now. All I know is that Arulius makes me feel like I exist. Here, now.

Maybe I also do it a little to spite Kastian too.

My lips meet his as I kiss the last of myself off him, and then he moves on me. He pushes his lips on mine and slips his tongue into my mouth. We are really doing this. My body aches for him, for anything.

"Is this really happening, love?" He smirks. I kiss his stupid smile and he growls sensually.

"I don't know what's happening." I pull away and exhale. "Can you tell me if this is real? If . . . I'm real." I don't think anything of it. Not with him. Saying the words shouldn't mean anything to someone I hardly know, right?

He nips at my soft ear. "Does this feel real?" His warmth fills my ear, making me shudder.

"Yes," I rasp.

He grins. His hand slides around my back and pulls me over his erect cock. "Does *this* feel real?" I let out a weak cry as his length strokes me. He no doubt feels the wetness that seeps from my thin pants. I nod. He pulls me away, earning a whine of protest. "So then why are you asking if you're real, lovely?" His expression softens. He's looking into me like he sees everything. Like he sees *me*.

Something sinks in me with the way he watches me. Like I'm broken. He asked with such a somber voice. It nearly breaks my heart. Why did I ask that? I guess because nothing feels real anymore. Or at least *I* don't. Is it because I was *in-between* for so long, as Wren said? Nothing seems to fit with anything anymore. My mind scrambles.

"I . . . I just needed to make sure." That's all I can say. It's the truth, after all.

He stares at me for a few moments and I thank the gods that he accepts that as an answer, though he raises a brow at me. He shifts me off his lap and stands, realigning his brackets that I rudely displaced when I fed.

"Can you . . . carry me so we can get to Margo sooner?" I reluctantly ask, gritting my teeth that I would ask him for *anything*. But the moment we just shared . . . it was enough for me to trust him a little more.

He stretches his golden wings and I marvel at how wide they spread. His span is much wider than Kastian's. I wonder if it has to do with age. He said he was around three hundred years old. Kastian is much, much younger, like me. We are birds that have hardly left the nest.

"Of course, lovely," he mutters. "But only on one condition."

I frown. "And what is that?"

"You tell me why you need to make sure you're real." He offers his arms and I let him scoop me up. I consider his words for a few moments. He's the first person to ask for a reason why. Most people just want to hear positive things—*Yes, I'm fine*—and be on with their day. They don't want to know what monsters lie in my heart . . . in my mind.

That's a hefty price to pay. Does he want me to unload all my baggage and woes on him? He doesn't seem like the kind of person who necessarily cares to hear them. But he's staring at me so expectantly. His amethyst eyes flicker with what I dare label concern.

"Fine, but as we fly."

"Good enough for me, love," he chirps as he propels us into the sky.

12

Arulius flies with the grace of a god of wind and sky. My cheeks warm as he flies above the clouds so the sun can reach me. How he knew I was cold is a mystery to me, but I bathe in it. I haven't felt the rays of sunshine in days, and being cooped up in the small cottage has made me rather restless. The light stimulates my skin and I allow myself to soak up the bliss. Even though I know what I have to tell Arulius isn't going to be warm and pleasant, I still feel a weight lift from me, as though the sky is washing the sorrows from my shallow shores.

I'm not even sure where to start, so I just begin where it makes sense.

"Aunt Maggie died . . . then Margo did too."

He raises a brow.

"Margo was my dog. She is why we are heading to the

Hollow Keeper. She was . . . well, she was *everything* to me. I thought I remembered every detail of Margo's death but I don't, or maybe I don't want to. I just know that she is dead and apparently so am I. I wandered the forest as if I was still alive for months. I was . . . searching for something. I knew Margo was gone but I still searched for something. I don't know what, though. Maybe I was hoping that she would find me again if I stayed a while. Each day, endlessly searching."

He's silent. I don't blame him—what's there to say?

"My aunt wore a long frown in death . . . and the vision of it has washed away the smile of hers that I remember, the smile that made her real. I've been so . . . different since then. And I don't even know how I died, and that is—it's pretty hard to accept. I don't *feel* dead." I raise my hand into the sky, the air rushing through my fingers. "But at the same time, I don't feel real either. So that's why I asked, because I desperately need someone to confirm that I'm real. If I'm not, then what's the point of anything?"

He frowns. It's an interesting sight—I've only ever seen him smirk or laugh, the cheeky bastard. He radiates a somber light off his sharp features. His sun-kissed skin glows with the oranges and yellows that prance in the clouds surrounding us.

My hand is still extended into the sky, desperately reaching for the strings of life that I pray will reach back out to me. Arulius dips his wings to the side and my hand plunges into the puffiness of the clouds beneath us. My fingers trickle with wet drops of rain that welcome my skin, the sensation of being caught in a rainstorm. Goosebumps shiver down my neck.

"Being real isn't determined by others saying so," he whispers, reaching his hand out to mine. His warmth and soft touch are as kind as the clouds. His tan skin presses against the back of my elbow. My hand is so small against his. Together our hands are enveloped in the clouds and I know he feels the rain and the kisses they grant just as I do, a million small wishes that live above the realm of Tomorrow. "This moment." His voice is soft in my ear. He clutches me tighter with his other arm, caressing me softly. "*No one* could convince me that this moment isn't real. Even if I'm not, then so be it. The rain greets me nonetheless. The sun warms me anyway. This moment means something to *me* . . . That is real enough."

I'm devoured by his words.

Everything he says makes sense. The rain greets me, the sun warms me, and this moment with him . . . it means something to me too. My heart throbs. I still have feelings about what he's done, but Arulius is so much deeper than he alludes. No one has ever said something so poetic and melancholic like this to me—so sincere. A tear flutters from my eye and is whisked away by the wind that carries us.

"You're smiling, aren't you?" He chuckles.

His voice brings me out of the ruins of myself. I *am* smiling. I let a giggle slip.

"I can tell by the way you tighten your stomach as if you have butterflies," he purrs. "It's cute, love."

My cheeks heat with his admission. "I didn't know I did that."

We arrive in a small village at sunset.

Arulius says it's the keeper's residence and that we will find him here rather than the Hollow's Grove at this hour. It's a quiet village, made up of only a handful of cottages and streets. Trees of what I consider a normal size surround the structures, making them hard to see from above unless you already knew the town is here. Though we are much further north now, the weather is still quite fair. The air is less sweet and holds scents of leaves and moss. A sort of dampness rests in the breeze.

As we fly closer to the ground, I catch a glimpse of Murph's black fur and two beat-to-shit males standing next to him.

"Gods." I roll my eyes and dread that we have to land. The fact that I'd prefer to be with Arulius speaks volumes for how mad I am at them.

"They arrived earlier than I thought," Arulius retorts with a hint of amusement in his tone.

I don't feel like seeing either of them right now. They nearly killed Murph *and* me with their recklessness. Does life mean so little here? Or maybe they just don't fucking care. What if Arulius hadn't healed me in time? I sigh.

Kastian droops his wings as they watch us descend. Good. He should feel bad. Wren watches us from the corner of his eyes. He leans against Murph with a joint in his mouth and his arms crossed over his chest. Arulius sets me down and I stretch my legs with a deep yawn. Saying that it was a long day would be an understatement.

"Hey, look at these." Arulius grabs something on my back. A sensation I don't recognize spreads on the spot he touches, sending a shiver down my spine.

"What *is* that?" I gape and spin, trying to see what he's grabbing. His purple eyes fill with amusement.

"They're so adorable," he purrs.

"What are?" I demand. I can't see what he's pulling on. It's weird to have another extension of my body just between my shoulder blades. My eyes widen as it dawns on me.

He laughs, his voice deep and soft. "Your wings have sprouted, lovely."

I still, excitement bursting through my chest. "Really? What color are they?" I'm not sure why it matters. Am I hoping for golden wings? Maybe dark twilight?

Kastian approaches cautiously as I glare at him and steps beside me. He observes my back. I look away from him. He . . . betrayed me in a way. He became someone entirely different earlier and I don't like it. I don't like *anything* about it. I hear him take a deep breath at my reluctance to speak with him. Good, I hope it stings.

"I'm sorry, Elodie." His voice is heavy. I say nothing—there's nothing *to* say.

"Cream." Fingers glide down my new short wings. "Like the wings of a dove as it faces a yellow and orange-hued dawn," Arulius says drearily, in a way that makes the somber feelings return to my heart. The words are too beautiful to say with such melancholy. He's back to his elusive self now that the others are around again. I feel the need to follow suit.

I turn to face my frenemy. His amethyst eyes dance in the twilight like the corners of the universe. "Thanks, Arulius." A weak smile tugs at my lips.

"Anytime, love." He keeps his face expressionless except for a slight smirk.

For the first time, I don't hate him for using that stupid nickname. Kastian furrows his brow at my new attitude toward the golden Eostrix. I can tell he senses the distance from me and I want it that way.

I ignore Kastian as the three of us walk up the small slope to where Wren leans on Murph. I don't bother looking at him as we come to a stop, but my hand does meet Murph's muzzle. The beast's deep brown eyes tell me he knows what I did for him. He presses his forehead into my chest. His head is easily the size of my entire body.

"You're welcome," I whisper against his forehead. Murph's shadow fur wisps and is cool on my skin. The Pine Hollow lets out a low grunt and I smile.

Wren clears his throat and looks me up and down, no

doubt seeing the blood-soaked clothes from my waist down. "Let's go." I scoff as he waves at me to walk beside him.

We parade through the village until we come upon the largest cottage tucked in the corner of a wall of immaculately thick trees. Their branches hang low and hide the cottage walls almost perfectly. The stones are embossed in ivy and I almost want to ask if I can take a clipping of it, but I have no place to keep it or plant it, so I just admire them silently as Wren knocks thrice on the old wooden door.

There's some rustling, and then a male, maybe a handful of years older than Wren, appears behind the door. He recognizes Wren and Arulius but his gaze lingers over Kastian and me suspiciously.

"Commander Bartholomew." The man dips his head and holds his bow until Wren speaks.

"Moro. It's nice to see you." He lifts his chin high, expression sharp. I raise a brow but choose to remain silent. Wren definitely fits the part of Violet's Commander. It's hard to remind myself that he's a high-performing part in her military. To me he's just Wren, the friend I hate right now. I want to believe that he truly is on my side. That's why we're here, isn't it?

"What can I do for you and your . . . guards?" Moro leans against his door to glance at Kastian and me again, giving us a thorough frisking with his eyes.

Wren nudges me forward. "This is Elodie, my current intake. We are here for her Pine Hollow." *Current intake.* I roll my eyes and bite my tongue to keep from saying something I'll regret.

I gaze up at Moro nervously. He seems nice enough, but I've been fooled before. His skin is dark and smooth, a stark contrast to his brilliant silver eyes and short, gold-speckled hair. He meets my gaze and raises a brow.

"New intake, huh?" he asks Wren like I'm not standing here. Wren nods and Moro tightens his lips in thought. "Might take a few days to find her Hollow. We've been experiencing huge influxes of them lately." His hand finds his scruffy chin. Gold stubble hairs bristle as he scratches his jaw.

My heart plummets. That means that large numbers of dogs are dying in my world. I clench my fists. Some thoughts are too horrible to think. I don't want to hear the soft whimpers of their passing. I can't let myself lose sight of what I need to focus on right now, so I shake the thoughts from my head.

Margo.

"That's fine. May we have quarters to rest in while we wait?" Wren unstraps his forearm brackets as if he's ready to rest this very instant. Kastian and Arulius both look eager to rest as well.

I can feel my shoulders slumping too. I've always hated traveling and how it saps the energy from my bones. Every time Mom and Dad managed to somehow pull me from our forest, I would mope the entire time. Mother used to get so frustrated with me when we traveled to Heirah for the annual festival held in Barkovah. I was only ten, but I felt weaker each day we were away from home. Away from my forest.

Moro lets us all sit at his dining table while he prepares a few rooms—*a few* meaning I have to share with someone, and I hate the idea of it being with *any* of them. I slump in my chair with nothing short of a bad attitude and glance around Moro's keep.

It's pleasantly normal. There are enormous harnesses on a hook near the front door and a few muzzles that I'm not sure would even fit Murph, they're so large. I ponder if Margo would fit in any of the harnesses. She was a formidable Shiba mix in my world, so why shouldn't she be just as perfect here too? I let my chin rest on my forearms as I study the room. The warmth from the hearth and the ambiance itself here makes me feel much lighter already. I can tell Moro is a good person just by his style of living.

The stairs creak under Moro's feet as he patters up and down them, bringing blankets and pillows to rooms upstairs. The scents of burning wood and cedar fill the space, making me think of home. The logs crackle and snap, luring me into an even wearier state than when we arrived.

Kastian and Wren try to talk to me a few times, but I refuse so much as to acknowledge them. Arulius finds this amusing and laughs hysterically each time they try. I have to bite back a smile each time he does, because dammit, his laugh is contagious. This leads to him getting a few punches in the arm and a haunting glare from Wren.

Once Moro finishes with the rooms, we are offered a hot

meal consisting of bread, cheese, and vegetation I don't recognize. Supper is quiet, awkward, and—oh, weird. Moro wasn't expecting anyone so he hardly has any room to sit in his messy entertaining room. More harnesses and grooming items are littered across his furniture. I question how bearable the stay will be, and how long.

Then comes the room assignments. I push for my own room, I really do, but Wren argues that I won't hesitate to run away again and that I've lost those privileges. Kastian offers but Wren and I both heavily disagree. I know it hurts his feelings when his eyes widen at my protest, but fuck him. How does he think I felt after him not even noticing a *tree* fall on me? Especially one that *he* made fall.

That leaves Arulius. I go to bat for him—if I have to stay anywhere, he is much better than my other options. Of course, Wren laughs me off. He makes it clear that I have no choice in the matter. That *he* is my caretaker, like I'm some Hollow. I haven't forgotten the collar that he put on me—the leash too. My fingers trail back to my neck, relieved it's still gone. I loathe the idea of obeying him but I have no choice.

The room reminds me of Wren's cottage in Caziel. It's empty and sort of somber, proof of a lonely life and nothing to fill it with. Does Moro not have a family? I picture his life just spent tending to the Hollows for centuries, coming home to no one. At least the Cypress has Marley to speak with. This place is . . . utterly empty. There's not a single photo to grace the walls.

Wren makes the bed and hangs his clothes on hooks by

the door. He opens the dresser and pulls out a large white shirt and tosses it to me. "Here, put that on. I'll have Moro's maids clean your uniform tomorrow." He keeps his amber gaze on the floor.

I narrow my eyes on him. "I'm not getting dressed with you in here."

He shrugs. "Then sleep in your bloody clothes, Elodie." He lies down in the bed and faces the other direction. I roll my eyes. Good enough.

My crimson uniform puddles at my ankles as I slip into the large white shirt. It fits me like a dress and I wonder what giant once lived here to have a shirt so enormous. I leave my clothes on the floor and frown at the blood that still clings to my legs and below my waist. It looks like I've bathed in the damn stuff.

Thankfully there's a bathroom in the hall next to our room with a tub and large bucket of warm water set there by Moro. I silently thank the keeper. He must have seen the state of my clothes. I sigh. *What a long fucking day.*

My skin thrills as the warm water engulfs me. How long has it been since I've had a bath? A few days at least. I sigh again and start scrubbing. When I finish, the water is murky with a pink hue. I drain the tub and dry my hair with a citrus-scented towel.

The shirt feels better against my skin now that I'm clean. I slip back into it and return to the room, then finally crawl into bed. Wren doesn't move and I send another silent thanks to whatever gods blessed this night so greatly. I don't realize how ready for sleep I am until my face sinks into my pillow. I nuzzle my cheeks into the soft fabric and the pull of rest has me before I can even think about the day's events for the hundredth time.

It's still dark when pain shoots through me, waking me from my dreamless sleep. I cover my mouth to keep my yelp silenced. My bones burn again, so horribly and violently. At one point I swear I can feel the flesh around them sizzling and melting. My back flinches near the stubs of my wings and I can hear it—the cracking and wet snaps. Smoldering pain ignites through me. I wrestle myself so that my face is buried in my pillow. I don't know how long I stay like that, but it feels like hours of excruciating agony.

Finally, the pain eases. My mind is exhausted from battling the screams that welled in the back of my throat. I slump back into the sheets. I can feel feathers against my back now. They rest just below my ribs, curling at the ends above my tailbone.

"That was *something*."

I flinch at his voice but don't have the energy to say anything back. Of course my painful growth spurt woke him up. I'm already facing him so I opt to keep my eyes closed. If I ignore him, maybe he'll just leave me alone. I'm really, *really* not in the mood.

The bed sinks as he moves closer. "You know, they say it can take up to two hundred years for an Eostrix's wings to fully come in." His calloused hands run over my left wing.

Interesting. I keep still, resisting the sarcasm that begs me to retort with obscene things. *Please just assume I'm asleep.*

"Are you feeling hungry?"

I'm fucking *starving.* But I'd rather rot in a cell than feed off Wren again. I can wait until morning and meet with Arulius. I can't believe he's my go-to now, but I refuse to feed from Kastian either after what he did. Same with Wren. And Arulius isn't so bad after all. I find that he's actually really kind, whether it's real or not. He's real enough for me.

Wren leans in closer and his breath warms my cheek. "Elodie. I know you're not sleeping. I need to talk to you."

He won't give up until he says whatever he needs to say. I sigh. "What?"

"See, I knew you weren't asleep," he murmurs. I can hear the sly smile on his lips and it pisses me off.

"What do you want to talk about?"

He lies nose to nose with me and it takes all I have to keep from rolling over. "I want to apologize for not helping you when the tree fell . . . I also want to thank you for saving Murph." His brows knit close together. "I can never repay you for saving him."

Oh, *now* I get an apology? When no one is listening? At least he knows I saved his Hollow. Prick.

"I couldn't just do nothing. He would have been smashed." I huff.

"Like you were?" he whispers painfully.

I flinch and gaze up at him. His long, dark hair rests across his neck and a few strands cross his face. His deep amber eyes are soft like they were last night. Why is he so different around others? To uphold his image as Commander?

"Why are you so cruel?"

His eyes widen at my words and a pang of hurt flickers in them. "Cruel? Ouch. I have a duty to uphold, Elodie. I can't let friendships and courtesies get in the way of that."

"It wasn't your duty to fight with Kastian," I counter.

Wren's face becomes expressionless.

"It wasn't your duty to let me and Arulius go off on our own. And what about your duty to Murph? Just letting your loyal companion die . . . Disgusting."

He wrinkles his nose in disdain as I say the latter. That's his weakness, his soft spot.

"You don't understand anything. You're just a stupid dead girl." He glares at me through the dim light.

Just a stupid dead girl. That one hits me deep and he sees it. He can see the break he causes in my walls. I bite down on my tongue to keep the tears in. No *friend* would ever say that.

"Shit, Elodie, I'm sorry—I shouldn't have—"

I push myself up even though my body screams at me. His words shake me to my core. I won't let him speak to me that way. I won't let *anyone* speak to me that way. Because what he just said is true . . . I *am* just some dead girl. *You're not real, you're not real.* The words cave in my mind once more, burying me further in myself, into the dark corners that I've managed to stay on the edge of for so long. The room seems to shake as I stumble to my feet and make for the door.

Wren crashes to the floor behind me but I'm determined to get as far from him as I can. I fumble with the doorknob, and when it opens I tear down the hall, each step more sure than the last. *I need to get air. I need to feel real. Anything. Anything but this dark emptiness.*

"Elodie! Stop!"

Doors open behind me as his shout no doubt wakes the others. Footsteps crash behind me and my stomach wrenches. I'm not trying to run away, I just want . . . I just need to be alone. To get some air. To feel real.

I'm halfway down the flight of stairs when arms wrap around my waist, sending me and my captor pummeling down the steps. A dreadful snap and burst of pain in my wing tell me immediately that I've broken it. Agony shoots up the spot between my shoulders. We slam into the main floor with more cracking and groaning. My heart pounds against my ribs with increasing fear. Wren pins me to the ground and presses on my broken wing with his palm.

I let out a cry that I never knew I could make. It's rotten and so is he. It's the act of a wolf in sheep's clothing.

"Just when I think you'll figure out you can't escape me," he snarls into my ear. There's a certain type of evil that Wren is. An evil that he will never face. He'd rather take it out on me instead.

"I just want to be alone!" I scream and try to lift myself, but I'm so weak and everything pounds with a vile, deep pain. "I wasn't trying to escape, Wren, I'm just trying to get away from *you!*" My voice is so loud in my ears and I continue to scream through gasps and tears. "You said . . . you said I'm just *some dead girl!*" Tears brim in my eyes. "I already know that I'm . . . I'm not real anymore."

Silence shrouds the dark entertaining room except for my gasping sobs.

Wren stares at me through bewildered eyes.

A light flicks on and my gaze meets our audience. Moro looks concerned, but it's Kastian and Arulius, to my surprise, that have horrified expressions written on their faces.

"What the fuck did you say to her?" Arulius's hand crunches something in his palm. His eyes are wide and he's not composed. It's the first time I've seen him without his gold armor. His features aren't nearly as intense or frightening without them. He's shirtless and wears black pants that hug his skin.

Wren flinches above me and snaps at them, "She was trying to leave . . . I—I couldn't let her escape again—"

Kastian's black wings blur through the thin space above and crash into Wren. I roll once with the force of his tackle. My body is slick and wet with hot crimson. Everything in me screams *run*, but I have business to finish. I'm not going to run away this time. Not when Margo is this close. My chest is tight with the chaos warring inside me.

The two males struggle violently across Moro's furniture and I hear him gasp from above at the mess they're making. Arulius is at my side in a matter of moments and helps me stand.

"Are you okay, love?" His amethyst eyes inspect me thoroughly and wince with every broken bone and cut he finds. "You're *not* okay—you need to come upstairs."

I rip my hand from his. He blinks in surprise at what little strength I have left. "No. We aren't replaying yesterday."

"Elodie," he mutters in a concerned voice, but lets me press on.

I approach them as Kastian clasps Wren's stupid neck in his powerful jaws in what I assume will be a deadly bite. I've put enough together at this point to realize that Kastian shows his affection and care through violence, but I don't need violence. I need comfort. So why is Arulius the only one . . .

"Stop."

Kastian's jaw muscles tense and his azure eyes reveal his distress. Wren grips at the Eostrix's hands that pin his body to the ground. He's done. I have the entire room's attention and it fucking sucks. I want to be alone and cry for hours at what Wren said to me, but I won't. Instead, I'm here and I'm going to make myself very fucking clear to them. All of them. But what will get through to them? Wren just wants to fulfill his *duty* to Violet. Kastian wants to help me, gods know why, and Arulius . . . I think Arulius just wants to be entertained. My lips sting as I set my teeth into them.

"All I want is Margo," I stammer. "I just want Margo. I *want* to room with Arulius while we stay here and I *want* to be left *alone*. I don't give a shit how we do it, but you two stop fucking fighting and just *find Margo*." I glare at them. Kastian lets a low growl out as he crunches into Wren's neck anyway.

The Cypress squirms under him as blood leaks from his throat.

I don't care. I said what I needed to. I'm done and am so godsdamn tired. I limp to Arulius.

"Elodie." He mutters my name carefully, as if I will break if he says it any other way. I lean into the golden Eostrix and let him carry me into his room.

He shuts the door with his hip and gently lays me on the bed. He curses several times as he examines my body. My wing and right wrist are broken, several lacerations spread across my ribs, and my ankles are swollen.

"Gods," he curses, shutting his eyes at the sight of my wing. "It'd just grown. You might never fly right." Arulius's finger glides gently across my feathers as his words sink into me.

I'm thankful that I haven't seen them yet. It hurts less since I don't know what my wings look like. Hurts less since I've never truly flown. But knowing that I've been robbed all the same instills great pain where my hope and excitement had grown.

He presses his palm to my cheek and I gaze into his purple eyes, I'm so, so tired. But my consciousness is wearier. What does it matter if I'm real or not? I'm *dead*. That much is true. Permanent. Not ever going to change. The only part of me left is my love for Margo and the hope to see her again.

"I need to heal you, love." Arulius lies close to me. I glance over and quickly find the thick artery in his neck.

Is this what my life is now? Pain, suffering, feeding, and

more pain? I flex my jaw, disgusted with myself and everything I've become. Tears fall over my cheeks. I clench my hand over my chest, wrinkling the white shirt that I now realize is torn in several places after the scuffle.

I have worse things to be worried about.

"Is it the only way to heal?" I rasp. He studies me for a moment and nods. "Okay," I murmur somberly.

He leans against the wall that his bed is pushed against and holds me. Oh gods, he holds me so delicately. He's considerate of my wounds, especially my wing. He seems the most upset about that. I purse my lips and press into his neck. He doesn't flinch.

He strokes my hair gently and sets his other hand across my stomach. I drink tenderly from him. I'm feeling fragile. Something about the violence Wren displayed makes a trauma I don't quite remember throb through my bones. It's there but . . . it also isn't. I can't figure out if it's because I don't want to remember this trauma or that I truly am not capable of it. I remember hurting so horribly. I remember blood and screaming. Fur and . . . Margo.

I consume him softly tonight. He makes me feel so safe. Why is Arulius being so nice? I suppose he never *wasn't* nice to me, he just accidentally almost *killed* me that one time. But ever since then he's been . . . like a missing part of me. I think of him showing me what it was to be real, my own definition of real. *Maybe I can be real again someday. Maybe I will feel the rain kiss my skin and the sun warm my weary soul . . . Someday, maybe.* I crack my eyes open. He's gazing down at me. Such a warm gaze. It pierces my heart with emotion. So much grief rests in his gaze, but why? I close my eyes. *Tonight, I wish I wasn't real.*

I pull my teeth out slowly and rest my chin on his shoulder.

I'm so damn tired.

"Here, lie down, love." Arulius brings his pillow over and tucks me in. I don't deserve his kindness and I don't have any words, not after what happened. He tugs a blanket over my shoulders and wraps an arm around me, pulling me close and placing a gentle kiss on my forehead.

This moment. *This moment matters.* His words soak back into me. A weak smile tingles on my lips. This moment matters. In a night of moments that don't, this one does.

"You *are* real," he whispers into the darkness. I don't reply. I can't conjure words that would thank him enough for his comfort. Instead, I nuzzle into his embrace and cry until the gods of sleep come for me.

13

I lie in bed until midday. I don't want to see Wren or Kastian or anyone except Arulius and the Hollow keeper. I want to see Margo desperately and Moro will be the one to deliver the news, so I wait impatiently. Moro stopped in for a moment hours ago to let me know he's headed out to start searching for her. He reminded me that it will be a few days at the least, so to not get my hopes up for the day.

Great. What are we going to do for a few days? I mull over how much empty time I'll have to worry my ass off about stupid things. Like what if I don't recognize Margo right away? What if she doesn't remember me? I let out a sigh. I can't just sit around and have this anxiety building up inside me.

I can just stay cooped up in this room, but that doesn't

make me feel better and it feels like Wren wins if I hide the entire time we're here.

Arulius gives me the space I need. He suits up early and mumbles that he's going to spend the day training. He didn't say I couldn't join, but he also didn't offer to teach me. So I decided not to say anything as he left.

Learning to fight is a double-edged sword. On the plus side, I can defend myself and kick Wren's ass. On the downside, I will probably lose more *privileges* and be put back in the Vernovian Thorn or lose my chance to get Margo back. I mull it over for a good few hours. I only stop fretting when a sharp knock rattles my door.

"Yes?"

"Elodie." It's Kastian. Good gods. "May I come in?"

I frown, but I've already moped most of the day and my rage is already subduing toward him.

I sigh. "Sure, come in."

The door cracks open and Kastian's white hair and ebony horns are the first to appear. He peeks in as if he thinks I'm armed with pillows and have them cocked and ready. As his blue eyes make it over the edge of the door, I can't hold my laugh any longer.

"You're *that* afraid of me, huh?" I settle on the side of the bed.

He curls a smile and enters the room, softly shutting the door behind him. "I just hope you know how bad I feel about yesterday . . . about *all* of yesterday." He regards me and I pat the spot next to me. Relief flickers across his eyes and he sits down.

"I know. I just wish *Arulius* hadn't been the one to help me. I thought you and I were closer than that." I hesitate. Gods, I can't even look at him. His sage scent fills my senses, reminding me of his lonely estate in the glades. My heart aches with the thought of his loneliness and how he tries so hard with me.

"I know, it's no excuse. Nothing could excuse how I acted."

"Well?"

"Well, what?"

"What's your excuse? I want to hear what it is at least," I retort.

He brings his gaze to the window. "It's not an excuse . . . It's just how I've always handled my problems." He pauses. "I try to stomp out the things that hurt or harm, instead of dealing with them. It's like a tick in my mind, and once I snap I just . . . I can't focus on anything else except the rage. I'm so sorry, Elodie."

I purse my lips. I wasn't expecting that. None of us are perfect. It's hard to admit to our flaws.

I give him a nod, accepting his apology and letting my mind trail back to Arulius. He's already been gone half the day. I decide to change the subject. "Is Arulius back from training?"

He raises a brow at me. "Why?"

"Do I *need* a reason? I'm just curious." I roll my eyes and tilt my head at him. He considers me with his ocean eyes before standing. The tension between us is still taut.

"Well, let's go see. You need to eat lunch anyway." He rises and stretches his wings. I haven't touched mine all morning. I'm too afraid to see if the damage remains from last night.

The stairway rails are reduced to shards of sharp wooden spears angling upward in an awful manner—evidence of the night's harrowing events. I tense as we carefully make our way down the steps and peer into the entertaining room. Thankfully, Wren isn't around.

I let a low breath of relief escape me. "What's for lunch?" I don't bother smiling at him.

He walks into the kitchen with a grin. I take a seat at Moro's small dining table, still a mess from supper last night. Poor Moro. We just barged into his house, ate his food, destroyed his staircase, and forced him to search for *one* Pine Hollow. *My* Pine Hollow.

My Margo.

Kastian sets down a jar of some sort of jam and a few different types of bread. I stare up at him. He has a proud smile stretched across his lips. I bite down on my lower lip and try to keep the mean things I want to say to him in my head. *Asshole. Bastard. You were going to let me die.* Something along those lines.

"Which do you like?" He doesn't notice my seething. He holds up one loaf that is covered in seeds and oats. I shake my head. He selects a lighter loaf. "This one?" he tries. I shrug.

"Sure."

We eat and make small talk about what the remainder of our stay will entail. Kastian offers to teach me the basics of flying, but with my wings being so small still and one severely injured, I don't think it will help. He insists, saying how important proper basics are. I roll my eyes but eventually agree.

I take my last bite of bread and sweet jam. "Arulius is training. Maybe he can teach me a few things?" I mutter. I glance at him and pause midbite. Stupid—such a stupid thing for me to ask. I let my shoulders droop. Arulius won't want to spend his time training *me*. I'm still really unsure of our relationship. Are we enemies, friends, guard and prisoner? He's so hard to get a read on.

"What's going on between you guys? I've never seen Arulius so . . . attentive," He mumbles as he shoves the last bite in his mouth. His cheeks are rosy from the afternoon cup of mead we indulge in. Turns out Moro had a stash under the kitchen sink and, well, we have nothing better to do. I take a deep sip of mine as well, allowing myself to smile in my cup as the flavor of honey soaks my tongue.

"We are on friendly talking terms, which is more than I can say for you."

He slumps in his chair. "I know, I know. And again, I'm really sorry." He sits still for a moment, his cup clenched between his hands. "I get so blinded by rage sometimes and I . . . I never spend much time around others, so it's hard for me to be socially appropriate. I care about you, Elodie, more than you know. I cared when the tree fell and when Wren hurt you last night . . . Instead of comforting you, I lashed out on Wren. It's my way of coping. I know I fucked up."

I soften my eyes. I'd be lying if I said a part of me didn't understand where he's coming from. I'm socially awkward, but he's been banished to the glades to live utterly alone. I *know* he cares and that he is trying, but it doesn't mean it didn't hurt.

I fold my arms. "Fine, it's fine. But I won't forgive you next time if you do it again. Got it?"

He gives me a weak smile and nods gratefully.

We clean up the table and kitchen in silence. I mend the broken stair rails as best I can, and Kastian promises we will ask Wren for money to buy material to properly fix it when he returns.

"Where did you say Wren went?" I ask. A bad feeling has been weighing on my stomach all morning. It's not like him to leave me alone with the one friend I have—correction, Arulius is my friend now too—but still. Something is off. Isn't that the entire reason he *attacked* me last night? To keep me from *escaping* him? I let my eyes roll. What a fucking hypocrite.

He probably left me here alone because he knows I won't run. He knows my only goal is Margo. But the real question that keeps me up at night is why he is helping me get her. I can't figure out what he is getting out of this.

"He said he was helping Moro in the search."

Kastian's horns gleam as he steps out into the sun. He

tucks his wings tightly to his back to avoid the heat seeping into them. I observe and try to copy, but gods, I never thought it would be so hard to control these things. I try flexing muscles down that are foreign, but my wing flaps up and smacks the side of my face instead. Kastian purses his lips, his blue eyes widening, and then he roars with laughter.

I flatten my ears and narrow my eyes at his amusement with me. "I don't see what's so funny."

"You." He lets another roar of laughter out. "You're like a newborn Eostrix testing your wings." I swear I see a tear roll from his eye and I just want to smack him.

"Oh my gods! Stop!" I shout and end up laughing as well. My cream-colored wing is still perked up as if I'll have to fight it back down.

After his laughing fit subsides, he helps me settle the wing down. "See, we are *definitely* going to need to go over the basics."

I hate that he's right. "Uh-huh." I grin nonetheless. I've never been one for grudges. Mom always said I had a big heart. I'm still angry with him, but I won't let the dreadful feelings drag down my day and he *is* trying to make up for it.

The village is more active now that it's midday. Still, with only a handful of cottages, it's pretty quiet, which I don't mind—not at all. With the few villagers that are stirring, I somehow manage to elicit an uncomfortable number of stares.

"Why are they looking at me?" I nudge Kastian with my elbow.

"Must be your odd wing color and ears." He hesitates.

"I'm sure mine doesn't help either." That's right, he is the only ebony Eostrix I've seen. My chest tightens as I think of how lonely that must be. My eyes trail his scars once more. His neck and arms hold the most. They are dull and blackened against his tan skin. I can't help but notice there are a few fresher ones too. *Wren.*

"You still owe me a story, you know." I twirl dark strands of my hair and keep my gaze ahead.

"Hmm? Oh yeah." He dips down and intertwines his fingers with mine. Stunned, I gaze up at him.

"What are you doing?"

A mischievous grin forms on his glinting lips. "I saw this once when I was a boy. Not many of us have elders that are willing to take us in when we arrive here, so I taught myself many things as I survived in the streets of Nesbrim. No one wanted a dark-winged Eostrix. They said I was bad luck. A bad omen . . . Anyway, a lord and his lady were walking through a crowded street one day and they held hands like this." My fingers grip a little tighter at the sadness in his voice. "It's not a common thing in Tomorrow, to hold hands, but I figured it must mean that they were close. Perhaps they found one another after arriving by miracle. It was a gesture of comfort and love."

I reach my free hand up to my chest, my heart breaking with the idea of him as a child all alone, not understanding love or kindness.

"Why were you a child when you arrived here?"

He glances down at our intertwined fingers. "Because I

died as a child in the human realm. I don't remember much. I was only five."

My feet stop before my heart does, tears fast behind. "Kastian . . . I'm so sorry." I search his face for the pain I feel, but his eyes are only filled with warmth.

"That's about as good of a story as I can muster up, I'm afraid." He rubs the back of his head and gives me a fake smile. I can see the hurt ebbing through it and my heart drops.

"Don't."

He raises a brow. "Don't what?"

"Don't pretend like you're okay." My eyes soften and I squeeze his hand. He stares at me for a few seconds.

"You don't miss anything, do you?" His smile fades. "I'm long past that pain. I'm okay now. Much better."

I furrow my brows. "Promise?"

He dips his head down and presses his forehead against mine. "I promise, Elodie."

"What are you two doing out here?"

We both fidget our fingers with a jolt, but Kastian doesn't let go. "Arulius. We are actually coming out to train with you." The golden Eostrix raises a brow at me and I shrink under his beautiful purple gaze. "Then some flying basics. You should have seen her slap her face with her own wing earlier." Kastian smirks. I shove him, our fingers still locked together. Arulius is acutely aware of this. His gaze lingers there, expressionless and distant.

He looks me over and after a few dreadful moments he finally mutters, "Fine." I can't help but feel a bit disappointed. There he goes, reverting back to his cold and callous demeanor.

Pots of flowers and vines cover the patios of every shop we pass. Some are even set around the stone pillars at the entrance of the Hollow village. I can't help but notice how Arulius admires them too. Maybe he also has an affinity for bright, cheerful plants and whimsical greens.

He leads us to a grouping of trees. They all bear deep cuts and bleed sap that's a deep shade of blue. I gawk at it, not just at the odd, thick sap, but also the depth of the cuts. I glance at Arulius. He doesn't look particularly impressed by it.

"I don't get it. Where are your weapons?" I examine them both. Neither has carried a sword or dagger this entire trip. They share an amused glance and look back at me.

"Eostrixes don't wield swords, lovely," Arulius muses. He lifts his right arm and I honestly don't know what I'm expecting. Giant claws? A blade to form from his palm? It's nothing like any of that.

A golden aura shrouds his arm and he slashes in the air towards the trees. The aura holds its arced form as it rips through the air and slices the bark deeply. Blue sap flicks across the grass and rocks.

My mouth gapes. Gods—what kind of power *was* that? I gawk at him. His body thrums, shimmering with the remnants of the aura. He stands tall and his amethyst eyes radiate with power. Golden wisps of energy flow through the purple waves. His brows furrow and he grabs my hand, making me flinch. His grip loosens and he sucks his lower lip in.

"Your turn, love," he mumbles as if he's annoyed with me. Kastian leans against a tree behind us. He doesn't seem that impressed, but I am shaking from the display. Do they expect *me* to be able to do that?

"I can't do *that*." I put my hands together nervously. I thought I'd be training with a weapon, not some power within me. Embarrassment fills my cheeks. I don't want them to watch me fail.

Arulius dips his head down over my shoulder so Kastian can't hear. "It's okay, love. I'll show you how, okay?" I clench my teeth. His breath is warm on my neck and it threatens to send heat through my core.

"I'm not some baby," I seethe and shake him off. He smirks and takes the same stance he did moments ago, waiting for me to replicate it.

"You need to focus. Push all your being into your hand and hone it." I copy his stance and frown as I'm already losing his instructions in my head.

"Focus, hand, hone," I repeat. He nods. I raise my arm and stare at my palm. I try to envision whatever the hell *honing aura* means. I try to push energy into my hand, but after a few minutes of utter nothingness, my arm is drained from holding it up rather than filled with aura.

I drop my hand to my side and let out a sigh. "It's not working." Arulius observes me closely.

"I think that's enough for today, love." He pats my head. I

narrow my eyes at him. "It takes practice. You're not some prodigy and you won't master it in one day." His purple gaze brims with amusement.

I don't need to be a prodigy. I just need something to keep me safe from Wren and Violet. I shudder thinking of that horrible woman. Her crimson eyes creep into my mind.

"Well, what about self-defense? I know you guys know how to do that," I retort. Kastian approaches me now.

"I can teach you while we work on your wings." A small beat of hope pulses through me. This I know I can manage for the day.

We train all afternoon and every second of it is grueling. The wing exercises are simple enough. I learn how to extend and retract them, feeling like a child learning how to walk. It's weird moving muscles that never existed before, but I make do. Self-defense is another task altogether. Kastian shows me a few moves, one to trip my attackers and another to pin them. Arulius comes at me more times than I can count and throws me on my ass more times than I'd like to admit. He isn't going easy on me, not even a little bit. *Fucking asshole.*

At one point I hook his ankle and think I have him, but he shifts his weight to his other leg with speed I didn't know he had and counters. I'm flat on my back and seething before I even know what he's done. The only satisfaction I get is watching a bead of sweat roll down his forehead and knowing I'm at least putting up a small fight.

The sun is setting and my stomach's empty. I can't tell if I need food or if I need blood. I haven't had any since last night.

The cottages have warm lights glowing from inside, and insects stir in the air. I think it's funny that insects even exist here in the afterlife. What purpose do they serve? Are they the souls of bugs who perished on the other side of Bresian? I ponder the thought, feeling a little bad for the ants my aunt helped me stomp on when I was five. We eradicated an entire army. Even still, they make this realm feel more like home. Perhaps they are purely for comforting those who've stumbled here like me. Those who need the simple comfort of their wings' low hum.

As Moro's cottage comes into view, I can make out Wren's figure leaning against the vines and Murph's fur casting shadows into the window light above.

"Kastian, how long will I need to feed on blood?"

The two Eostrixes turn in unison and gawk at me. Oh gods, maybe I shouldn't have asked at all. Is it a weird topic for them? I lace my fingers to keep them from trembling.

Arulius lets out a snide chuckle and Kastian looks like he's about to just pretend he didn't even hear me ask. My cheeks heat.

"Love, you will need to feed for the rest of your life. More now because you're transitioning, but it won't ever go away," Arulius purrs.

What? That can't be . . .

"But why?" I whisper. "I don't understand why."

Kastian gives me his famous expression of pity. "Eostrixes are just made that way. It's in our nature. We feed to keep our aura complete and our bodies strong. It's also how we . . ." His voice chokes up.

"How we fuck." Arulius hums.

I swallow my spit down the wrong tube and cough violently. What the hell! Arulius cackles and Kastian covers his face with his hand. I feel as ashamed as he looks. I've fed on three males already . . . three! A well of shame and embarrassment fills me. My stomach twists and I just want to hide.

"No need to be shy, love. It's natural here. Whether it be feeding, healing or . . . you get it." He grins. It's the first genuine smile he's made all day. I can't help but soak it in. It's too beautiful to ignore.

"I'm not a . . . trollop, am I?" I mutter between tightly closed lips.

Arulius lets another roar of laughter fall over us and I—oh gods—I want to disappear.

"A trollop? Love, I'll say it clearer for you. It's *normal* for Eostrixes to feed on one another and others. Just not Cypresses and those of the High Court. We don't touch those." His eyes graze over me.

"I guess it's just all really different for me." I sigh.

Kastian tugs on my floppy ear and grins. "It's okay, don't feel weird. Just let your instincts guide you." I nod and try to push the conversation out of my mind. The way Arulius spoke sends waves of urges through me, and I repress a smile as I think of feeding on him tonight.

Wren is grumpy, as *always*.

He eats his supper with silent fury and doesn't talk much. I avoid his gaze just as much as he avoids mine.

Arulius breaks the silence first. "Where have you been all day?" He pushes a small potato-looking vegetable around on his plate.

Wren shrugs and mutters, "I was helping Moro search for the Pine Hollow."

Moro shifts in his seat uneasily at that and I know he's lying. The remainder of dinner is quiet and everyone is exhausted. I don't bother even glancing at Wren as everyone makes their way back into the bedrooms. I am to room with Arulius for the remainder of our stay because Wren hates Kastian and assumes we would try to escape or plan something elaborate, which I'm not capable of, especially after training all day.

I plop onto the bed and tear my boots off first. My feet are blistered and sore from kicking and tripping all damn day. Arulius takes a bath first. I explore the room and dig through the dresser until I find another oversized shirt to sleep in. I sit and wait for what feels like hours for Arulius to finish up. When he finally opens the bathroom door, he rubs a towel against his wet hair and grins at me.

"Your turn, lovely."

"Stop calling me that," I hiss. "My name is *Elodie*."

He raises a brow and pouts. "I don't want to call you by your name."

"Too bad."

"Hmm. How about Ellie?" He clutches his chin with his hand in thought.

I scoff.

"Odie?" I roll my eyes and push him. "Got it—El."

"No nicknames!" I snarl. He covers his head as I toss the shirt I found at him.

He laughs. "Okay—see? Love isn't so bad, so just deal with it. *Love.*" I seethe at him, but after hearing all the names he *could* pick, I will settle.

"Whatever." I stride into the bathroom and shut the door.

I let the heat soak into my weary body and think of Margo. For the first time since leaving the room this morning, I realize, I haven't had thoughts of my existence. I let myself slip into the tub until the water sits just below my nose. Today was nice.

Once I finish up, I pull the overly large shirt on and set my dirty clothes in the hamper for Moro's maids. They must've been in earlier in the day because my uniform is clean and folded nicely on the vanity.

Arulius is in bed with a book in his hands and doesn't so much as glance at me as I creep into bed. *Thank the gods.* The shirt is nearly see-through. I snuggle the sheets over myself and keep my back to him. He reads for a while longer before turning off his light.

I'm nearly asleep when I feel his arm slide under mine and over my stomach. I still and heat instantly flushes across my face.

"What are you doing?" I whisper. He brings his lips to my

neck and I flinch. A deep, dull ache throbs between my thighs. He pauses and pecks a kiss against my skin.

"I'm hungry."

I smile. It's dark enough, so I hope he can't see my expression, but I've been waiting all day for this. *I'm hungry too.* I push my neck up toward him and he purrs.

He slides his tongue along my neck, eliciting a breath from me. I hate how he makes me feel, but at the same time I want to devour the feeling, because no one has ever made my heart beat as furiously as he does.

I press my hand against his, warmly splayed over my stomach. He gives my neck another lick and then embeds his teeth into me softly. He makes me feel everything. I can feel the rain against us as he held me in the sky that evening, and so much warmth. My skin tingles with the brush of his. I let out a soft moan and he tightens his hold on me, inhaling deeply and pushing his hips against me. There's hardly anything between us and the shirt is already riding up.

Gods.

I pant and moan uncontrollably. He grinds himself into my backside ruthlessly and I devour the sensation of it . . . of him. His erection makes itself known and—gods I think he is bigger than Kastian. He takes one last deep pull of my blood and something happens when he does. I cup my hand over my mouth to keep from screaming out as my entire body thrills with rain and sun and *him*.

He remains still and our breaths sync, long and staggered. I can't think and I don't want to. I just want to *feel*. I want to know that I am real and this . . . this is real. I bite my cheek and blood pools in my mouth as he slowly withdraws his fangs. He swipes his tongue over my wound and cleans me thoroughly, sending ripples of pleasure and lust through me.

I roll to face him and his purple eyes radiate warmth. The way he looks at me makes my heart pulse faster and slower at the same time. I want to . . . *No. He doesn't care about me. This is just normal Eostrix behavior.* I reel my feelings back in. It's going to take some getting used to, to not feel what these moments tear from my heart.

We don't say anything. In a way, we don't need to. I slide over him and press my mouth against his shoulder. I'm tired of the neck and want something new tonight. I bite into his flesh above his collar bone. He yelps. I wonder what it feels like. Good—more than good, I'm sure. I draw him in with long, slow pulls and his blood spills into me. He tastes like aged wine, each sip sinking me further into a state that will surely leave me dizzy.

He whimpers beneath me and sets his hands on my hips —my bare hips. The shirt has tugged up in our frenzy and my body is flush against him. I release him with the realization and gasp.

"No undergarments, love?"

"I . . . They were dirty." He hums a low laugh and I tear into his shoulder again to get him to shut up. The bastard is always laughing at me.

It works. Maybe a little too well.

His body jerks at my rabid bite, and in that moment I

realize how foolish I am. So very, stupidly foolish. His tip nudges my entrance as he jerks forward, and fucking hell, if it wasn't for his thin underwear he would have . . . gods. No more playing.

I pull my fangs out and we both have the most ridiculous expressions painted on our faces. His cheeks are blooming with red and I know that we crossed the line of *normal*. I roll to my side, embarrassment pinching my cheeks, and he does too. We'll hopefully forget that happened with a fresh blanket of sleep.

I ball my hand over my chest, my heart fluttering like a caged bird. Why do I get the feeling that we are trouble for one another?

Gods.

I'm in over my head with him, and by the look on his face, he knows it too.

14

I wake to soft breathing. Deep inhales and slow exhales tell me he's still asleep. I roll under the covers to face Arulius. The night we shared is still fresh on my mind, and I bite my lip to quell the heat that's rising to my cheeks and between my thighs.

Arulius's lashes are dark against his sun-kissed skin. I still find it odd to see him out of his golden armor. His nightshirt is a simple black fabric that hugs his muscles graciously. His golden tipped hair is messy across his forehead. I stifle a giggle. Normally he is so put together and stoic, but I suppose we all have moments of vulnerability.

I reach my hand up to his forehead to brush his hair back. I don't know what possesses me to do so, but I am all in at this point. As my arm passes my view I'm met by his eyes, amethyst gems that are staring back at me with amusement.

Gods be damned. I pull my hand back quickly and grip it with the other as if I've touched something sacred, something forbidden.

The corner of his lip kicks up and I can't think of anything else to do except close my eyes. *Of course he won't believe you are sleeping! What are you doing?!* I frown as my thoughts whirl. When have I ever been this struck by a male? He will be my undoing.

"Love."

"Yeah?" I rasp.

"Go put some underwear on."

The following days fall into a routine.

Moro leaves before sunrise to continue the search for Margo, Wren disappears somewhere for the majority of the day, and I'm left with Kastian until around noon. We help clean up the cottage and walk the village until Arulius is ready for training. He still gets up awfully early each morning to go train before the sun even rises. I don't understand how *anyone* can have that sort of devotion.

I keep practicing honing my aura to no avail. I can't even feel it forming, so half the time I just give myself a headache trying to focus *anything* into my hand. My wings haven't grown any more since that first night, so flying is still not in the stars for me. Kastian makes me practice my stretches and then we move on to self-defense, where I have my ass thrown, beat, and tossed around by Arulius every single damn time.

Supper follows—an uncomfortable time at the table with Wren—and then bed. The days keep coming and going.

Still no news of Margo.

I can't help but think something is holding up the process. After a little over a week, I wake up early, before even Arulius. It's the first morning in a while that I'm able to catch his sleeping features. His lashes are heavy and thick. They lie delicately across his cheeks and give me butterflies. I shake the sense back into my head and slip out of bed, tiptoeing down the stairs. Moro has a small light on in his kitchen and is pouring himself a cup of tea. It's still dark outside and his lean figure is silent in the dim light. He never did speak much. I wonder if it's because of Wren's daunting presence always looming around.

"Good morning," I whisper, trying not to spook him.

Moro turns and smiles at me. To my surprise, he has two cups of tea ready. I raise a brow, not knowing how he could have possibly known that I got up early. I knit my brows and smile back.

"Good morning, Elodie." He hands me a mug and settles himself at the head of his dining table. I take the seat next to him and blow on the tea. The steam swirls around my cheeks and smells of honey and lemons, much like the tea my mother used to make me when I was sick as a child. Cold winter mornings were spent wrapped in a warm blanket, blowing across the top of my mug while my mother nestled next to me in the window seat. We would watch the snow dance across the ponderosas while she told me the lore of the gods and spirits of the forest. I credited her storytelling and lore to Old Man Bruno.

I hum low, my lips turning up at the corners at the tender memories.

I glance up at him. "Moro, I was wondering if I can accompany you on your search today." I grip the mug tightly, bracing myself for his rejection. "It's just . . . it's already been over a week and I think I might be of help to you."

He's quiet for a few minutes and sips his tea thoughtfully. "I don't see why not," he finally mutters. His silver eyes flick to me with a smile.

"Really?" I blurt and set my mug down swiftly, earning a splash of bitter liquid on the front of my shirt. "When do we head out?" My heart races and my entire body thrums with excitement.

He turns and looks at a clock near his sink. "In about five minutes, so drink up." He chuckles. I down my tea, nearly choking on the hot sips, and set my mug in the sink.

"I'll get dressed and be right back down." I dip my head quickly and rush up the stairs.

I can't believe he is going to let me help. *Margo.* Today might be the day we meet again. Here, in another life sure, but we will meet again. I feel the doubts and worries of *what ifs* rise up within me once more, but I fight them down. There's no room in my heart for such thoughts. Not when today should be positive.

I nudge the door open quietly and dress in the dark. Arulius lets soft snores escape with his breath and I know he's still fast asleep. I bend over and snatch my boots, pulling them on carefully and slipping back out of the room.

Moro's just setting his mug in the sink when I return, and he tilts his head towards the door. I nod in understanding and we step outside. The four moons are large in the sky. The galaxy above us shivers in purple and blue waves as speckled white dots of stars and distant suns twinkle. I take in a deep breath of the morning air. It's cold and damp with morning dew, coaxing my lungs with fresh scents. So similar to my world, yet so different.

This moment is real.

Moro's dark skin glimmers under the cosmos and his silver eyes twinkle as the stars themselves do. *What creature is he?* I wonder. He's different from the others, the most human-looking but also the most mystical and secretive. The only magical physical appearance on him is a bright blue tattoo that lines the back of his head and trails down his temples. It contrasts his short gold hair marvelously.

His aura is richer than the others'. I can feel it shrill through the ground and air whenever he's near. No wonder he is the Hollow's Keeper—he's as brilliant as the creatures themselves are.

As I stare in awe of him, he snaps his fingers lightly and

two Pine Hollows creep around the corner of the cottage. I was right, he has a way with the beasts. He mounts the larger, pitch-black Hollow. Its eyes are gold and they're the only visible part of him in the darkness.

"Your Hollow is beautiful," I mutter, amazed at how different it looks from Murph. Do they all look so different from one another? Perhaps they take after their riders. Wren's Hollow bears the same translucent leaves that he has. And I catch a glimpse of the neon arc around Moro's Hollow's ears

I bring my attention to the other Hollow and sip in a breath. It's smaller than Moro's but beyond beautiful in comparison. Its fur bristles white, tipped with gold flakes. Its eyes are a deep ebony with small streaks of white pearly lines that tell me where its pupils are. I bring my hand to its muzzle, mesmerized by everything this Hollow is.

"What's this one's name?"

Moro raises a brow and leans forward to stroke the white Hollow's forehead. "This is Ceres. She is among my favorites." The Hollow hums in his hand and I smile.

"Ceres," I mumble, running my hand down her neck. She greets me with a subtle gaze and leans her head into me. "You have the best job here, Moro." I grin at him. His eyes widen.

"Job? This is my duty to the High Court. It's my purpose."

"Yeah, that's what I meant." I remind myself that I'm not in the human world anymore, and jobs aren't really a thing here. "You have the best duty to the court."

He smirks. "You're right. I do love the beasts. Anyhow, let's get going before the Commander or your Eostrix guard wake and try to stop you from helping," he mumbles and pats his Hollow on the neck. It leaps forward and Ceres nudges me to climb up. I mount and we are off in a blur. The Hollows move like water through the village and bound over branches and rocks smoothly.

We ride for just a few minutes before a dip in the valley leads us into a thicket of underbrush. There's a clear path here, no doubt trailed by Moro daily. The twigs snap under Ceres's paws and the scent of fresh rain and moss tickles my senses. This is real. My fingers press into her fur—real.

The thicket gives way and we emerge into a wide grove of enormous trees, the trunks of which span as far as I can see. The branches all remain hundreds of feet above. It would be pitch black in here from the covering leaf canopy if it wasn't for the million orbs of mushrooms that cling to the bark. A soft turquoise glow pulses through the soft air we breathe. A scent of damp moss and earth fills my senses. It's oddly quiet here. There's nothing more than the stir of the wind and pads of the Hollows we ride.

I gasp at the sight of this place. "Moro."

"Amazing, isn't it?" he mutters, bringing his Hollow to a trot. I nod dumbly as I continue to gawk at the beauty. "I remember my first time seeing this place. I was as much an awestruck fool as you." He chuckles and a smile crosses my face too.

"I don't know how you're able to leave at the end of the day." I bring my gaze back to Ceres. Her fur responds to the grove, like she belongs here and everything in her blood sings and swoons for the air of this place.

We go on for quite some time. As we continue, I begin to notice something that makes my heart sink more and more.

There are no Hollows. The space beneath where I envisioned there being hundreds of Hollows is . . . utterly empty.

I furrow my brow and look at Moro. He's watching me expectantly. Does he want me to ask about it? His expression seems to be telling me he wants me to see that something is amiss.

"Um, Moro," I begin, "where are all the Pine Hollows?" A sinking feeling plops into my stomach. His silver eyes flicker with pain just for a moment before he schools his features.

"What do you see, Elodie?" he asks carefully, as if he has to piece the sentence together tactfully. I narrow my eyes and search the barren plains once more.

"I see nothing." I shift my wary gaze back to him. Something is definitely wrong. Panic itches along my spine and it takes everything I have to keep it from showing.

"Yes, that's right. Peculiar, isn't it?" He considers his next words. "What do you think it means?" I raise a brow. I think I understand what he's doing. He's trying to lead me to an answer that he can't say aloud . . . Is he cursed from speaking it?

I curl my lips and goosebumps shudder across my skin.

"I'm not sure." He frowns. I rake my mind for anything I can ask to let him lead me to the right answer. "Were they taken?" I whisper. The thought seems so awful. So horrible. Who would take the mystical beasts? And why?

His eyes light up, and he nods slowly.

Okay, closer. I go on. "By the High Court?"

Another curt nod.

"Are we safe?" I blurt and become acutely aware of how silent the forest is. His eyes freeze on me and he gives a slow shake of his head, subtle enough so no one else can see except me. My veins chill with ice. "Moro . . ."

"Shh—listen to the forest, Elodie. Listen to Ceres." His silver eyes flick behind us and return to my gaze.

Fear tugs under my skin. I take a slow breath and keep my eyes forward. Is he saying there's someone behind us? This certainly is *not* the morning I was hoping for. What do we do? Continue forward like idiots? My heart thrusts against my ribs and pounds in my ears. I hear a snap behind us and can't keep my eyes forward any longer.

I whirl and gasp as my eyes meet Wren's darkness. His expression is cold and as he opens his mouth to shout something to me—then the heavens above us crash down.

Light explodes into the grove and branches and mushrooms fall heavily from the sky. I shriek and time seems to slow and speed up all at once. I'm in a hurricane of shouts and debris. Heavy bodies land around us, growling like savage animals.

I welcome the panic now, it ripples through me, and in

the chaos, I'm thrown from Ceres. My back hits the ground roughly and I roll until gravity stops me. I lift my head and gaze at the imperial armor that covers several daunting soldiers of the High Court.

My mind shatters with the picture that all of this chaos paints. Wren said we could come here. Was this entire *finding Margo* thing just bullshit? I tighten my jaw as I push myself off the ground. The soldiers consist of Eostrixes, Crypresses, Moss Sparrows, and . . . Dreadiuses. Their horns are different, pointed straight back, and rather than two they bear three, with one down the center of their foreheads. I recall seeing a few in Caziel.

Dust and debris cloud the air. I haven't been spotted yet. This might be the only chance I get to escape. I rise to my feet and bolt to my left, the trees are darkening as if the sun's rays are toxic to them. The turquoise light fades into a dim glow. My lungs ignite and I try to open my wings to fly. Pain flares through my new bones, but I clench my teeth through it. I know they are still small, but I have to try. They took Margo and all the other Pine Hollows. Moro tried to warn me. My mind whirls fast as my eyes search for a break in the soldiers that are getting their bearings. One spots me and my heart drops. They're chasing me.

Wren. He's been planning this all along. He's been taking the Pine Hollows and lied about letting me reunite with Margo . . . but why? What in the name of the gods did I ever do to deserve this? I'm just some nobody. Violet wants me dead and contained, but why? *Who the fuck is she really trying to find?*

I stretch my wings like Kastian showed me and I try to raise them to catch the air one more time. It's no use. I can't fly. I lose my breath after a few strokes of my wings. Pain continues to sear through the injured wing and the dizziness it wrings from me makes me sway. A roar echoes behind me and I know they're right on my ass.

"Elodie!" Wren shouts from my left. Murph crashes into the brambles in front of me, cutting off my path of escape. "Get on—now!" His eyes dart to the warriors exploding through the grove behind us. Fear laces his eyes like a rapid poison.

"Y-you did this!" I scream. I have to escape him. I have to get away. Murph raises his head and growls loudly as the warriors are nearly on us now.

Wren's dark eyes widen with an invisible wound. "Elodie —I didn't—"

Kastian's dark aura arcs through the chaos and slices through Wren's chest, stopping any words he planned on saying from spilling from his sinful lips. He shrieks in pain and dark crimson expels from his wound. Murph rears and leaps with his teeth bared. The poor Hollow is still trying to protect his master.

Wren's blood splatters across my face. Its hot stickiness instantly makes my stomach churn. I whirl to see Kastian's ebony wings break the light above as he crashes into the ground with thunder on his heels. The earth shrills under his power. He's enraged, and the entirety of the world will know it. My eyes widen at his strength.

He's an angry god sent from the depths of heaven and the close border of hell. But more than anything, he's here for me. I rise to my feet and run to him with tears brimming my eyes. *Real. This is real.* Each step I take sounds like a drum through my bones.

"Kastian!" I cry. The warriors are here, mere feet from where we stand. I don't think he can hold them all back alone.

"Elodie, stay behind me. Remember your training." He snarls and readies his aura as the imperial soldiers close around us. Black sands swirl around his arms and feet.

"Where's Arulius?" I shout, eyes jumping from each warrior. Their expressions are hardened with the willingness to draw blood. I desperately search for Moro's face, but I see no trace of him or the Hollows. *Fuck!*

Kastian lashes out with his arm and an arc of black shadows races for three warriors. One jumps out of the way, but the shadows catch the other two. Tearing and gushing sounds shake my core as I watch their bodies fall. I tremble as the metallic scent fills me. The air is so fucking heavy. My wings are sticky, and I realize they too are drenched in crimson.

"He's on his way. We woke late," Kastian growls and sends another arc towards our right. Shouts and roars erode the earth around us as more soldiers stream in from above. My heart sinks. There's no way we can keep them off of us.

We're trapped.

Kastian's inhales deep, ragged breaths as he grows weary from exerting so much of his aura. His skin pales and his wings slump behind him as if they've grown too heavy to lift. I can't just sit here. I have to do *something*. I hold my arm up like Arulius taught me and focus on my palm.

Please . . . please. Something—anything. Please do *something*! I desperately clutch my chest with my other hand and tears spill from my eyes. Nothing is working. I can't fucking do *anything*, and the helplessness of that thought shatters me.

Helpless. Real. This is a horrible reality I don't want.

The warriors circle closer to us and Kastian's spent, I can feel it. Why aren't they all just attacking us at once? I shudder —they want to take me alive. They might as well just be playing with us.

One of the three-horned warriors lunges forward with a sword of ruby- and onyx-encrusted steel. Horrified, I watch as it sinks deeply into Kastian's chest. He jerks back and blood spews from his lips on a sharp cough. His white hair smudged from the debris and his azure eyes meet mine as he slams into the ground.

"Kol," he mutters through gritted teeth, and blood bubbles at his lips. Kol snickers and tears his sword back, slinging Kastian's blood over me in the process. I embrace Kastian and ignore the laughs and shouts of bloodthirstiness behind me.

I press my hands onto his chest and cover the wound. Hot pools of his blood cover my hands, and I know it's too deep to stop what comes next.

No. No. No. Heal. Please . . . please heal.

My eyes burn, my chest seizes, and my body is cold.

"You're okay, you're going to be fine." I smile, my eyes wide. Why am I lying? He's *not* okay. "We've been through worse." No, we haven't. But I say the words anyway.

A hand grabs the back of my arm and I rip it from their grasp, whirling with fangs drawn. "Don't *fucking* touch me!"

Kol's eyes are black, darker than any night one could get lost in. His soldiers rally around him, ready to grab me, but he turns his jaw at them and shakes his head. "Let her grieve," he says soullessly.

Kastian's breath weakens. The warriors around us lower their weapons and let me embrace him. I can hear a few laughs and muffled snide comments still rising between them.

"Elo . . . die . . ." Kastian rasps, coughing violently as he tries to say more. "I remember y-you . . . I-I'm so s-sorry for not t-telling you s-sooner."

My tears drip onto his cheeks and merge with his. He's angelically beautiful with tears brimming in his eyes, but it's the love in his gaze that seizes me, a pain so raw and unfinished. My voice is entirely stuck in my throat. I'm drowning.

"I r-remember you . . . Tal—" He chokes on fresh blood as it courses past his paling lips.

"No!" I scream, my voice raspy and raw. "Wren! Wren! Please!" I know how erratic I'm acting, but I don't care. "Wren! Heal him!" My heart savagely bangs against my ribs, drowning out the sounds around me except for my screaming.

I find what I'm looking for. Wren's body lies still on the

ground, blood still oozing from the wound that Kastian inflicted. He won't be moving anytime soon if he isn't already dead.

Alone . . . I'm alone.

I take a shallow breath and gulp the knot down in my throat. I can do this. I can help Kastian.

I bring my eyes back to the weak Eostrix in my arms and do the only thing I can think of. I bite into my arm and tear at my flesh until the better part of the soft portions of my arm are on the ground beside me. Blood gushes from me and I tilt his head, pressing my throbbing arm into his mouth. There's so much crimson pulsing everywhere, covering the entirety of his face.

Please work. Please. Please work.

Kastian's eyes open weakly, caressing me softly, touching every part of my face before they begin to glaze on a slow exhale.

"Kastian?" I whisper.

It's so quiet.

That whisper becomes stale in the air. It's a whisper just for him but I know it never reaches its destination.

Nothing. His eyes slowly fade into gray, into nothingness, until he is no longer looking at me, but through me. The oceans of him calm into a hush until there are no more soft echoes of the life I once stared into.

"Grab her. Let's get back to Nesbrim," a soldier calls out.

I whirl and scream at the shorter warrior who tries to grab my arm. He backs up and glances at Kol, who waves him off.

"Give her another minute." His smirk is proof he's enjoying the pain I'm feeling.

"Kastian, you're okay. You're still here. It's okay." I pull my arm out and blood pools in his mouth, undrunk, much like his unspoken words. I press my nose against his. "I'm here, it's okay." My voice cracks. "I'll let you rest for a few minutes but then you have to get back up, okay?" I brush my hand through his white hair. It's still so soft and airy. His cheeks are still red with the heat of battle.

"Gods," a deep voice murmurs behind me.

I turn. My eyes are so weary. Arulius stands with his shoulders slumped. I smile at him. Finally, he's here—he can help.

"Arulius! It's okay." I tug Kastian's limp body for him to look and I wipe my tears as a smile of hope spreads across my lips. "See? He's okay, he just needs rest. Can you help me heal him? We need to—"

"*Elodie*, stop." His eyes are wide with horror, voice sharp. I can see my reflection in the distant fields of them, the shock that engulfs my eyes. That's the first time he's snapped at me.

"What?"

He kneels beside me. The warriors still stare at us from behind, glancing at Kol, waiting for direction with confused expressions. "Love, he is . . ."

"*No.*" I glare at him. "He's *fine!*" I scream. "Look at him. He's just tired. I already gave him some blood and he is . . . he is . . ." I gaze at Kastian's cold eyes. They are so empty . . . like Margo's. My blood streams from his lifeless lips. A lump too thick to swallow forms in my throat and my heart squeezes inside my chest. My eyes burn with denial.

"He is dead, love."

I . . .

I feel everything.

Everything.

15

Dead?

I stare into Kastian's eyes, his once-beautiful blue eyes filled with kindness and life. He's dead. He is dead and his last few moments of life I spent shoving my bloody arm into his mouth.

I let my grip on his body loosen. His skin isn't as warm as it once was. Arulius is still kneeling next to me and sets his hand on my shoulder, sending a shudder through my bones. "I will take care of this." I don't look at him.

I just stare endlessly at Kastian's body. His beautiful black wings, his face, *everything* is covered in blood. This isn't how today was supposed to go.

Please. I think of Margo. *Please.* I dip down and press my hands against his chest. On the gash that no longer bleeds between his ribs. I focus my aura into my chest. I know I was taught to use it as a weapon, but I have an instinct to focus it on my heart. As I meet his cooling skin, I focus it on him.

Nothing.

Not real.

He isn't real anymore. No matter how much I want him to be. Tears roll down my face. I care for Kastian so dearly. Even though we had our arguments . . . he was still my dark Eostrix. We were just standing here moments ago. Visions of his bones and feathers lying here in the glowing cavern of the Hollow's Grove for the remainder of eternity sends shivers up the crevices of my soul, weighing me down like anchors deep in an abyss.

Arulius plucks me from the ground, bringing my consciousness back to the *now*, and holds me close to his chest.

I gaze at the soldiers who watch us with expressionless eyes. Why are they waiting? Do they think Arulius still serves Violet? I find the black pair that belongs to the one that reaped Kastian and stole his life. Kol. I burn an image of his sharp features into my mind. Skin as smooth and youthful as Kastian's was. Hair like midnight fire, a dark crimson amongst his three ivory horns. But it's his wicked smile that I will remember for the rest of eternity, his sharp teeth and the thirst they carry.

They raise their weapons as Arulius opens his wings to take flight. I stare emptily at Kol. I'll never forget his face. I will walk to the ends of this earth and take everything he's ever cared about. If there's anything I've learned from this world, it's that I'm no longer the soft, kind girl I was. I'll never be the same.

As they leap to attack, realizing that he's no longer serving Violet, Arulius opens his wings with such force that it blows most of them over. Helmets and horns alike collide and clank loudly through the grove. My black hair waves angrily in the wind he casts. Arulius clutches me tightly.

Kol stands steady, reangling his sword in his grip and ready to slice Arulius like he did Kastian. I relish the look of betrayal that flickers across the motherfucker's eyes.

Arulius's purple gaze is already locked onto the beast. He holds me with one arm, and with his other, he clenches his fist instead of lashing out with an arc. He roars as a golden aura raises around us like drops of water trapped in a cylinder of glass. The sheer power tickles my skin and the fury in his eyes is fanatical. I can see the pain in them. He and Kastian weren't close, but I think they formed some sort of bond over our time together. My heart wrenches as I stare down at Kastian's body for what will be the last time. Small traces of his white hair blow in the gusts. His eyes still reach into the nothingness above him. Wren lies just as still.

My heart lurches and I know I'll never heal. Not from this.

Kol curses and his eyes widen with fury. "You fucking bastard!" he shouts. "Why drag this out?"

Arulius narrows his eyes and releases his balled fist. An explosion of power isn't even the tip of the iceberg of what it's like. His aura rains down like the hellfire of gods, pelting the warriors as if an army of demons and angels alike let loose every last golden arrow in their hilts. It's continuous anger until his brilliant wings break the light barrier at the top of the canopy. I pretend like I don't hear the screams and wails of undiluted fear from below us. I wrap myself in their cries and a wry smile tugs at my lips. It starts small but erupts into hysterical laughter. I laugh until Arulius reaches his hand up and gently covers my mouth to silence me.

We left too much behind us.

We left *everything*.

Wren, Murph, Moro, Ceres, Kastian . . . and every secret that remains buried in that grove. Why did they attack like that? My mind is on the cusp of breaking, on the edge of an already crumbling cliff.

"Why did they attack us?" My voice is raspy from the screaming. It scorns my throat just to speak.

Arulius tightens his jaw but doesn't respond. He just continues to fly.

I press him. "Where are we going now?"

"We are going to Kastian's glade." I still, my heart beating slow, pain-filled pulses into my soul. "They won't come to his realm."

I sleep in Kastian's bed tonight. Arulius takes the couch in the corner of the room. He wants to be close in case we were followed, but allows me my space. We didn't talk on the flight here and we aren't talking now either. We're exhausted and I'm still trembling from all of it. There are no words to soothe what just happened.

I don't think I'll be able to sleep. An overwhelming amount of nothing spins in my head. But I find sleep eventually. I wake the next morning not knowing how I fell asleep nor how long I've been sleeping. Arulius isn't on the couch and I'm glad for it.

I need the peace of silence. To mourn.

I need to make everything that has happened make sense, because none of it does. I walk around the estate with my blanket wrapped tightly around my shoulders. The soft fabric smells like *him*. Sage fills my senses and I clench the cloth desperately. Kastian's face is still fresh in my mind, his blue eyes still not yet gray in my illusion of him. The swells of the blanket wash across the floor as I make my way from wing to wing, aimlessly walking like a ghost, nothing more than a whisper in this dreadful place. I stop at the large windows in the conservatory. I linger there and just gaze out into the endless dead forest.

Dead. Like Kastian is. Like Wren could be. Moro and the others possibly too . . . Maybe . . . maybe I should be too. A poison prickles my mind, a thought so cursed crawling beneath my skin like an insect, whispering to me, telling me that I don't belong. That I never did. That I should wake up now because none of this could possibly be real. The hours tick by and I feel the weight and burden of loss. Alone. All alone.

Not real.

I roam the corridors back to Kastian's room. The walls are white and the drapes are black. My footsteps echo somberly through the rafters above.

I draw a bath, the water cold and unwelcoming. There are so few things I press on for. What more can I lose?

I lost Margo *again*. Or rather the chance to have her.

I lost Kastian.

My suspicions of Wren were right, but I fucking lost him too.

I lost . . . myself.

I'm already *dead*. Already not real. So why do I have to keep pretending? The itch tugs and calls me. I cup my hands over my ears, trying to block out the voices in my head. *You're just a stupid dead girl.*

I'm so fucking tired.

I slip into the bath and cold water fills my body with something other than the vast void. My bones go numb and my very marrow pacifies. I rest my head back into the water, letting it take me from the pain and hurt. I let it take every part of me away into the darkness of an unknown lake of dread and rest, one filled with the skeletons of my past and sorrows I will never be able to overcome.

I want to wake up. I want to be real again. I just want to be real.

I inhale.

A sharp sting grips me and shakes my entire body. Ice so cold and taxing fills me. I've never been so cold inside.

So . . .

16

"Elodie."

      Huh? Who is that . . .

        "It's time to wake up, love."

I open my eyes. My lashes are wet, leaving blurry drops of sleepy rain behind on my cheeks. Arulius gazes down at me, his face pale. His amethyst eyes are tainted with pain.

I remember what I did . . . or tried to do. He's going to want some sort of answer, but all I can manage is, "I'm awake."

I am. And no matter how much I wish I wasn't still in Tomorrow, there's nothing I can do. I'm awake and I'm unfortunately still here.

His purple eyes well with anguish. "What were you thinking?" He clutches me tightly. My foot slips on the tile as I try to sit up. Are we in the bathroom still? "Elodie, it's my fault. I should have been here. Gods—I thought I'd never see your beautiful brown eyes open again." He brings my wet body closer and hugs me tightly.

"Is . . . is Kastian here?" I mutter. This is his bathroom after all. Maybe it was all just a dream. He grasps handfuls of my shirt in his trembling palms. "Arulius?"

"Elodie. You know he is dead . . . You know that."

Ah. That's right.

I do know that.

This is real.

Days pass in a flurry.

I spend most of my time moping and lying in bed. Everything feels like a big task: getting up to eat or bathe, walks, talking, eating. Everything is torture. Arulius doesn't leave anymore after he found me that night. I promised him I don't feel as broken now, but he won't take that chance. He's always nearby. I'm not allowed to take baths alone, which is interesting. He will either lie on the floor or bring a chair and face the corner, talking to me the entire time. I have to admit, his efforts mean a lot to me. Especially in this time of finding myself again. Nothing is ever rushed with him.

Time heals everything, right?

After a few weeks, I begin to feel the chords of time lessen my pain. We take walks through the forest daily and our combat lessons keep us busy in the afternoons. I find solace in the hush of Kastian's lands. Death is always a whisper here, constantly in the wind and always peaceful.

We of course feed daily, each one more painfully sensual than the last. After a week of it just being us, I realize how soft and kind Arulius really is. I see it in the times when he gazes at the sky and in the moments after drinking my blood. He has a habit of pushing my hair from my face gently and pecking small kisses along my cheeks.

He's impossibly easy to love.

Sharing the bed was my idea. I can't just let him keep sleeping on the couch. We stay up into the early hours of the morning sharing stories of our lives. I tell him about my mom and dad, all the things they taught me, and how kind they were. Even after I lost touch with reality, they loved me fiercely. I tell him how much I miss them. I even tell him about adventures I shared with Margo through our forest. The time we spent renovating my shed and all the existential moments in between.

My Aunt Maggie is harder to share about, but eventually I do. Arulius is the only person in the realms that knows how I struggle with determining what's real and not. The only one who wants to carry some of the weight with me. So I share the memories, so painful to reminisce on, but with him I realize that the most important thing to remember about her was how unapologetically real she was. She was a woman who made you feel happiness with just her smile alone.

I want to smile that brightly. With him, I find that I can.

I'm finally able to wield aura.

During one of our late-night sparring matches, I tap into something deep within me. All of a sudden it just snaps and the aura flows as I wish. It's not nearly as strong as Arulius's, but I'm so relieved that it finally revealed itself. If I had been able to fight that morning in the grove . . . maybe things would have turned out differently.

I use that fury to push myself harder each day. I will *never* let another person or creature I care about be hurt on my behalf again. Never.

I let out a long exasperated sigh. "Arulius!"

His gray, gold-tipped hair peeks over the tub. His purple eyes do as well, only far enough to see my eyes. "Yes, lovely?" He smiles.

I lean in closer to his face. "When are my wings going to grow more? I want to fly but I don't think they're big enough yet," I mutter, puckering my lips out with frustration. They haven't grown an inch since the night with Wren all those weeks ago. I gaze at Arulius's brilliant gold feathers with jealousy.

"Sometimes it just takes time, love. You can't rush these things."

I stare at him with an annoyed expression. "That's all you've got? An excuse?" I tease.

He scoffs. "Don't make me come in there, love." He narrows his eyes at me. I can't help but smile. Over the last month, we've bonded so much more than I ever thought we could. I felt so torn between him and Kastian before . . . Well, now that it's just us, the walls of my heart have begun to feel immensely less brittle. With him I feel entirely complete.

"I *am* hungry," I mumble. "Maybe I can have a bath snack?" His eyes widen.

"Did you just say *bath snack?*" He grins. "Are you referring to *me?* As food?"

I sip in a breath, giving into my lust that's been stirring me since the moment he and I collided. "Would you be mad if I said yes?"

He slips a hand into the tub. "Only if you don't eat me," he murmurs. "Mind if I come in?"

Gods. I stare at him. I knew when I suggested it that it would lead to this. I inhale deeply and the scent of the lavender aroma fills me. I nod, keeping my lips tightly pursed together.

His eyes flicker with eagerness and he pulls his shirt off and tosses it on the floor. He leaves his underwear on and carefully dips his feet in. I pull my knees up to my chest and watch as the water line nearly spills over the tub's edge. I've seen him shirtless plenty of times, but for some reason, he looks different in the tub. He looks more vulnerable.

He stretches out his legs on each side of me and I move through the water to him, putting a knee on each side of his hips. His cheeks redden and he sucks in a breath at our closeness. We've yet to feed in the tub, and while we've been feeding regularly, it's been rather difficult to keep our *needs* held back. I can tell he is waiting for me to make the first move. Arulius is a gentleman in that aspect.

And I fucking love that about him.

He rests his hands on my lower back and props me up on his lap. I'm straddling him and I try to focus on feeding rather than the cock that lies needy between my thighs. I run my tongue up his throat and down the right side of his neck, placing my teeth between his neck and shoulder. I've discovered that this is his sensitive spot. I push in and his blood enters me with sweet, welcoming bliss. I let a soft moan slip through my lips and clutch his neck a little tighter. Each time I drink from him I can feel the sky on my skin, and wisps of warmth flutter through me with each tug. His hands run up my back gently and he pants. I know he wants to feed too. I've felt the same urge plenty of times, to feed at the same time.

Retracting my teeth, I glance at him. "It's okay. We can feed together," I murmur against his ear and he shudders beneath me. His cock twitches, letting its presence be known and I have to suppress a lewd tremble just above him. *It's just instincts. It's normal.* Actually, you know what? Fuck that.

246

This draw we have is far beyond that. It's more than instincts with him.

He pulls his head back. "Love . . ." He moans as I let myself rest on him, his underwear the only barrier between us.

"Yes?"

"Remember when I told you about how Eostrixes . . ."

"How they fuck?" I retort, recalling exactly how he'd said it before.

He coughs. "I was going to say *make love*, but yes." I can't help but enjoy the way my chest squeezes at his reform. His skin teems with warmth and I don't think it's just because of the bath.

"I remember, but you never got into the specifics." I shrug, dipping my head back down to stroke his neck with my tongue. I suck on his soft skin and fully intend on leaving bruises.

He trembles. "Right, well, Eostrixes don't feed on one another at the same time unless they intend to make love. It's how they blood bond . . . so I can wait until you are finished."

A pang of disappointment floods through me. "Do you not want to bond with me?" We are in a tub, I'm naked, and he is damn near there himself . . . Maybe I misread the signals he's been sending me. My cheeks heat. I'm so stupid to have asked, but my heart yearns for him. He's my everything in Tomorrow, and now that we've grown so close . . . I know he's the one for me. He's so beautiful, the most striking man I'll ever know. Inside and out. Sure, he has his flaws, and I have mine. He and I just click. We fit so perfectly.

He pulls me back and looks into my eyes. "What? No. Gods, no. That's not what I meant at all by that, love." His cheeks are as flushed as mine feel. "I . . . I would be honored to bond." He rubs the back of his neck and relief flows over me. My heart pounds. That means he wants me too, right? "I think you're the most beautiful Eostrix to ever have graced this realm." He studies my face affectionately.

"You would? I am?" I smile. "You're the most stunning creature I've ever seen. I thought so the moment I saw you in Nesbrim."

He grins but it quickly fades. "I thought you regarded Kastian in that light." He isn't trying to sting me, he's being truthful, and I appreciate his honesty. His brow furrows and he looks at me longingly. Is that why he's held back for so long?

My smile withers. "It's true, I . . . I had feelings for him. But he is gone and I've accepted it. We were never . . ." I murmur, blinking long and slow. "I've had feelings for you for some time too, you know."

He flinches. "Really?"

"Is it really so unbelievable?" I tilt my head and set my palm against his cheek. He leans into it and purses his lips on my skin.

"I mean . . . I'm *me*. The Eostrix of Nesbrim. Everyone either fears me or despises me greatly."

I let a soft chuckle slip out. "Don't get me wrong, I *hated* you." He quirks his lips. "But then you showed me another side of you, and I think I can understand you more. You are kind and caring, you help your friends rather than serve Violet with undying loyalty, and you're also sort of shy."

His eyes narrow and cloud. "Shy?"

"Yeah, you always change around others. Like you're keeping your sensitive side hidden from the world." I rest my head on his shoulder again. "Like you're afraid to be seen for what you really are."

He tenses as the latter words leave my lips. He bends me back before I can ask what's wrong and the water rushes from the tub's edge. Our eyes meet briefly and he smiles the saddest smile I've ever seen. I can't tell what elicited such pain from him, but he dips down to my neck, pulling my thoughts to his touch. His teeth pierce into my shoulder and a deep pain surges through me, drawing forth a shout. The pain shifts into pleasure as he pulls my blood into him. I let out a short cry and place my mouth on his neck once more. I hesitate, unsure if he intends for me to feed too. But his hand cradles the back of my head and coaxes me softly into his neck. I give in. His blood smells of honey and I want him. I want all of him.

We feed together, selfishly and entirely. We've suffered enough, haven't we? Now we just want to enjoy this simple and affection-covered world we've built around ourselves.

I'm not gentle and neither is he. The pull of feeding together sends a frenzy through my body. The tub begins to overflow as our blood spills over our backs and mouths, turning the water maroon and rendering the purpose of the bath pointless.

The sensation from feeding together is different than when it's done one at a time. I'm sinking—no, soaring. Our blood burns together and becomes one. His hands explore me and I realize I'm doing the same. His palms brush against my breasts, my nipples peaked and sensitive. I pull from him and he releases me too, glancing down at my body, following the curves and dips. "So fucking beautiful, love." I return the favor and when I see his hard cock, I bite my lip. A prick of blood trickles and he leans in to catch it.

His lips press onto mine, a sweet embrace of the rain and sun, like he once showed me. Each kiss we share feels as sensual as the first.

Real—he's real. I want all this and more. Him. I want him.

Is it really okay for me to be this happy? At one point I thought only finding Margo would make me happy again . . . and though it would, I've found another supplement of happiness that I didn't see coming. Arulius.

I press into his mouth harder. Arulius moans deeply against my lips, and our tongues dance and pull one another. He leans me further back until my body is submerged in the maroon water. My hair, entirely behind me, swirls in the crimson tub.

His hand glides down to my slick pussy. It throbs and aches so horribly, and has been for weeks. He rubs his finger against my clit and pauses, glancing up at me. I sip in a breath. His amethyst eyes are just mere inches from mine. So beautiful.

Tension tightens between our breaths. I thrust my hips to let him know I'm waiting. That's all he needs. His fingers trace me and then he's inside me, making me cry out. I buck my hips as he rubs my clit and thrums his finger inside me. I grip his back tightly, digging my nails into his skin. His wings tuck tightly against his back. He lets out a moan, pushing his fingers deeper into me. I moan in tandem and we spiral together, falling into one another like we know nothing else but each other.

He slowly pulls his finger out of me and I let out a whine in defiance. He smirks and lets an amused laugh out. "Let's move to the bed, love." I raise a brow and smile.

Arulius lifts me out of the tub and carries my naked body to the bed, hair dripping and all. Our wings are heavy with the crimson bathwater. Somewhere along the way he loses his underwear, because by the time we reach the sheets he is completely bare. I gawk at his length and he smirks at me again. I've had my fair share of men, but Arulius really is a god.

I reach for his cock and he twitches with a soft breath as I let my hands wrap around his girth. He bridges himself over me and pants with pleasure as I move my hands in rhythm with our breaths. My cheeks are hot—gods, they are so hot. I stare at his expression above me. His brows are furrowed and his eyes fill with a longing that makes my heart nearly split open. If hearts can bleed from feeling too much, then mine is gushing at every seam and filling my core with him.

He leans in closer to me, nudging me with his swollen erection.

"Tell me you still want this," he whispers against my lips. I taste our mixed blood on his. My heart thumps wildly.

"Yes." I shudder and all I know is him. All I know in this moment is us. Here and now.

His face softens and he nuzzles into my neck, moving his hips up, pressing his tip into me. I suck in a breath at the intensity of him.

This is happening. This is real.

As if his beautiful mind can read me like an open book, he brushes my hair back. "You are real. This moment—this moment means *everything* to me. Real or not."

I smile and brush his hair back. "It means everything to me too. Real or not." His amethyst eyes shimmer in the dark. My heart warms, as if he's reached inside and embraced my wounded organ. It flutters and twists for only him.

He presses in until our stomachs meet. His cock stretches me and I cry out. I wince and bite his neck to suppress a moan. He stills and kisses me deeply. We belong to one another. Maybe we always have. His eyes fill with lust. He moves his hips and pulls nearly all the way out before thrusting himself back in hard. I'm filled with ecstasy and sink my teeth into him once more. His neck is taut and veined from his frenzy. His blood trails down my neck and pools in the crests of my collarbones. I can't hold him close enough. I never want this moment to end.

His thrusts build and my moans grow louder. I release his neck and he grabs my wrists and holds them with one hand above my head. I purr at his rougher side. All the boys at home were too afraid to even try the gray acts. His amethyst eyes shimmer at the sound I make. His other arm arcs beneath my back, making me raise my stomach up toward him.

"Elodie," he moans and I glance up at him, his purple eyes glowing in the dark.

"Yes?"

"You're so fucking beautiful. So—" He groans as he thrusts in deeper. His hand finds my clit once more and rubs circles that send me over the edge. His eyebrows knit together. I moan in tandem with him and we move in sync as we peak together in a wet and intimate explosion. The sun and rain are nothing compared to how tenderly he touches me, how much life he elicits in me. This moment matters. Our bond is real.

I let out a shrill cry of pleasure as I come undone at his mercy. He pushes his engorged cock once more to the hilt and holds himself there as he comes, throbbing inside me. His body shudders and he lets out a moan equally as long as mine. His cock pulses against my inner walls and heat fills my core. He bends his head down and presses his lips on mine. I kiss him back and brush my hand against his cheek. He leans into it and closes his eyes. His lashes brush my palm softly and tug at my heart.

I take in his beauty. Every single drop of him. He looks soft now, tamed and calm. Maybe it's because I know him now, but he looks so different from the night we met. I'm even more struck by his beauty now than when I first laid eyes on him, because his eyes hold an immeasurable amount of sunlight and rain in them. I can feel the heat of them against my cheeks and I'm . . . I'm in love with him.

"I know this will probably sound silly to you," Arulius murmurs into my hand, sweat still beading down his forehead, "but I love you, Elodie." My eyes widen.

"Why would I think that sounds silly?" Tears brim my eyes. He loves me?

He withdraws from me slowly and I take a short breath. He rests his body next to me and wraps his arms around me. I'm consumed by his warmth. I love him too. My heart thrums against his, and in this moment I feel something different. A soft stir ignites my chest with a weight.

"Do you feel that?" he whispers into my ear. I nod, head tucked safely into his chest. "It's the bond."

I clutch over my heart. I can feel his heartbeat within my own chest. "I can feel your heart," I breathe out incredulously.

Arulius runs his hand gently down my spine. "And I can feel yours, love." His hand clutches my back as if he can feel a sharp pain. "You've suffered for so long. I want to take that away from you." His embrace grows tighter. Can he feel my lingering pain? I won't tell him this is the tail end of it.

"Arulius . . . thank you for saving me." He flinches at my

sudden admittance. "Not just a month ago in the Hollow Grove. I never thanked you for saving me from my mind. For showing me that I decide what's real. When I felt the rain kiss my skin and the sun warm my weary soul, I think that's when I started to fall in love with you."

A warmth spreads through my chest at the same time that a soft laugh escapes his lips. "Even though you still resented me?" I nudge him with my elbow. I haven't forgotten that our first encounter ended with my body being broken.

"Even then." I push away and glance up at his face. He has the grin I suspected he'd have. He brushes his nose against mine. Gods, my heart flutters again. He's so soft with me, raw and gentle.

"Well, love, believe it or not, I think I started to fall for you the moment I saw you in Nesbrim. Violet's court had never seen a woman of your beauty bless its halls before." His purple eyes narrow. "I was devastated when I heard her ruling . . ."

I remember seeing his face as Wren and I left in a hurry that night. But if he felt that way ..."Why did you help Wren that day?" I whisper.

He considers his words for a moment. "I'm duty-bound to Lady Violet, love. I am sworn to do as she commands." His voice trails off in thought.

I furrow my brow. "But what about when you helped me escape the Hollow grove? That wasn't her command."

A weight forms in my chest. He lets out a long sigh. "It's complicated . . . I—"

"Is anyone here?" A voice calls out from the foyer of the estate.

We both flinch at the sound of another's voice. Someone's here.

"Hello?" the voice calls out again and I recognize it. It's been weeks, but I remember his voice.

Moro.

17

Arulius tenses with surprise.

"It's Moro!" My eyes brim with relief.

He nods, the stern callous look that I haven't seen in weeks taking its place back over his features. There goes my sweet, gentle Arulius, to be hidden behind a warrior's guise.

We quickly get dressed. I throw on a beige nightgown. There's no time to waste with pants and shirts. I glide down the stairs before Arulius even has his pants pulled up. As I reach the lower floor, I see two males soaked with rain.

Moro's silver eyes widen as I appear. His skin is paler than usual and he has heavy bags under his eyes. "Elodie! Thank the gods you are okay." He meets me halfway into the foyer and I hug him tightly. His wet clothes soak my nightgown in seconds but I don't care. I thought he was dead. I thought we lost everyone.

I pull my face back to meet his and tears fill my eyes. "I thought we lost you." My lower lip trembles as I try to hold back the wail that rises in my throat. He's here, he is okay. He is *real*.

His dark skin softens around his eyes. "I thought we'd lost you too." I freeze at the word *we*. I forgot there are two males in the foyer. I tilt my head past his shoulder and see the man that makes my blood chill.

"*Wren*." His name is like nails in my tongue.

His body is slumped. He tenderly holds his chest where Kastian slashed him. He's still every bit as beautiful as the night I followed him into Tomorrow. Rain drips from his sleeves and his dark eyes watch me warily. I really thought he was dead. Are they ghosts?

I take a few staggering steps backward, glancing from him to Moro with fear. I'm not sure how to feel. Part of me is relieved, but . . .

"Elodie, I know you think Wren brought Violet's soldiers to the grove, but you're wrong," Moro insists with a frown.

I shake my head, tears now streaming down my hot cheeks. "Moro . . . Kastian is *dead* because of him!" I scream.

Wren gives me an aghast expression. "Elodie—"

The walls I've built in the past weeks for my sanity start to crumble. Why are they here? How did they escape the warriors? Why is Moro *defending the Cypress*?

Why did we let Kastian die?

Why did *I* let Kastian die . . .

I feel a heavy hand plop on my shoulder and I glance up to see Arulius's leery gaze set on Wren. It flicks to Moro and then back to the Cypress. He flexes his jaw like he's ready to kill Wren. My heart thumps against the walls of my chest. No more death. Please, no more.

"Wren? Did you send those warriors to the Hollow Grove?" The Eostrix's voice is vile. He raises his upper lip in a snarl to bare his sharp fangs—taking a step in front of me protectively as his golden wings cover me. I can feel his fury welling in my chest, a taut pull. Unpleasant emotions rise against the walls of my ribs. I glance at Arulius. My eyes widen at how the bond works.

Wren stands taller and lets his hand fall to his side. His eyes are unreadable and sinister. He stares at Arulius like . . . like *he* is the villain here. "I could ask the same of you, Arulius."

A feral growl escapes Arulius's throat and his golden wings stretch wildly in the spacious foyer. Wren clenches his fists and translucent thorns and vines crawl down his arms. The air thickens with hatred and anxiety. Moro stomps his foot firmly against the tiles, sending echoes through the space above us. Turquoise wisps cloud by his feet. The Pine Hollow Keeper has a mysterious magic about him and it catches both of the quarreling males' attention.

"Stop it, you two!" he growls. "We can't go throwing accusations like this at one another. What's important is that we are all here, and we need to regroup and make a plan."

My heart sinks into my stomach, curling into a somber plea. "Not *all* of us are here." The air pacifies and the three males look at me with empathetic eyes. "Kastian . . . I—I tried to save him."

Moro approaches and bends down to look me in the eyes. "Elodie." Light fills his silver gaze, and a weary smile tugs the corners of his lips. "Kastian is alive."

What?

He's . . . alive? I sink to the floor, letting my knees hit the tile, dropping my hands next to them. "Are you—"

"He's alive, Elodie." Wren steps closer, cautiously eyeing Arulius, who returns a scowl. "I saw him with my own eyes. After you two broke free, whatever you did . . . he breathed once more."

The stones that pillaged my inner walls shatter, trembling and breaking, but not with despair—with relief and hope. An unbearable amount of solace and emotional strings pull me from the rubble that I'd been sent to rot away in. I can see the light again, and in it is Kastian. His kind azure eyes—I need to see them again to erase the gray, horrible ones that haunt my dreams. My conscience has been so, so heavy with the guilt of him dying.

"He's . . . really alive?"

Moro and Wren's smiles hold only hope. I flinch when Wren upturns his lips. I haven't seen him smile since before we left for the Hollow Keeper's cottage.

I know their words are the truth.

I let out a cry that has long since nestled into my soul. I let it out because I will never have to hold onto that despair again. The guilt of his death is washed from my hands—and I saved his life? But how—no, I don't care how. All I care about is that my friends are alive.

"W-where is he?"

Wren extends his hand in an offer of peace and helps me up off the ground. "Violet has him. We couldn't stop them from taking him. They would have taken me too if they hadn't thought I was already dying."

"By *they*, you mean Kol?" I seethe as the tri-horned creature's face brushes my memory. Wren raises a brow and nods. Arulius flicks a surprised glance at me too.

"How do you know his name?" the Eostrix asks, his purple eyes wavering.

"Kastian said his name before he . . ." I stop myself there. No need to dredge those memories up again. I'm going to see my ebony-winged Eostrix again, no matter what.

Moro peels his wet coat from his arms. The water has already formed a formidable puddle beneath him. "We need to rescue him." A grim expression passes his eyes. "Violet is more than likely holding him there to lure you in, but I doubt that means she is treating him well."

I consider his words. "And the Pine Hollows?" Why did she have them all taken from the grove? To keep me away from Margo? What did I ever do to deserve such wrath from her?

Moro furrows his brow. Arulius sets a blanket around my shoulders and I flinch under the weight of it. "Moro is bewitched, love. He cannot say what has become of the Hollows," he mutters and Moro nods reluctantly.

I knew it. Something was off with him in the grove that morning, like he was trying to show me what was amiss. I shake my head. We don't have time to go over the past again. We need to save Kastian. A pang of guilt spreads through me. I've been here . . . moving on and finding happiness with Arulius, while he could be being tortured as we speak.

We decide to leave the planning for the morning. Everyone is exhausted—Arulius and I for a different reason— but we need fresh minds to devise a scheme for infiltrating Nesbrim. They look weary and in desperate need of a change of clothes. I show them rooms that I'm sure Kastian wouldn't mind me allowing them to use. Spare shirts and pants are already in the dressers.

I let Moro take a bath while I take care of Murph and Ceres. I'm surprised that they miraculously made it out of the grove, but it makes sense. Moro practically disappeared once the Nesbrim soldiers broke through the trees. Now that I think about it, he probably took the two Hollows the moment Kastian attacked Wren. I send a silent prayer of thanks to all the gods that guided him to do so. He wouldn't have been able to fight against all the soldiers, and he is the reason Wren and the Hollows are alive.

I bring bowls of food out for the two Hollows and they both wag their tails at the sight of me. A pang throbs through me when I realize that Moro's magnificent Hollow is not among them. I won't ask him about it. His eyes carry the pain

I now realize he is harboring. I can't take any more pain tonight, the good or bad kind.

I spend a good thirty minutes petting the Hollows and praising them for how much they've undoubtedly overcome and helped out. Ceres wags her white and gold-tipped tail and nuzzles me as if thanking me. She has no idea how much I need it. I hug her tightly until my tears dry.

I make my way back to Kastian's room with a new fire ignited in my soul. I feel like a person again, one with a chance to right my wrongs. I need to save Kastian. Not just because he saved me, but because I . . . I care for him, and in a way I always will. I swear to find Margo too. She's the end goal, always, even though I've found a new path with Arulius. I take in a deep sigh, praying and hoping that she will understand if it takes a bit longer for me to find her. Our friend is in trouble and I won't leave him behind. Not again.

When I reach the room, Arulius is already waiting for me. I flinch as I anxiously become aware of what we were doing in this room just an hour ago. He remains fully clothed as he rests with his arm propped up, but he has a tormented expression that glosses his eyes.

I sit on the edge of the bed and remove my boots. I'm not sure if he wants to talk or not, but my stomach curls at the questions he might have for me. I hope he doesn't feel threatened by the fact that Kastian is alive. I care for the dark-winged Eostrix, but he will *never* be Arulius. He'll never call me nicknames that make my heart leap and make me *feel* like he does.

"Well tonight was . . . unexpected," he murmurs behind me. "Wasn't it, love?"

"Which part?" I whisper back. It's an honest question —really.

He sits up in bed as I lie back, turning my head towards him. His black shirt clings tightly to his body, making it hard to focus on anything else. I manage to force my eyes to his face where he has already noticed my gawking and has a weak smirk. He's back to his kind and gentle self again. My heart swoons as his amethyst eyes caress me with affection.

"All of it. It was honestly all very unexpected," he mutters as he sets his hand on my stomach and draws lazy circles, sending waves of desire through me.

"I . . . I can't believe that Kastian is alive." The words are lighter than I expect them to be, sounding like a breath of hope and relief.

He evades my eyes. His anxious feelings twirl in my chest. "Do you regret what we did tonight? Or what we admitted to one another?" Arulius wraps his right hand over his left arm in what looks like an attempt to comfort himself for what might be coming.

"No. I don't regret it." That's the truth. "I meant what I said, Arulius. I love you."

He turns to face me and leans in closer. His gold-tipped hair tickles my forehead as our eyes line up. Amethyst fire-like stones left on the hearth are all I see. And just like that I know my heart has aligned with his. He has to be feeling the same fluttering I'm experiencing in my heart. I really hope he is. He'll know my words are true. His eyes soften and a warm smile spreads across his beautiful lips.

I thought I'd feel the same warmth I know I'm sending him, but instead I'm filled with a churning weight. I raise a brow at him.

"Are you sure you love me?" His voice lowers.

I don't answer, not for a full few moments. Is this a test? "Of course, Arulius," I finally murmur. "Why are you asking?" I push him over and he lets his body fall softly against the pillows and sheets beside me. He's still gazing at me with everything he is. His features are weary and defeated.

His throat bobs. "Because I don't think you realize how much you mean to me." He reaches his hand up and presses it against his eyes. "We bonded, love." His voice breaks.

"I know," I mumble into his arm, pressing soft kisses against his skin to hopefully lighten up his mood. How can he think I'd forget? I clutch my heart. I can still feel his heartbeat within me. It's the most comforting sensation I've ever felt.

"I don't think you do know."

I raise a brow at him. "What do you mean?"

"We bonded . . . shared blood. We are connected now, love." He reaches a hand to my cheek and brushes my skin softly. I blink twice.

"And what does being connected entail?" Did I miss something? Why didn't he bring this up earlier? I know I can feel some of his emotions and he can feel mine, but . . .

He glides his calloused hand across my back and pulls me

close until my face is resting in the crook of his neck and chest. "It means we are one. We are bonded Eostrixes and our fates are tied." My heart skips a beat. Our fates are tied? "If something should happen to either of us, the other will know."

Okay—we would just know? Is that all?

"Oh," is all I can muster. I don't regret it . . . I like being bonded to him. Being this intimately close to him is something no one else will ever have. He is mine.

Why didn't he tell me this earlier though? A baleful thought ruptures the silver lining.

What does he intend for me if he didn't tell me something clearly so important?

Breathe, I remind myself. I sip in a breath and am thankful my face is buried in his chest. Otherwise, he'd see the confusion and dismay I feel. Well, maybe he can feel the weight of it on his chest through the bond.

His warm hand finds my stomach again and stirs a question that I'd let slip my mind. "Arulius, are there contraceptives in this realm?" I mumble with heat rising to my cheeks.

A laugh stirs deep in his chest. "Love, the beings of Tomorrow cannot bear children. There has only ever been one being born into this cruel realm." I raise my face to him, lifting a brow in question.

"Only one?" Why? I think briefly about it.

He lets out another curt laugh. "I wish I could sire a child with you though, love." He brushes his fingers through my hair and my eyes widen at his admittance.

Gods. My face heats and I can't think of anything to say in response to that.

"Let's get some sleep, lovely. Tomorrow will be an unforgiving day." He presses his lips against mine and combs his fingers through my hair. A warmth spreads across my chest and I know he's found rest with his warring emotions.

I, on the other hand, do not fall asleep for a long time. His ominous words echo in my head and bring an incessant anxiety that circulates through me.

Tomorrow will be an unforgiving day.

18

I wake early, much like I did the morning that Moro and I went to the Hollow's Grove. I didn't sleep well at all. Not surprising, given everything that happened in one godsforsaken day. I try to keep my mind clear as I quietly get dressed, and sail through the halls and down the stairs with stealth. Arulius held me tightly through the night. It was the first time we'd embraced so tenderly while we slept. My chest stirs thinking about our blood bond.

Warmth and the knowledge that he's *mine* make my heart swoon with bliss.

I have an inkling that Moro will be up too, and the soft light that radiates from the dining hall tells me I'm right. I step into the opening with a large smile tacked on my lips like a fool, thinking that I will see my friend making tea for the both of us, but no. What I get instead is a weary and ragged-looking Wren.

Startled, I clasp my hands together and hold my breath, hoping he won't see me, but of course, he does.

"Elodie," he says abruptly, as if I interrupted his thoughts. "Couldn't sleep?" He has dark circles under his eyes and his beautiful face is simply exhausted. Is he still in pain?

I still don't trust him, but Moro does . . . and I have to believe that means *something*.

"Yeah." I sigh, stepping forward to take the seat across from him. "You?"

He props his chin on his palm and gazes at me sadly. "Yes, unfortunately. My mind is plagued with the attack on Hollow's Grove." His dark amber eyes rest on me with deep thoughts. "I really don't know what happened. I've been running everything through my head three times over hourly, and still, nothing sheds light on any of it. Moro was bewitched, but by whom? Then there's the matter of Margo—I don't know how Lady Violet could have possibly known." He shuts his eyes as if he can picture the answers if he just forces them into being.

"I thought you asked her if you could bring me there to find Margo?" I say wryly.

He frowns. "I told *you* that, yes. Though I told Lady Violet that I was simply moving you back to Caziel where it would be easier for me to keep an eye on you until she decided what she wanted to do with you."

He lied for me? To the one he is loyal to and serves before

anyone? *Wait—I shouldn't trust him so loosely.* I sharpen my mind to not be so open.

"Why would you lie to Violet if she changed her mind about killing me?" I ask, raising my brow in suspicion.

His eyes narrow and his already tight jawline tenses. "Because you are my friend, Elodie." I flinch. "As I told you weeks ago, I don't intend to harm you or let anyone else inflict it on you. No matter what you think of me. I can't let you sink in your ship alone. Violet claimed she received news that may change her intentions for you, so she wanted me to keep you safe but away from Nesbrim."

My eyes sting with the threat of tears but I hold them back. I've been on a rollercoaster with Wren, but I've always wanted to trust him—yet I also have a million and four reasons to *not* trust him. My broken wing throbs. My Cypress friend—I hoped we could be that, but in the grove . . . how did he nearly catch up to us right as the warriors attacked?

I rest my eyes on him like stones. "What I think of you is that you're sly. You needn't reason to take people from their realms. And you're not loyal to anyone in particular." He shrugs and shakes his head slowly, as if there is no befriending me. "Tell me, Wren, how did you know to warn Moro and me in the grove that morning?"

He considers me for the length of a long draw of breath. "I'd been searching for the hidden village you spoke of when you were still but healing. Liasium." Crap, I completely forgot about that . . . the archives that may or may not hold the reasons Violet seeks me so tirelessly. "It took days to find the dwellings, and once I did—Gods, Elodie. I didn't expect to find what I did."

I lean into the table. "What did you find?" I try to ruminate on what Kastian had told me over a month ago now.

He sits back in his chair and lets his arms fall on the wooden armrests. "I'm not sure you're ready to hear it, Elodie. But it's the reason that, once Violet realized we weren't in Caziel, she immediately sent her warriors for you. Her source of intel is beyond me, but once I discovered her motive . . . I raced for the forest."

I hold my breath. A lump forms in my throat at the memories that threaten to resurface.

"Not because I thought I'd find you or Moro that morning, but because I knew she would be after the Hollows, and by the time I burst through the thicket and saw vast emptiness . . ." He brings his hands to his eyes and covers them, as if the memories steep pain back into him. "I knew they were already in our midst. Then I saw you two. I tried—I tried to warn you, but Kastian was already on me."

"Wren—Wren, oh my gods." My hands clench my mouth tightly as I let the words slip out. He didn't betray us . . . we betrayed *him*, and he still came back for me. I press my eyelids together securely and the rain from my soul flows out of me, tears as salty and guilty as I feel.

"He got me good, Elodie." His hand glides to his chest and I can tell he's tried to heal it, but darkness is spreading across where the cut landed. My eyes widen. Is he *dying*?

"Wren, are you okay?"

He smiles easily. "Let me finish. After you two escaped, Kastian rose. I hated the fucking bastard for cutting me down like he did . . . but I cried when I saw him rise, Elodie." Wren crying? Laughable—not the time, but it was laughable. "Not because I valued his life as much as you do, but because I knew what I'd found in the archives was true at that moment. The Goddess of Dawn has returned to us, Elodie." His dark eyes gaze at me solemnly. "The Goddess of Life who will bring the forest back from its dying light and reincarnate all those who've slept for far too long."

My mind traces back to my time in the forest. Over the years it held fewer and fewer creatures, as if they were stolen from our world. The ponderosas blackened and their needles tanned with dreary death. I thought it was just a sickness passing through the forest. I didn't think my sanctuary was dying.

Don't say it. Please, gods—don't say it.

"You. Elodie." Wren isn't smiling. In fact, he looks really fucking sad for me. "*You* are the Goddess of Dawn."

19

No, no, no, no, no, this is *not* happening. I'm nothing. Especially not some fancy god of the realm. I hardly even know if I'm real or not. I can't be a god of *anything*.

I stare at Wren for the better part of five minutes. There are no words I can form. He just laid out an entire pile of emotional events that already passed and bestowed the weight of seven suns on me. What the fuck am I supposed to say to that? I worry my lip and say the only thing that comes to mind.

"Are you okay?" I ask again in a voice just above a whisper, hoping that he will answer me this time.

He tilts his head at me but I can see the understanding in his eyes. Wren has always been wise and forgiving. Even so, nothing could make me feel better about what has come to pass. I can't forgive myself for not trusting him after everything he's sacrificed for me. He may have been cruel at times, but his intentions were always good.

"I'm fine." He gently touches his chest, winces, and tries to smile it off.

I frown and narrow my eyes. "I don't believe you. Let me see." I walk around the table and stand over him. He groans and knows I will have my way one way or the other. He lifts his shirt and I grit my teeth at what lies beneath.

Black ink covers his torso, twirling like shadows around his heart and spreading to his limbs. It looks like a haunting tattoo of a tree, outlining all the veins and arteries that lie beneath his skin. My fingers fall to his chest and he winces in pain.

"Wren, you are *not* okay." I take the seat next to him and press my palm over the initial cut inflicted by Kastian. No wonder he looked so tired and like he was dying.

He quirks a weak smile. "I didn't want to worry you or Moro."

"How were you not able to heal it? You can heal practically anything."

"I suspect that Kastian is the God of Death, and that includes illness. A curse to any he inflicts with his cut. Unfortunately it can't be healed easily," Wren mutters as if it is common knowledge. I pause at this. The God of Death? The one I always claimed to have hated and despised? Wished horrible things upon? My heart breaks, because his life has been every bit as awful as I hoped.

I clench my fists. "And yet all this time you pestered him like that?" He laughs softly. "I'm serious, Wren." I try to stay focused.

"You're always serious, Elodie." He scoffs. "Always so serious and so sad." His long, dark hair lost a lot of its luster, though his attitude is still strong. He looks more drained by the second.

My lips tighten. "Can it be reversed? Tell me how to help. Do you need blood?"

Wren sets his soft hands against mine. "I don't think so. I've done everything in my ability to heal it to no avail. I think I'm done for."

No.

His weak smile makes me tremble with all the feelings I've been pushing out for so long. No more death. No more grief and sadness. I want to be real. For Wren and Kastian. Moro and Arulius. For Margo and . . . and for *me*.

"No," I hiss in a low breath. "You don't get to give up."

"I'm sorry, Elodie, no isn't an option. I will perish."

"No." I rest both of my hands against his chest. He flinches under my touch. I focus all my aura on the black line that pulses with the heat of infection, and pull the magic within me from my heart like I did when I apparently healed Kastian.

Please.

My aura tugs inside my cavity and fills me with the warmth of a tight embrace. Love? It's a pleasant feeling. I focus on it and my entire body thrills with the lovely feeling. I watch my hands carefully as a soft glow spreads from beneath my fingertips and into his chest. The light fills every crack and wisp of the shadows that loom along his skin, flushing out all the curse's dark whispers until there is nothing left but my light.

My heart soars. Rain kisses my skin and sunlight brushes my face. A whisper from someone echoes in my conscience. I don't recognize it though. I'm quickly brought out of my deep internal plummet by Wren's sharp gasp.

"Elodie." He gawks at me with wide eyes, staring down at his shadowless skin. "You blessed the curse." His breath leaves his chest with a sigh of relief.

A wave of riveting weariness washes over my bones. It feels like all my energy has been sapped, and a knot grows in my stomach. Hunger brims within me. I clench my stomach and know Arulius must feel this sudden shift in my body as the floor above us creaks.

I don't want to believe that I can be the goddess he spoke of, but if this wasn't proof enough, I don't know what would be. If I truly brought Kastian back from the permanent death, I ponder what else might I be able to do. But also, what duty it requires of me . . .

"Thank you, Elodie."

Wren pulls his shirt down and stands. His face is already showing the relief I know he feels. "I'm going to wake Moro. We need to start planning early. Kastian needs us." I gather my hands up to my chest, the aura still warm and thrumming against the walls of my heart.

"Yeah." I smile. "He does."

We spend the better part of the morning going over the details of our plan. Moro and Arulius are much slower to fully wake than Wren and me. After our conversation this morning, I have a stronger fire burning within me. I won't let my friends down anymore. They are all here for *me*. I have to match their efforts with my own.

Moro shares where he assumes they are keeping all the Pine Hollows within Nesbrim. According to him, there really are only a handful of places where they have the space to maintain and care for hundreds of the beasts. He suspects they are in the High Court's atrium. He describes it as a glass dome that stretches over a few acres. Arulius twirls his cup of tea as he listens to the discussion. He doesn't have much input and looks bored out of his mind. I'm sure he could easily storm in there himself with the power he displayed before in the grove. His strength surpasses all of the rest of ours without a doubt.

After we eat and pack some food, we all get dressed for the journey ahead. I strap on my golden war brackets and black underclothes. I still admire the way the attire fits me. I truly look like a goddess. We don't skip the discussion of how few combat skills I still have, but with all the training I've had in the prior weeks with Arulius, it makes me confident I can kill if I need to. My wings now drape just beneath my knees but are still far too small to get any air, and with the break still being sensitive, it isn't an option for me. I can *maybe* glide, but I've been too afraid to try. For now, though, I will play defense and heal any injuries that may occur.

This is risky, and we are probably heading straight into the depths of Lady Violet's scheme. She knows we will come for Kastian. All she has to do now is wait.

We ride the Hollows out of the dead forest by noon. The sun peaks in the center of the sky and a soft gust of the wind brings the scent of ash and death. Wren rides with Moro on Murph's back. Ceres is only large enough for one rider. Arulius flies close by, glancing at me often, and a stir of warmth fills me every time. Once in a while he glides higher up to get a better vantage point of the lands ahead.

After traveling for hours, we finally clear the glades of Kastian's court. The Hollows can run for days at a time so we aren't concerned with their vigor as much as we are our own. Moro is hoping to reach the Moss Forest before nightfall, but we are still hours away. Wren suggests we stop in a small bundle of trees for the night and make camp.

I don't realize how weary my legs are until after I stretch them out and sit sorely on a fallen log. Ceres circles me and rests her head at my side. I already love her. She partially fills the hole that Margo left me with. I pet her and lean back into her white wisping fur. She did so well today, Murph too. Carrying two males couldn't have been an easy feat. The dark Hollow sits next to Wren as the Cypress tries to get a fire started. Arulius flies off to make sure our perimeters are safe from any enemies, while Moro spreads out some bed rolls.

I watch comfortably, leaning against Ceres. "Wren, can't you just use your power to make the fire?" It takes everything in me not to laugh at him. He has every ability in the books but can't start a small fire?

He shoots me an annoyed glance. "Elodie, fire magic is not something Cypresses can perform."

"How the hell would I know that?"

He grins. "I just thought you were smart and may have picked that up by now." I roll my eyes and rest my head on Ceres, nuzzling into her fur. It's nice to have everyone back together. Our little band of misfits.

Arulius returns after his rounds and helps with the fire. He finds it as laughable as I do, and he doesn't hold back his amusement with it. After everyone nestles into their small nests, Arulius and I take the far corner of the camp so we can feed. We don't want to . . . disturb anyone, especially since it's so sensual—more so now that we are bonded. I noticed Wren and Moro casting us questioning glances all day, but thank the fucking gods, they are too reluctant to ask about us.

I pull my teeth from his neck and he releases me at the same time. We clean one another's skin with a brush of our tongues. When he pushes away, he stops his face just inches from mine. My breath hitches and I hold it. I stare into his amethyst eyes and before I can mutter a word, he presses his lips onto mine. My chest ignites with waves of emotions. I can't tell which ones are coming from him or me but I soak it all in.

He breaks the kiss and leans his forehead against mine. "Gods, you're so perfect, love. So beautiful. I missed you so much."

"Missed me? We've been eye fucking each other all day." I smirk.

His eyes glimmer. "I can still miss you."

I puddle in his arms. No one has ever loved me as fiercely as he does. No one.

He brushes my cheek gently with his hand and nudges me to lay down for rest. I nuzzle into his chest and he wraps his strong arms around me, pulling me close until all I can hear are his heartbeats. The last thing I remember before falling asleep is the sound of him breathing.

We wake early. Dawn brings the warmth of the sun and renews our spirits. The Moss Forest only takes an hour to reach from our rest stop. I wonder why it's named after moss, but it doesn't take long to figure out. The trees look like sticks with gigantic balls of green fluffy foliage on the tops and sides. The underbrush is the same. Moss *everything*. I think of Marley back in Caziel. He must come from this forest.

"Stop," Wren calls back to me and Ceres. Moro shifts uneasily on Murph's back as the Hollow slams his paws into the earth, bringing them to an immediate halt.

Ceres makes a more graceful stop and flicks her ivory ears

back in irritation. I lift my ears to try and listen. Why did we stop moving? Arulius flies down and lands silently by me.

"What's going on?" He crosses his arms and glances at me, a flicker of concern glimmering in his amethyst eyes.

I tighten my lips. "I'm not sure." We both look at Wren, who's sitting at attention on Murph's shoulders. He's so still. He heard something, I'm sure of it.

"Wren," I whisper, but he doesn't respond or move a muscle. Moro turns and looks at me with the same confusion.

I dismount from Ceres and creep up to stand next to Murph's wisping shadows of fur. The Hollow glances back at me and grunts to acknowledge my presence. I stroke his muzzle and set a hand on Wren's arm. He flinches but remains eerily still.

"Wren," I whisper again, a familiar panic and fear moving through me. His amber eyes are set on the darkness of the moss's thicket, searching for something unseen. I shudder, remembering this ominous sensation from the grove.

"Elodie," he finally speaks, calmly but with such a grim tone. I bring my eyes to his. The same nervousness flickers across his gaze. "Get ready. Right fucking *now!*" he shouts.

His words are silenced with Murph's booming roar. The Pine Hollow whirls in front of me as an arsenal of black inky shards pierce into his side. Black liquid oozes from his fur and the Hollow falls to the ground with a heavy *thud*.

No.

"Murph!" Wren screams as he's thrown to the ground. Murph yelps in agony, spitting blackened blood across the forest's floor. My veins thicken and send pain into my limbs with each pulse. Chaos ripples through the trees, and gold and black and crimson armor sings a horrible song that twists and churns my bones, painting the bark and greens of the leaves with everything I fear in this realm. Death.

Moro charges for Ceres and mounts her quickly. He leads her to attack a group of Violet's soldiers. Her sharp teeth snap onto a soldier's arm while Moro has a short sword drawn and slashes through the air at another. The soldiers' guts spew and cries boom in my ears.

I cling to Murph's side. The sounds of fighting and dread are not sounds I'll ever get used to. Arulius roars and crashes into their ranks, his golden aura blading around his hands like arced swords.

I look up to Wren as he stands above Murph and me. His gaze is distant as he stares at Murph's seizing body. I snap out of my trance and furrow my brows. *No more. No more being useless.*

"Wren, I'll heal Murph. You protect us while I fix him," I say confidently. Wren seems to remember that I possess the powers of the Goddess of Life and a weak smile of hope crosses his face. He nods curtly and leaps into the warriors that unsheathe their swords a few feet away, cursing as he lashes out a whip of thorns in rage.

I run my hands across Murph's trembling side, his shadows becoming less wispy with each moment that passes. I bite my lips and shove the part of me that's uncertain if I'll be able to heal him into the back of my mind. I *will* heal him.

"Murph, it's okay, shh. I'm here. I'm right here."

The black splinters are difficult to pull out, but I suffuse my aura around my hands to help grip them. They're slick with ebony ink. I push my hands against the Hollow's side. His breath is weakening. He's feeble under my palms. I hold back tears at the sight of him. He's such a strong beast, reduced to a shivering pup within the span of a minute. The worst part is that the shards were meant for me . . . No longer, it seems, is Violet willing to take me alive. These shards would have killed me in seconds.

Murph lets out a low whine, slicing the air with high-pitched, heart-wrenching cries. I hold him tenderly and comfort him.

"You're such a good boy, Murph. I know it hurts, but I'm going to heal you up. You're okay."

I focus my energy in the wells of my heart and push the strings through my arms and into him. After a few minutes, I release him and check the wounds. Something's wrong. I don't see the lights and glow as I did with Wren.

They aren't healing. A stone drops in my chest, into an endless pit.

Horror—pure, undiluted horror envelopes me.

"Wren," I whisper. I need help. I need help. "WREN!" I scream.

His black hair pops up from the bushes as he lashes behind him with an arc of dark green thorns that embed in and animate the trees forward, grabbing the warriors with their branches. He charges toward me with blood and cuts covering his entire body. Crimson leaks down into his left eye and he keeps it shut. Anxiety fills his remaining eye, as he surely knows what I couldn't do to have screamed in such a way.

"I—I can't . . . s-something isn't right, Wren." Salty tears trickle into the corners of my mouth and I rub Murph's side to show him the black ooze that won't wash away. "S-something is wrong."

He slumps down next to me, his knees thudding with his weight. A warrior charges behind him and raises his sword to cut into the both of us. Arulius appears over the warrior's shoulder and clasps his neck from both sides with such force that the neck is gone before I can blink. Blood rains down on us and Arulius's luminous purple eyes burn into the dim forest air. "What's wrong, Elodie?" He clenches his chest painfully. He must feel my anguish as deeply as I do through the bond.

Wren doesn't seem to notice the hot crimson running down his neck or across his lashes, dripping into his eyes. The decapitated warrior's confused heart still pulses violently, showering us with the sin of this morbid day. Wren blinks slowly and leans over Murph's body.

No, no, no, no. Not again. Please.

He brings the Hollow's muzzle to his nose. Murph lets out a low whine, so weary and raspy it tears my heart. Someone's crying. Others are shouting and cutting flesh. But all I can hear are Murph's last labored breaths and soft whimpers.

My heart begins to thrum in an uneven, erratic beat. My

eyes blur with the vision of blood and whimpers . . . crying and screaming. Not again . . . I shrivel into myself, bringing my knees to my chest and covering my ears with my hands. I scream as my mind breaks with the unbearable traumas, ones I'd forgotten and the ones now. Arulius wraps an arm around me and breathes soothingly into my ear.

"You need to calm down, love."

I don't acknowledge his words. All I can do is stare unblinking at the Pine Hollow and the Cypress.

Please.

"Murph!" I cry. Why, gods? What did he ever fucking do?

Wren doesn't say a word. He keeps his forehead pressed on Murph's until the breaths slow. They come in deep, whiny draws, slower and slower until the universe stills. Until the last light in his eyes fades into a hush, into the quiet corners of our dark reality.

"Goodbye, my friend," Wren speaks softly, eliciting throbs from my heart. "You . . . were a good boy."

20

Murph's translucent leaves fade from his fur, orbing into the sky like fireflies ascending into the universe above. His wisping shadows disappear, leaving his body just as his soul has. Wren sits back on his haunches and slumps his arms to his sides, staring endlessly into the sky, following the orbs into oblivion.

A storm wells behind my eyes and in my temples, dark clouds of trembling despair, a squall of rage so soaked in hate that my vision blurs. All I can see and hear is Murph's dying breath repeating in my ears. So similar to Margo's. Too similar. I clench my heart. It was *my* fault.

The rhythm of my heart soothes my mind as something deep and heavy clicks open within me, like a door that was meant to stay locked has been shattered open. A lullaby that my mother once sang to me, one of dread and sorrow. The music box of my pain, it played when Margo died too. How fitting it should strum again.

I stand, not consciously. I'm simply a bystander in my own body at this point. Just watching, curled up in a ball inside. Broken. My eyes graze over the warriors that still fight against Arulius and Moro. Ceres is wounded but continues to fight too. All for me. They die, they bleed, they suffer. For me.

I can bleed too. I can die and suffer for my friends too. A force within me raises my arms, hands cold and bare. My chin tips up to the treetops above and a light warms my neck.

Crunching bones and flesh ignite through the thicket in a flurry. Black hot rain pelts down on my face as I continue to stare up to the heavens. My eyes scorn the gods for what they've done. The patter of the blood soothes my rage, strokes it like a beast that has sought to be tamed.

I'll kill all of them. *All* of them.

Through the ticking sounds of drops on the forest's leaves and moss, I hear Moro gasp behind me. He's but a few feet away. I turn my head and let my heavy eyes, filled with unbearable grief, stare at him. His face is smeared with crimson and a deep anguish crosses his features as he sees Murph's lifeless body. Tears stream down his face, washing blood from his cheeks.

"No," he whispers, much too quietly for me to hear, but I see the word leave his lips.

Arulius walks over to me and tries to comfort me once

more. His golden wings are drenched and brush the forest floor heavily behind him.

"Holy hell," he mutters at what I made of the soldiers. Their limbs dangle from the branches and teeth lay scattered across the mossy forest floor.

Moro kneels by Murph's side and sets his hand on the Hollow's neck. "Be in peace, my friend." He sends a prayer to some god, whatever god that would allow such a horrible unfair fate to unfold. My heart thrums with rage.

Guilt starts to seep in and the part of me that is curled and hiding deep within myself dies.

"I . . . I tried to save him." I fall to my knees at the Hollow's side. "I tried. I did what I had before and nothing happened. I tried and tried and nothing would work. It's . . . it's my fault." I choke on my words. The three males covered in red glance at me with sorrow still stinging their eyes. Arulius clenches his chest and winces as my grief grows. "It was my fault . . . and now Murph is gone." My voice quivers and twists within my throat.

The Eostrix hugs me tightly, a weight that I'm not sure I can bear. "It wasn't your fault, love." A wisp of warmth brushes against my ribs and I let my tears fall.

Wren's gaze is nearly as empty as his Hollow's. His dark eyes are not quite as contrasted as they once were. The translucent leaves have faded from his black hair as they did from Murph's.

Ceres, spattered in blood, limps up to Wren and presses her muzzle into his shoulder. Such a kind and caring creature.

My eyes blur with tears. Her gesture wrings tears from the Cypress as well.

My dear Wren.

I've never heard anything wail the way he does for Murph.

And I never want to hear such tender pain ever again.

21

We barely make it to the end of the forest by nightfall.

The warriors had been waiting for us, that much was clear. We pursue carefully and in silence. No one utters a word except for Arulius checking in on me constantly. He can feel my pain through our bond. He clenches his heart and walks beside me for the remainder of the day.

The forest seems to mourn with us. The creatures that swing in the trees make small cooing sounds and the birds sing a song of rest. We are tired and sticky with blood, slowly losing sight of the goal we once had. With the loss of Murph, things don't seem to mean as much anymore, but we can't let his death be in vain. We have to keep pushing. For Margo, for Kastian . . . but at what cost?

At what cost . . . The price is the lives of others, it seems. But no one asked me if I'm willing to pay. I'm not, not with their lives.

We break the treeline just as the final rays of sunset bead and splinter across the expansive sky. Even Arulius seems to be worn thin.

"Are you okay?" He glances over at me. His golden wings are tacky with dried blood, but his amethyst eyes glow against the dimming sky. "You look tired, love," he mumbles and furrows his brows, rubbing my sticky cheek affectionately. He settles next to me as we get ready to set up camp. Only no one is setting anything up. I think we all find it useless to dirty the clean bed rolls with our crusted bodies, and we are all so fucking tired.

We eat in silence and find sleep the same way. Ceres wraps around me. Arulius is smushed in too. He holds me so gently. He'll never know how much I need it, his comfort, his love. His heart flutters through the bond. We feed softly tonight, so tenderly it almost makes me tear up because I didn't know it could be so soothing after such distress. His blood warms my mouth and fills me with ambrosial flavors of honey. I smile at the warm memories his blood stirs within me. The happiness that he makes me feel in my darkest of times and the love he constantly showers me in.

I pull my teeth out. "Arulius."

"Yeah?"

"I love you."

I feel his lips turn upward on my neck. "I love you too."

We settle and don't speak for a few minutes. My weary body is already taking me into my dreams when he softly nudges me. I raise my head to peer at him.

"Do you ever wonder why these types of things happen?" he whispers.

I nod somberly.

"I wonder that more and more often. That Pine Hollow didn't do anything wrong. You've done nothing wrong, and yet the gods come after you like wolves after a rabbit." He glances at me. I take in his sharp features. Even in the dark, and under all the blood, he is iridescent in the moon's pale light. "You deserve more than *this*." His hand crests the back of my weary head.

"I keep wanting to wake up," I admit. "Because how can any of these awful things be happening? But I'm awake . . . No matter how much it hurts, I know I am awake. I don't know why my magic didn't work on Murph." I clench my fists against his chest. "I tried everything I could. It's like a curse follows me wherever I go, bringing suffering and death to those around me."

That's a hard pill to swallow.

Arulius flinches. "None of it was your fault, love." His voice is filled with anguish. There's a tug on the bond. My chest feels heavy with his grief.

I let his words soak in, but they don't bring any relief. My eyes trail to Wren, who is curled in a ball by himself across the small clearing. His Hollow usually curled by his side, but now that spot is cold next to him. His lone silhouette steals my sleep and drives the knife of guilt further into my bleeding heart.

In the morning we all make small conversation while preparing to set out again. Arulius spots a creek for us to get cleaned up in, and thank the gods for it. I've been carrying around who knows how many people on my skin. The thought sends a shudder through me.

Moro's been acting odd all morning. At first, I thought it was because he was still bothered by the day prior. We all were. But something else seems to be tugging at him, wearing on him until midday. He slows his pace to walk beside me and Ceres. Arulius glances back and raises a brow but I just nod to him. He flies ahead a bit to give us some space.

"Are you ready for Nesbrim?" Moro asks with a gentle frown. "You very well might have to fight against Violet."

I look down at my hands, Ceres's white fur bristling between my fingers. I know that's a possibility but I really hope I won't have to. I can only seem to use my power when in extreme emotional distress. How many have I already killed? I don't even know . . . I let out a sigh, glancing over to Wren. He walks with a slump to his shoulders. He shares the walk that I took on as I wandered the forests in the in-between.

"I'm ready," I reply. "Is Wren okay? Moro . . . I tried my best to save Murph. I don't know why, but my healing didn't work on him like it did Kastian and Wren." I hold back the tears that fight to break free and swallow the lump that's been stuck in my throat all day.

Moro's silver eyes consider me. He brings his hand to mine, his dark skin smooth against the sunlight. "Elodie, you may be the Goddess of Life, but even you cannot save a Pine Hollow once it begins to die in Tomorrow." He speaks with wisdom from his time in this realm.

My eyes widen. "But why?"

"Because they are not meant to stay here for eons like us. The Pine Hollows bring us joy and friendship, but their true duty is to the humans on the other side. That's where they thrive. Where they are meant to serve their true roles."

"And what is that?"

He smiles. "To bring happiness to the weary."

"Is Murph on the other side?"

His mouth tightens. "No . . . Creatures have not been reborn to the other side for hundreds of years. Once they die here now, they remain asleep. They are not completely gone, just . . . away."

The hope I briefly held slips away. "Hundreds of years . . . What happened to change that?" I glance back at Wren. If we can fix the Rhythm, then maybe . . .

"No doubt you've seen the doors of the High Court." I nod. "Talia and Borvon. Life and Death. Dawn and Rest.

They kept the Rhythm of the worlds. Give and take, in perfect tandem."

Kastian said something similar weeks ago. "Talia, the Goddess of Dawn, of Life and Rebirth. Kastian told me that she and Violet hated one another."

Moro nods, staring distantly into the hills we approach. "Talia did not hate Violet, she just wouldn't break her code of resurrection to fulfill Violet's wishes. Her highness was ruined when Lucius was taken from her. She couldn't understand why Talia refused to reunite them on the other side."

"Not gonna lie to you, Moro, I'm with Violet on that one." He shoots me an astonished look. I shrug. "It's such a sad love story. She only wanted to be with her lover. She wanted it so desperately that she would war against the realms and gods to be with him once more . . . It makes my heart hurt, to be honest. I can't despise her for just that because I probably would have done the same." The world can only break you so many times before you become a monster . . . the villain.

Moro's eyes soften. "Ah, then you only know the beginning of her pain. Violet had Borvon killed, did you know that?" My eyes widen and a pit falls in my stomach. *I did not know that.* "That's what I thought. She hated Talia and wanted her to feel the same pain she did. Of course, being the Goddess of Life, she resurrected Borvon into the human realm, where he lived a mortal life without her."

My heart burns. "But what happened to her? I know she died too . . ."

"Yes—she died in such a horrible way, Elodie. Violet

swore to stop the resurrection of all beings and she did . . . It ruined life here in *Tomorrow*. She bound Talia's powers with the help of an Eostrix. Not just any—he was the God of Wrath." He pauses. "Once her powers were bound, Talia could no longer resurrect the Pine Hollows, the Moss Sparrows, the Cypresses, or any creature. They all fell into the rest that waits after. Talia became so melancholic and dull, the life left her, like her power to grant it had."

My heart fumbles into my lap. "Did she . . . did she kill herse—"

"No," he says sharply and I take a breath of relief. "She went back to Nesbrim, stormed Violet's court, and begged for her to reconsider. She said that Violet's love, Lucius, had a path to walk and would return again one day." His silver eyes flicker with sadness. "Under orders of her highness, the God of Wrath struck Talia down. He killed her on the very floors of Violet's throne room."

I shudder and goosebumps envelope my arms. I remember when Wren and I kneeled before her on those very floors. "So after Talia's powers were taken, the Pine Hollows could no longer be saved after a mortal wound?"

He nods somberly. "But you are here now, Elodie. You can start the rhythm of life again. The pain that is wrought doesn't have to be eternal. It can be just a bittersweet kiss that means *we'll meet again* instead of *goodbye forever*." Moro brings his eyes to the sky, and I follow suit.

Orange and pink hues dance on the clouds, reminding me of the lullaby my mother would sing to me, the one with death and dread, but now I remember that it has a soft and kind ending to it. One that reminds me of this sky, a right to the wrong.

Hope.

I smile at Moro, teary-eyed. "I *will* bring them back. Everyone."

He beams back at me and nods with purpose. "I know you will, Elodie. You *are* the reincarnation of Goddess Talia. You can do everything she could and more."

My heart flutters uncomfortably and Arulius glances back at me with concern in his eyes. I know he feels my distress. "What do you mean . . ." I'm not sure I want the answer to that. If it's true, does that mean I'm not really *me*?

"You are the reincarnation of Talia. While Kastian—"

"Is the resurrected god Borvon . . ." I mumble, putting the pieces together. Moro nods. "I . . . I can't believe it." My mind whirls. Is that why I'm so attracted to him? So . . . drawn to him like I've known him for eons and lifetimes. Like we were crafted from the same stones. But are those feelings my own? I have a connection with Arulius unlike any other. We are bonded, but even before that, we just fit together so well. Does this mean that I *have* to love Kastian? If Borvon was death and Talia was life . . . they are yin and yang. Push and pull. Moon and sun. Destined . . .

But what if I don't want to push or pull . . . Do I get a choice?

My eyes search for the golden Eostrix, desperate for his amethyst gaze to warm me. I want *him*.

My heart sinks.

Chest tightening, I feel like I'm being suffocated. I can't be Talia . . . I am Elodie.

Moro sees my warring emotions. "Don't fret about it, Elodie. You are still *you*. I'm a reincarnation as well—we all are."

I appreciate his attempt to make me feel better, but I still need to process this. "Do you know who you used to be, Moro?" He seems so wise and old at heart. He has to have lived for hundreds of years here.

A brief smile crosses his chapped lips. "I've been on this plane for two hundred and ten years." *Gods, I was right.* "I can't speak to who I was prior, but I have a strong hold on who I am now." Riddles . . . He always speaks in riddles and it pisses me off.

"Oh, I see," I mutter, trying to imagine how long the Rhythm of the Realms has been in motion. Another question piques my curiosity though. "And what of Lucius?"

Moro's eyes search the sky. "Some say that he walks among us, others say he died here long ago, never to be rein- carnated and sleeping among the bones of Kastian's glades. I've heard rumors that Violet waits every evening, watching the sun crescendo beyond the hills, hoping that he will return one day."

"But he never has," I mutter. Moro shakes his head slowly. I don't like how Violet acted after losing Lucius but gods, I can understand it. Even still she longs endlessly for his return and that breaks my heart.

Nevertheless, I'm thankful for his conversation this afternoon. "Thank you, Moro, for that. It gives me hope knowing that, in a way, I might have a chance to save Murph someday."

Moro grins, his teeth bright white, his silver eyes gleaming. "Always a pleasure. We share a love for the Hollows. Our fight is for them and so much more."

I like that. No—I love that about Moro. I kick up the corners of my lips with a hopeful smile.

For the Hollows. For the Hollows and so much more.

22

We stay close to the ground, under the bushes of the valleys nearing Nesbrim. Night has been around us for nearly four hours already. My mind is weary from the long day of travel, but we don't have any time left to burn. My body aches from head to toe, but my stomach churns heavily with the information Moro burdened me with. I want to save Kastian and be reunited, but I will never leave Arulius's side. The yin and yang chain will have to be broken. I just don't know what it will mean for the worlds once I do . . . I glance over to the Eostrix as he walks beside me, his hair glinting in the moonlight, bristling in the breeze. He notices me looking at him and shifts his gaze on me. His iridescent purple eyes burn into me with life.

"Are you ready, love?"

I smile and nod.

We are freeing Kastian *tonight.*

The first time I was brought here it was through the southern pass, a nice trail that led right up to the court and the imperial estate. But since we are sneaking in and coming from the northern mountains, we don't have the luxury of a nice blazed path or even steady ground.

Wren is smart. He knows the High Court inside and out. If he says this is the best way in, then all be damned, it is. Arulius isn't allowed to fly anymore now that we are so close to the court. He could easily give us away with his bright golden feathers. He agrees it is the best plan and stays close to my side through the evening.

I grip his hand. He flinches in surprise at me. I grin softly at him and his fingers squeeze mine with the same affection. The patter of both our hearts warms my chest. We are going into Nesbrim together. I pray we will leave the same.

As we reach the northern walls, we put our plan into action. Of course, we have to change it up a little now that Murph isn't here. Moro and Wren are to take the west side of the court to find Margo and the other Hollows, while Arulius and I take the east side to find Kastian. Ceres remains at the meeting spot in the safety of the forest. Wren and Arulius both have extensive knowledge of Violet's court since they served her for hundreds of years, if not more, which gives me hope that this will work. It has to.

"You're sure you know where they are keeping Kastian?"

I whisper to the Eostrix as Wren and Moro sneak their way across the wall to the western gates. He raises an annoyed brow at me.

"Are you seriously questioning my knowledge? The *one* duty that I had when I served Violet?" We are both tense, but his voice carries a hint of humor. I kick up a corner of my mouth and shrug. "You're the worst," he mumbles playfully. He grips my hand tighter and my heart clenches with it.

We move along the wall quietly in the other direction. Arulius's golden wings are tucked back tightly to make himself as small as he can. I do the same. Thank the gods Kastian insisted on teaching me the basics.

As the eastern gates appear, the anxious feeling that has been worrying me all day climaxes. What if we get caught and can't save Kastian? What if *we* die? What if Wren and Moro can't find Margo? There are so many *what if*s that plague my mind today, and of course just after I thought I contained them, they come flooding in all at once.

Arulius stops and I crouch next to his right side, the wall to my other. He glances over at me and rakes me from head to toe with his beautiful amethyst eyes as if it might be the last time he can look at me. I find myself doing the same to him, memorizing every inch of his face.

Our eyes meet and I feel a painful tug on my heart through the bond. *I know, I feel it too.* I fall forward and catch myself with my hand. Wincing, I glance back up to Arulius.

"Are you okay?" His eyes widen.

I push myself back to my stable crouch and grasp my chest. "Nothing—I just lost focus," I lie. He stares at me like he doesn't buy it, but thank the gods, he doesn't push any further. I'm probably sending the same painful throbs to his chest as well . . . but this one feels especially heavy and sharp. I shake my head to refocus.

We inch closer to the gate. There are a few guards chatting on the edge across from us. The stone walls aren't lit, so at least we have *something* in our favor. Arulius turns to me. "You stay here. These guards probably don't know that I've been outcast from the court yet, so I'll go distract them. You sneak through when they turn away and wait for me on the other side, okay?" I nod nervously, feeling sick that we are about to breach Nesbrim. He narrows his eyes at me. "You *have* to wait. Promise me that you will, love."

"I promise, Arulius. I'm not going to run around like a lost kitten in there." I roll my eyes at him. He smirks, presses a kiss to my lips, and disappears into the bushes on our left.

I hold my breath for a few minutes as the night treks on, with only the low whispers of the guards to break the slow stir of impending doom that I feel building with each second that passes. Arulius's gray and gold-tipped hair pops out of the bush on the other side of the gate and I stiffen. I watch as he prowls out as if he's just been on a nightly stroll.

Please let this work. I bite my lip with anticipation.

He approaches them easily and the guards both immediately recognize him drawing up their hands in salutes just as

303

the Eostrix predicted they would. I let a silent sigh out. He chats with the guards and has them looking at him entirely. I see his luminous purple eyes flick to me and I know that I have to move now.

My legs tremble as I force them to advance into the light. The gates are two heavy-looking stone doors. They bear the same carvings that the high court estate had, and I hesitate at the foot of them. Two gods reach for one another in a somber attempt to connect. I examine the stones. There's no way I can get these things to budge on my own.

Panic hits me and I shoot a fearful glance at Arulius. He notices that I've stopped moving and his smile becomes more strained.

Shit shit shit. I look to the left and see nothing that can help me, then to my right, and thank all the fucking gods, there is a small drainage hole that I'll fit in. I pace over to it quickly and slip inside. I was expecting it to be wet and smelly, but they must not use these drains anymore because they are dry and dusty. I crawl on my hands and knees for a few minutes until I break through the other side.

It's dim here. Arulius was right about the east side of the court being the slums and prison quarters. There are no fancy, sparkling buildings and cottages like there are in the southern side. Everything is stone and no vines grow here. Does the sun even reach past the walls here? I entertain the thought.

Arulius is taking longer than I expected. I wait for what feels like hours but could be only twenty minutes. Either way, it's *too* long. I try to spend my time thinking of what I'll say to Kastian when I see his azure eyes once more and his kind, soft smile. Does he know that he is the reincarnation of Borvon? A small part of me hopes not . . . I don't want there to be expectations that I have to break.

I sigh at the headache that the frenzied thoughts give me.

While I'm busy contemplating, I hear a *snap* behind me. A shiver shoots up my spine and I whirl to look into the dark tunnel behind me.

Darkness, there's nothing but darkness, and a soft breeze from the other side. I *know* I heard something. I narrow my eyes more and a large rat-looking creature comes barreling at me. I nearly let out a shriek when I remember where I am. My hand flies to cover my mouth and I bolt out of the drain and race silently across the cobblestone street.

I take a few deep breaths and stare at the drain. The rat didn't bother following me out, but now there's a new problem: I'm out in the open. *Fuck.*

I let out a slew of curse words and pray that Arulius will understand why I didn't wait for him like I promised. I dart off in the direction that Arulius explained earlier is where we'll find Kastian.

The stones remain blank and somber as I make my way around corners and dash across empty streets. It must be awfully late because I don't see a soul. I foolishly gain a bit of courage from this, taking longer peeks around the edges and slower trots across the roads. I eye a tall, dark building and have an inkling that it is the prison, not because of its sheer size but more so because of the bars that are clamped on the windows and the despair I can feel emanating from the place.

Kastian is here. My bones thrum and my marrow tingles. Every fiber of my being is on edge, and at the same time filled with ecstasy with the thought of embracing him once more.

I circle my way to the back. We went over how we'll break in a million times, but as I am about to prop open the window, I still. *Maybe I should wait for Arulius.* I worry my lip, but Kastian could be just on the other side of this window. I look back up into the dark streets and stone cottages, the air still and silent. There's no sign of Arulius and I can't risk being found here.

I nudge the window open and slip inside. Just as my feet hit the ground, an overwhelming feeling of dread and rage thrusts against my chest. Heavy—it's so fucking heavy. And I know that Arulius has discovered that I wasn't where I promised I'd be. His rage sends fear through me. I'll have to face the repercussions later.

I shake the feeling and take in my surroundings. The room is dark. I can smell the dust and mildew in here from years of disuse. The door in the corner is only visible thanks to the low light that trickles in beneath it.

I push the door open slowly and look down each hallway, gray and dark just like the rest of the court right now. Almost *too* quiet. I push down the bad feeling and continue forward. I stop at each door and peer in cautiously. The bars are thick and cold, each cell holding equally chilling prisoners. I'm thankful it's so late and that I've been so quiet, because otherwise each of these prisoners might be awake and shouting at me.

I check every cage on the first floor, but Kastian isn't here. I pass by a dark and gloomy stairwell halfway through my search and decide that he will probably be kept underground rather than above.

I gaze at the shadows that seem to dance below the fifth step leading down. My stomach lurches and goosebumps ripple across my arms. I swallow my fear and take each step with wide eyes. Into the darkness I go.

The bottom floor is the closest to the physical embodiment of despair that I ever want to experience. The walls ooze with black mud. Cracks that break from the stones stretch feet at times, and the floors haven't been maintained in gods know how long. The moisture in the air stings my lungs. I cover my nose with my shirt but it doesn't seem to help.

I finally come across a cell and peek in carefully. There's a prisoner sitting up against the back wall. She's awake and keenly aware of my presence. I flinch. *Maybe I can just keep walking and she won't say anything.*

I straighten and begin walking ahead. "What are you doing down here?" Her voice is low and sharp. I freeze on my right foot and hesitantly face the cell again.

I try to keep my head. She isn't shouting or yelling. This can still be okay. "I . . . I am just here to find a bucket . . . Yeah, the Commander needs one—gods, it's a mess upstairs." It's perhaps the worst lie I've ever spun. I cringe at my efforts.

The prisoner leans forward. I can see her long brown hair braided down the left side of her head and her yellow eyes glow in the dim light. She's older than me and stunning for a prisoner. "Gods, that was awful." I can make out a smile that passes over her lips. "What are you *really* doing down here, little one?"

I tense. Again, at least she didn't reveal my presence. What harm can the truth do? She might even help me find Kastian.

I let out a sigh. "I'm trying to find my friend . . . He was taken a few weeks ago."

She doesn't say anything for a few minutes and I almost just keep walking. "You're here for the Eostrix." The female isn't asking, she plainly states it.

I furrow my brow and nod.

"Hmm. Well, he is at the very end. Best be careful, little one. There's a reason why you snuck in here so effortlessly. I assume it's the same reason that my night guard has taken an absence tonight." Her voice sends a shiver down my spine, and her warning rings ominously in my ears.

They knew we were coming. I knew it seemed oddly quiet. Everything has been too easy. "Thank you . . ."

"Nox."

"Thank you, Nox." I dip my head to her and make my way down the hallway hastily. If this is a setup, then I need to be quick. My chances are much better if I can free Kastian. We can still escape, we just need to be careful.

The door at the end of the hallway is made of bars, just like the rest behind me. I peer in. This room is bigger and the prisoner inside rests all the way in the back. I can barely make out their silhouette and I don't have time to guess. Biting my lip, I force myself to speak out. "Kastian?"

No reply.

"Kastian," I hiss a little louder. Hands fly to the bars and I fall backwards, landing on my butt and losing my breath. A scream catches in my throat by my better judgment. "Who—"

I'm stopped by the familiar wave of white hair, the beaming blue eyes that graze mine so desperately. My heart breaks, like a jar tossed from a window, shattering across the world until there's no way to possibly fit the pieces together again. I'm broken as I stare at the damaged Kastian before me. So wounded and bruised. Weeks' worth of torture glistens on his paled skin. His eyes are sunken and his lips swollen.

Tears roll down my cheeks with the heat of guilt. It's my fault he's here. *I* left him behind. Even though I thought he was dead, I still left him behind. I crawl to the bars. Kastian slumps down to greet me on the wet, mildewed floor, tears trickling down his bruised, beautiful face.

"Elo—Elodie." he rasps. It's so painful that he winces and shuts his eyes. I tremble, not out of fear for myself but with a fury that *anyone* could harm Kastian in this way. The kind and caring Eostrix of night. God of Death and keeper of the things that sleep. Burning rage fuels my tears now and I clench my teeth tightly together.

I'll fucking kill her. I thought I understood her pain. I thought I knew . . . but *this.* She is pure evil. Malice that this world doesn't need to plague it any longer.

"Kastian." I press my hand softly against his cheek through the bars. He leans into my palm, his cheeks sunken and pale. "I'm so sorry, Kastian." He smiles weakly.

"Not your . . . fault." His vocal cords rasp, making me shudder again.

I pull up my sleeve and hold my wrist to his mouth. "Here, drink. We need to get out of here now." His eyes meet mine and flicker with hope. I flinch as his teeth sink into my flesh, but relief flows as the bruises and swelling vanish from his face as if it was just paint all along. I take a deep sigh and am filled with solace.

He releases my wrist and wipes his mouth with his dirty sleeve. His brows knit together and he looks at me with a somber expression. A knot grows in my throat as I just now worry that he might be able to taste the bonded blood. I should have asked Arulius . . .

Kastian murmurs, "I have to tell you something, Elodie."

"What?" I ask as I stand and try to open the door. Locked, of course.

He hesitates. "Do you remember?"

I pause, chills running down my spine, knowing what he's asking. "I don't . . . I'm not Talia." He smiles anyway, nodding nostalgically and accepting my response.

"Can you break the bars?" he whispers, his voice returning to the familiar softness I remember.

"I'll try." I furrow my brow. *I have to break them.* As I focus my aura in my hands, a familiar voice calls from behind me, raising every hair on my neck.

"Elodie, love, I thought I told you to *wait*," Arulius snarls. His purple eyes are the only part of him visible in the gloom as his footsteps near us.

23

"Arulius! I'm so sorry, I was chased out by a rat." I beam at him, trying to coax him with my charm. He crosses his arms, clearly not impressed with me. That heavy weight I felt earlier by the gate presses on my chest, making me wince. I try to ignore it. "Hurry, we need to get this door open." I move out of the way for him to break down the door. For a moment, only a moment, he regards me, and for the smallest second a thought flickers through me.

What if he doesn't open the door?

He raises a brow at me. "You really are cruel, you know that?" He casts his hand in a golden aura and lashes out against the door. The hinges break with a clean cut and the door falls forward, crashing against the ground and rattling my bones with the vibrations. I breathe a sigh of relief and feel a bit remorseful for thinking he wouldn't do it.

I smile at him. "Thank you. And . . . sorry again." He rolls his eyes. I hop into the cell and embrace Kastian with all my strength. "I'm so happy you're okay. I've missed you so much," I mumble, face buried into his shoulder.

His cold arms wrap around me tightly. "I missed you too," he whispers. We stay like this in a silent hug for a few moments until I hear Arulius's throat clear. We both step back and look at him.

"Let's get going. We need to meet up with Wren and Moro." Arulius tightens his gold wings to his back as he glances around the damp walls. "You two can hug later." His voice holds his usual distance but I can feel the tang of jealousy throbbing across my chest.

A sting burns my heart. I'm not sure how I will tell Kastian everything that has happened since the attack in the Hollow Grove . . . Now certainly isn't the time to think about it. I shake my head and help Kastian out of the cell. Although my blood healed most of his wounds, he's still awfully weak. They must have starved him in these weeks. The cruelty leaves a horrible taste in my mouth. I want to cry again but I know we have much more important things to do than rejoice at our reunion.

We follow Arulius back the way I came—through the window. I make it through easily but Arulius and Kastian have a bit of trouble with their large wings. The streets are still relatively quiet and Nox's words ring in my ears. *Best be careful, little one. There's a reason why you snuck in here so effortlessly. I assume it's the same reason that my night guard has taken an absence tonight.*

It doesn't matter, not now that we have Kastian. Wren and Moro should have Margo by now too. My heart flutters like a leaf in a soft gust of wind at the thought. Her soft fur, her deep gaze and her loving heart. I will be with her and it can't come soon enough. How long have I waited for this . . . how long I've yearned.

Arulius and Kastian are able to push the stone doors effortlessly and in silent unison. The east gate opens, and the guards are under the impression we are just citizens with Arulius. I can't fathom the tale he spun to trick them, but it worked and my weary mind doesn't have the imagination to picture his tricks.

From the gates, we follow the wall through the bushes back to our meeting spot north of the wall. We don't mutter a single word until we reach the treeline leagues away from the wall. Ceres is waiting for us and wags her tail happily for our return. The three of us wait uneasily and chat idly for a better part of an hour. Wren and Moro are still nowhere to be seen.

"Something isn't right." Arulius wrinkles his nose at the night sky. The stars are still glimmering amidst the four crescent moons but dawn is brimming the hills in the east.

They are running out of time.

I glance nervously at the golden Eostrix. "What do we do?" I look at Kastian, who rests leaning against a fallen log. His beautiful ebony horns turn towards the sky as he sips in tight breaths. His skin is pale and beading with sweat, making his complexion clammy, and I know his wounds are still hurting him.

"I'm not sure, but we are running out of options. If they were captured . . ."

"No—they weren't captured," I snap. Arulius raises a brow at my tone. "They couldn't have been. Wren is too witty and Moro is wise. They will be here." I clench my hands as we gaze at the court from the hill.

Arulius doesn't try to push me with his taunts. He is likely as exhausted as I am and the sun's rays are forming on the tops of the cottages and towers. Every fiber of my being fills with angst at the sight of the warm light. Below, the fields remain empty. No Wren. No Moro.

No Margo.

When the sun's rays hit me, I start moving forward. We can't wait a single moment longer. Something is definitely wrong and each second we wait is another second that they could be in danger.

"Elodie." Kastian wraps his hand around mine and his quick movement startles me. Fire stretches across my ribs and I glance over to Arulius, whose teeth are clenched tightly. His amethyst eyes burn on the spot where Kastian touches me.

I meet Kastian's gaze. He isn't trying to stop me, but I need to make sure he understands my intentions. "I'm going to go back and get them. We can't let them fall prey to Violet." I seethe as her name spills from my lips. I resent her with everything I am.

Kastian grips my hand tighter with resolve. "I'm coming

with you," he says sternly, his blue eyes fierce and the strength seeming to return to him. A smile passes my lips. Even in his state, he will stand next to me and fight. For *our* friends.

Arulius lets out a sigh. "You two will be the death of me. Gods." His steps follow behind us. Ceres lets out a grunt and walks beside me. The sun beams on the sides of our faces as dawn is fully upon us. We each stretch our wings as we trudge down the hill toward the west wall.

I try to picture what the four of us look like storming down this hill, our golden armor and Kastian's ebony clothes. Have there ever been three Eostrixes like us to attack at once? Plus a Pine Hollow, I note as Ceres strides boldly behind us. We are a pretty formidable team and I wouldn't want to mess with us if I were a Nesbrim soldier.

This time will be different. It has to be.

We don't waste time trying to sneak in the bushes. The time for sneaking and being quiet has passed. Now we will have to rely on luck and how quickly we can take out a soldier if it comes down to it.

The stones that make up the wall are entirely smooth, perfect—cut from the cleanest mountains in Tomorrow. The forest tapers back near the north wall, along the clean-cut stones. We have no cover. We're completely in the open and vulnerable.

We move with stealth and speed. Arulius takes up the lead, followed by Kastian, then me. I watch as Arulius's muscles stretch and bound with sheer robustness. His body is made for war and fighting. I don't realize I'm gawking at his form until he looks back at me, just to glance into my soul. His amethyst eyes glimmer at me and I remember what it felt like to bond with him just a few nights ago . . . I blink the thoughts from my mind. I can't let myself think of anything else right now except the task at hand.

Save our friends.

The west gate comes into view after a few more minutes of dead sprinting across the barren field, but Arulius slows. He stops and signals for us to do the same. His golden wings are tucked tightly behind him. I copy and tuck my wings close to my back.

"What's wrong?" Kastian murmurs.

I crouch next to him and shake my head. "I don't know." I look around but don't see anything. "Arulius, why did we stop?"

He doesn't move to look at me, offers not even a curt reply. That makes a well of emotions trudge up from a dark pit in my stomach. I recall that Wren did the same thing just before Murph met his end . . . I try to follow his gaze to where he is looking ahead, but can't find any clues in the empty field.

"Get ready to fight," the golden Eostrix finally whispers, drawing forth his aura blades.

I flinch. "What?"

"They're coming—get ready!" He shouts the last part as an invisible veil lifts at the swing of a familiar creature's sword. A blade swings down on Arulius like I've seen it do before on Kastian.

Kol.

"Arulius!" I scream. He's more nimble than Kastian was that day. The golden Eostrix dodges out of the way and sends an aura arc out, taking Kol by surprise. The tri-horned creature shrieks as his severed arm casts blood over his torso.

I survey the field that is no longer empty and vast. No, now it's messy with the armor and weapons of the beasts that bear them. Dreadiuses, Cypresses, Eostrixes, Moss Sparrows, and smaller creatures that I can't even fathom. They are all here to fight for Violet. But my eyes don't stop there, I continue to search until I find what I'm looking for.

There. Moro and Wren are bound and gagged in the center of the mass of soldiers. Wren's hair is wild and wispy with the thick morning breeze, his dark eyes clouded with horror. Moro looks calmer but much more hopeless, like the fight has been wrung from him. Both of their clothes are tattered and ripped from an intimate fight. One of Moro's eyes is purple and swollen shut. His other silver one falls on us.

Run, I can hear him saying. Because there's no fucking way we can take on the hundreds of soldiers before us.

Then my eye catches on something else. *Someone* else. My heart drops deep into a dark pit in my cavity. Her black hair waves angrily across her crimson war uniform. Ivory brackets cover her throat and chest plate. Her red eyes are pinned on me and I feel the weight of the world under them.

Horrible. Suffocating. Hatred.

"Violet is here," I mumble, more to myself than anything, because Kastian is already fighting five other soldiers to my right. Arulius is battling it out with Kol to my left. I can't peel my eyes from her bending gaze. "She is here . . . here for me."

Hot liquid slaps across my cheek from the right. Kastian fells one of the Moss Sparrows. They don't die right away, because the shouting and pain-struck wails that follow are worse than the blood that I wipe from my cheek.

Something, I have to do something. I don't dare close my eyes to focus like I normally do, so instead I watch Violet dismount the largest Pine Hollow I've ever seen. It is a volatile, black wisping ghost. It shares with her its red eyes of anger and hatred. Its neck and wrists are translucent voids of space, where instead of the dark wisping fur there is dripping gold, like the light within its body is holding the joints together. It's a creature of the night. Of wrathful wishes, as is Violet as she stalks toward me. She pushes past the guards keeping Wren and Moro kneeling before them.

I glance down to my hand and am pleased to find a sword of golden aura already in my grasp, a nifty trick Arulius taught me in our weeks of training. I can see the flicker in her gaze as she shoots Arulius a glare while he continues to kill her soldiers. She must know now, if she didn't already, that her golden warrior has betrayed her in more than one way. That makes me feel a tickle of joy, because I'm not sure anyone else can make this bitch feel anything short of wrath.

A stray soldier leaps for me off to my left and I blindly

slash my arm into the creature, a Cypress, I think, because of their Vernovian Thorn, and their blood casts into the sky with my arc. The only things we had to practice on within the glades were the trees and dead things. So how was I supposed to know that my aura would cleave straight through the poor creature's body? My stomach lurches as the eyes of the soldier roll into their skull. I've never killed so intimately before, and never in my wildest dreams did I think that I'd have to, but gods be damned. Here I am.

Blood can't rest on the aura blade—physical things simply pass through. I'm thankful that at least one part of me isn't covered in the hot, crimson liquid.

"Goddess of Life and Rebirth. Goddess of *Dawn*. You deal death so easily for a being of divinity," Violet hisses. I whirl to find her within striking distance. I grit my teeth and clench my aura sword tightly. She's so close I can see the tinge of fear in her eyes. I can smell the lavender on her skin. Sure, she wants *me* dead, but I won't be the first one to attack. I don't *want* to kill Violet just for the sake of it. She's still a person. If she just can understand that I'm not Talia, not really, I'm Elodie. This stupid old grudge she has is for someone who isn't me. For someone she already killed a long fucking time ago.

I point my sword to her. "Violet, I don't—"

"Shut up!" She bares her sharp teeth. "I'm not here to talk with you, you vile wench. I will *never* forgive you. Never." She lashes out.

I stagger back. She doesn't even want to hear me out or

anything. "I'm *not* her! I'm not Talia. I have no grudge against you!" I scream, spit falling down my chin. If she'd let Moro and Wren go . . . I can forgive her for Kastian . . . for Murph. No more people or creatures have to die. Violet narrows her red eyes and sneers at me with malice.

"Of course you do . . . wait . . . You don't know?" Her smile is so wicked it sends chills up my neck.

I don't know what? I glance at Kastian and Arulius on each side of me. The fighting slows, more eyes beginning to pin on the confrontation Violet and I are having. My heart twists like it did earlier . . . Is it the blood bond again? My chest wells with pain and anguish. I meet Arulius's amethyst eyes and dread fills the parts that are normally so bright.

What do I not know? Clearly, they know something I don't.

Violet's lips part a bit and her grin curls more. "Ah, you are piecing things together, darling." I don't realize how fast and powerful she is. Not until her aura blade is inches from my face.

Margo.

Her name wisps through my mind and Ceres's white fur blazes before my eyes, throwing me back and making Violet lose her footing. The mighty Pine Hollow lands on the ground between us, causing the earth to shudder beneath her feet.

On my elbows and bottom, my eyes widen as I stare at Ceres. She looks back at me with desolate eyes, filled with warmth and . . . and . . .

Margo.

"Margo?" I whisper. Her eyes gleam as if to tell me *yes, I'm here.* The entire time—and I didn't even know it. My eyes meet Moro's and he nods with tears. He had her the whole time, keeping her a secret from even me. Was it to keep her safe?

"Margo." My voice shakes with emotion.

Tears roll down my cheeks. Why is this so familiar? Why . . . why do I feel like Margo has protected me like this before . . . with knowing pain and sorrow clouding her eyes.

When Arulius's figure appears behind her, everything pieces together. The image is a perfect, horrible re-enactment of what I'd forgotten. A piece of me that I accidentally left behind.

Margo.

An angry god.

And my bewitched parents with knives in their hands.

24

"Margo. Do you hear that?" I whispered.

A rustling sound woke me from the makeshift bed that I'd created for the summer months. I'd decided to keep the bed in my shed since I loved being close to the forest. Like a calling. I never wanted to stray far. Margo stayed with me every night, guarding the edge of my bed and keeping my feet warm.

Margo stood and a deep growl rolled out of her throat. She raised a lip, which was odd. She never bared her teeth . . . ever.

The sounds came again, louder this time. Hungrier, like they'd only be satisfied with us as their silencing act. Goosebumps traveled up the skin on my arms and I sat up to peer out the window. It was pitch black outside still. It couldn't be past two a.m.

"Hello?" I whispered, not entirely sure I wanted any sort of answer, but going back to sleep wasn't an option either. There was no response, so I figured it would be safe to peer above the windowsill. I tipped my nose on the trim of the frame.

Two pairs of eyes bored into me. I felt my blood chill. It became colder and pulsed slower than it should. Their eyes were dead, like the fish at the bottom of a bowl, waving into oblivion and looking into the great nothing beyond its shallow, watery grave.

"Mom? Dad?" I said the words but gods, I didn't mean them. There was no way these two people in the night were Mom and Dad. They couldn't be. Their features were blank. Scary . . . and expressionless. But my mother's hair was pulled back into the tight ponytail she'd worn it in earlier, her brown eyes peering so horridly into mine. My father's short brown hair met the shadows of the moonlight, and his round glasses caught the glare perfectly so I couldn't see his hazel eyes.

My jaw tightened and Margo let another growl escape her throat.

What the fuck was going on?

"Love," the woman who looked like my mom muttered, "Open the door, love." Her voice had no emotion to it, just hollow echoes of an empty shell. My heart pounded against my ribs like a drum. The beat was that of a horror climax in a thriller where the dumb bitch was supposed to run and get help.

Me. I was the dumb bitch.

"Margo . . ." was all I could manage as the two ghastly people stared in through the window with awful smiles. There was only one exit and they were already trying the handle. What was I supposed to do? I was stuck in a small shed with my dog. There was no way out. They would surely find a way in if I didn't run . . . if I didn't escape . . . .

Would we die?

No. No, that was stupid. We wouldn't die. Dying wasn't something that would happen to us. I straightened my thoughts. But we did need to get away.

After what felt like hours, the two people who looked like my parents finally left. I waited for ten, twenty, maybe thirty minutes before peering out the window. The only trace of them was a lone handprint on the sill. Margo had stopped growling and the coast looked clear. We had one shot, and I was going to run straight for Old Man Bruno's cabin.

I flipped the latch and opened the door quickly, bolting the second the door swung free. Margo was at my heels. I didn't look back, not once, because I didn't want to know if they were still there waiting to attack or give chase.

I just ran.

I just fucking ran until my lungs were burning and stabbing my insides. Margo panted heavily at my side. We couldn't keep this pace forever, but we were almost to Bruno's cabin and I'd be damned if I slowed before slamming my fists against his splintery door. And that's just what I did.

"Bruno!" I shouted, sending my pummeling fists against his door until a light flicked on and a worried old man opened the door. His eyes were filled with shock. I didn't blame him. I was cut all over from crashing through the forest and falling down a time or two, only to roll and then get back to the dead sprint. His eyes immediately trailed down to my shoeless feet and our hard breaths made him quickly wave us inside, no questions asked.

"Dear heavens, Elodie! What happened?" he asked nervously, hobbling over to his kitchen to pour me a cup of water. He was such a small and frail old man. Such a kind heart with a love of the forest as I had.

"M . . . M-Mom and . . . and D-D-Dad, they . . . a-are o—" I stilled myself and took in a deep breath. Bruno's worrying eyes returned to me as he sat the glass of water on the table and eyed the front door. He knew. He knew I was running from something.

"Your mom and dad what?" he said warily, still staring at his front door.

"They aren't themselves," I managed. "They . . . were at my door . . . just watching me and trying to get in. They weren't themselves." I shuddered as I thought of their hollow, glazed eyes, looking beyond me.

His eyes widened with sickening fear. "The forest has them," he murmured so quietly I almost didn't catch it. "The forest has come to claim them." His voice grimly glided across my ears. The wrinkles around his eyes seemed less aged as fear filled the spaces between.

What the hell was Old Man Bruno saying? What did I expect from a crazy old man, though? He always went off

*about the forest and the gods that ruled them. Spirits and crea-
tures that we couldn't fathom, he'd say.*

*"Um, Bruno?" I hesitated. He looked at me with wild eyes,
making me flinch and retreat to my seat. "What do you mean?"*

*"I know you think I'm just some crazy old man, but you
listen here, Elodie. The creatures I speak of are real. They are
dangerous."*

*He stood and hobbled to his room, returning with a shoe
box. He handed it to me and nodded for me to open it. I did.
Inside was a small dagger. The blade was gold and etched with
symbols, and the hilt was stunning ebony with a green gem on
the pommel. I looked up at him with a raised brow.*

*"You must protect yourself, Elodie," Bruno whispered, his
eyes searching his walls now. Great, I made the old man lose it.*

*"Mr. Bruno, I can't use this on anyone. We need to call the
police. At least have them come check out my parents' house."
I turned and tried to look for a phone on the wall somewhere.
No luck. Did he even have a phone? Worry dug into me and I
bit my cheek.*

*"You need to protect—" was all he managed to mutter
before a knife was pushed through his throat, the blade
protruding just from under his chin. Gurgling blood spattered
over his lips.*

"Elodie. There you are, love."

*I screamed a bloodcurdling scream that made my senses
blur. Margo snarled and barked wickedly as Old Man Bruno's
body crashed on the coffee table and let out a few fleeting
gurgles before falling silent. His old weary eyes watched me. I*

saw the light leave him and I knew his death was my fault. For bringing them here.

My mother and father stepped around Bruno's body, faces still void of any expression, and I broke for the door. Margo dipped between my legs and we were in the forest again, my mind screaming and my blood pulsing so thickly with fear.

They killed him. They killed him.

The insects were silent. Not even they dared hum on a night like this one. I let out another scream as something sharp pierced my calf, sending me tumbling into the leaves and pinecones below.

I gripped my ankle and pulled my leg up so I could see what caused such pain. A small knife protruded from my flesh, gushing hot red liquid onto my face and neck.

Panic. Horrible, dreadful panic burst through me. This couldn't be real. This couldn't be happening. Not real, not real, not real.

Margo turned around and leaped in front of me, snarling at my parents as they walked towards us, obscenely horrid smiles across their lips.

"Margo," I whispered, tears falling.

I knew what was going to happen next.

I knew.

Margo turned her head back and gazed at me with somber eyes filled with fear and love. She'd defend me until the end.

"Go! Margo, run!" I screamed, throwing a handful of leaves and forest debris at her. "Run!" I thrashed my unwounded leg at her.

But my loyal dog, my foolish Margo, stood steady, like a mast against the stormy sea. Unmoving. She let out a ferocious bark as my father lunged for her. She bit his shoulder with viscous and angry twists of her head.

My eyes locked on a figure standing beyond them, behind mother even. Someone was standing there, watching, waiting. Speaking in a hushed tone. Who was that? It didn't matter.

Because father brought his knife down.

He brought his knife down and plunged it into Margo's back. Blood sheened on his blade as he pulled it out and stabbed her again three times over. Her whimpers slipped through her teeth as she held on.

"Nooooo!" I shrieked. It was a cry I'd never wrought out of my throat before. It was filled with anguish and terror. "No! Not Margo! Please!"

She held on for so long. She didn't let go of his shoulder until he stood and shoved her off like she was nothing. Like she didn't even faze him. I kept my eyes on her body, the slow breaths that began to ease and ebb away from her. I crawled to her and embraced her trembling body in my arms.

"Why?" I screamed at my parents. "Why!"

They betrayed me. They killed Margo.

My mother knelt down next to me, scooped her hand behind my head, and cradled my neck.

I knew what was coming next.

I knew.

"Because she has called for you, love."

Then Old Man Bruno's golden blade found me. It found the softness of my weary heart.

My body jerked horribly. I didn't . . . I didn't feel anything at first other than the intense fear, and I suppose my adrenaline pumped so wildly through me that I wouldn't have felt anything.

But I did feel something.

Margo lifted her head feebly with her last thread of life and licked my hand gently, letting me know I wouldn't go alone.

A sweet goodbye. One that should never have come to be.

Goodbye, goodbye. We will meet again.

A weak smile cursed my chapped lips because at least we were going together.

At least we would walk through the forest side by side.

Together, into a better tomorrow.

I sipped in a ragged breath, the pain now ebbing into my chest. She stabbed me between the ribs, just under my breast. My lungs filled with my blood, drowning me in a hot, throbbing ache. Slow and agonizing. My breaths cracked and wheezed through the air.

Margo's head dropped softly into the brush, and she was gone. I could feel the coolness of the earth take her warm breath. How odd it was to feel no air leave her mouth. No more soft whimpers to sing me the lullaby of somber death. Now there's just emptiness.

I was next. My mother continued to cradle my head, shock now covering her face. She seemed back to herself again. As did father, his hands now trembling with his phone and disgust at the mess they'd made in the forest sweeping across his eyes.

I glanced down at Margo. I could feel my blood pumping slower through my arteries. Even slower through my veins. The pain eased. Her fur bristled in a soft breeze and I looked up, surprised to find another set of eyes.

A beautiful male god held Margo in his arms. Though it was another version of her, her ghost perhaps . . . His wings were dark and ebony horns pricked through his white hair. Such a solemn creature he was. His azure eyes met mine as he lifted Margo and he gave me a weak frown as he carried her away, deep into the forest, until my vision turned to black.

Margo. Please don't take her without me, I wanted to cry. Please don't leave me behind.

When I woke, I was safely tucked in bed in my shed. Only Margo wasn't there. So I wandered, I wandered the forest until I remembered her passing.

But I'd lost the parts that hurt the most. The parts that included our horrible demise. My parents were our attackers. Old Man Bruno dying. The ethereal male that took Margo deep into the forest. The one that stood and whispered odd things from afar . . .

I wandered through the silence of the ponderosas.

Waiting.

Waiting for anything but the endless cold and empty forest I wandered.

25

Time seems to slow.

Margo's eyes are still on mine. Her white fur bristles with the shouts of soldiers and Violet raises her aura blade once more. This time its intended target is the Pine Hollow before me.

My Margo.

My eyes slide to the golden Eostrix behind them, so similar to the shadow I saw *that* night. Why are things lining up like this? My mind sharpens back to Violet and her arching arm. The pain in my chest, over my heart where my mother stabbed me, pulses with the agony of the truth and the things I forgot.

How could I forget... how did I not recognize Ceres was Margo? Was the pain too much? My warring heart chases my feeble mind.

This time I won't let Margo die to save me. Never again will she have that fate. I stand and let out a cry as I lurch forward. I raise my hand to Violet's throat and will my aura to pass through her like she undoubtedly would have done to us. Mercilessly and without hesitation, I thrust my blade to her flesh with every intention to decapitate the bitch.

Only, she's cast backward with the tug of one of her favored soldiers. One that I should have been aware of as they moved behind her to pull her back. He deflects my blade like he knows how. Like he was the one to show me the way of aura. As if he was the one who taught it to me.

Because he was.

Arulius.

His amethyst eyes blaze with anguish and hesitation. A blade of his own presses just above my heart. The swell of emotions and stinging pain burns my ribs. I push him away through the bond. My mind snaps at what this appears to be.

No.

"Arulius... what are you doing?" I grit my teeth and try to ignore how my heart seizes under his gaze.

He considers me for a long moment. We stand there eyeing one another. His grasp on my bladed hand tightens as he takes a shallow breath.

In this moment I know what he is—what he's *done.*

"You... you were the one... the one who..." My eyes study his desperately. I don't know if it's because I want him to stop me and tell me that I'm wrong, that everything I'm about to accuse him of is wrong, and to joke around with me again. I want it so badly to be a misunderstanding, but everything in my head screams at me that it's the truth. It's my heart—my stupid, foolish heart that cries that it's all a lie, and there's nothing more that I want to believe.

But he just stands there with his stupid, anguished expression, as if *he* is the one hurting. He has no words to spare for me.

"Arulius." I turn my head and glance at Kastian, his eyes wide with the same horror. I turn to meet Arulius's gaze once more but he's a mere inch from my face, burning purple eyes of the beautiful creature he is staring into me so hollowly.

"It was me, love," he says somberly, running a hand down my cheek.

My eyes widen. "Why..." I clench my hands into tight fists at my sides. My world is collapsing. My heart breaks into billions of shards that will never be whole again. Ruined. My heart is ruined.

Why, Arulius.

He frowns weakly and I flinch. "Because she called for you, love." His hand glides down my neck and softly brushes where he used to bite me.

Those words... *Because she has called for you, love.* That's what my mother said moments before. My eyes fill with painful hot tears. Mom called me *love* multiple times that night.

"*You* bewitched my parents."

"Yes." He says it so simply like it's nothing. Nothing.

This isn't happening. Arulius *can't* be a traitor... my murderer.

"Arulius." I rip my wrist from his hand. "Stop. Lying." I glare at him. *Please, you can't be a traitor... Please lie to me. Please.*

His gaze hardens. I frantically step away from him and look at Kastian, who bares his teeth with hate at the golden Eostrix. He clearly doesn't think Arulius is lying, and as I gaze upon my blood-bonded male once more... neither do I.

"Why?" My voice breaks.

He keeps his steely expression. "Because I can only serve Lady Violet, love. I cannot let you kill her." Despair swirls in my chest and I know it's not my own. Mine has been burning ruinously for a few minutes already and this is... older pain, a guilty pain. "But I can keep you, Elodie. We can be together as bonded partners. Violet can never change my love for you." Kastian flinches at the mention of a bond but remains silent.

I scoff at him. "I will never love you! No creature in this world or the next could *ever* love you," I snarl at him. He winces at my words but says nothing in response. I feel a sharp tug in my chest and I hate it, I fucking hate him.

I'm falling apart. How can one of the closest people I trusted turn on me like this? My heart throbs. I hate this. I hate this so, so, so much because I... I loved him. I loved Arulius for saving *me* in so many different ways, at my lowest moments, showing me what being real truly meant and why it matters. To whom it matters... But he was the one who killed me, Margo, and Bruno... and that's *not* love.

I let out a laugh I don't recognize, sending shivers up my own spinal cord. "You were the one who sent word for Violet to take the Pine Hollows."

He nods. "Only Moro and you could tell which was Margo. Violet decided it was best to take them all. We knew you'd come to her on your own this way."

Bile rises in the back of my throat. "The reason that Kastian was slain and died in the grove." He gives another nod and a hint of a wry grin.

My blood boils, spilling into parts of my soul I didn't know existed, wrathful and filled with darkness, sinister energy that isn't my own but resides within me now.

Hate.

"You're the reason Murph is dead," I see Wren's eyes flicker with agony at the sound of his Hollow's name.

He pauses at that one. "I did not intend for the Pine Hollow to die, love. I didn't want any harm to come to anyone. I just—"

"You just what?" I scream, throwing my arms in the air. Arulius flinches and his eyes widen.

"I was just following orders." He eyes me carefully. The anguish wells in my heart again. I push it out with resentment. Stop. I want it to fucking stop.

"The reason Margo and *I* are dead!" I scream, so close to his face that I can see his pupils dilate. "The reason why she... she bled for me and suffered incredibly. Why I felt so much pain for such a long time." Tears freely run down my cheeks, making it hard to see clearly. "The reason why I didn't want to be real anymore!" I raise my free hand to his throat and bring my blade out once more. It glimmers hot on his skin. He doesn't even flinch. "Why did you make me suffer? And then why the fuck would you befriend me... and make me... make me fall in love with you?"

His eyes narrow in pain, and that feeling of unbearable sorrow pushes heavier on my heart.

"Why would you... would you bond with me... after everything? *Everything* you've made me endure. Why didn't you just take *me*? Why did you have to draw this out with death?!"

His jaw tightens. "I had to get your trust. It was necessary... I had to bond with you to have control—"

I can't bear to look at him anymore. Hate brims in every fiber of me and I tear my hand down his throat. His golden brackets don't block the cut I make. His eyes are still watching mine. He doesn't flinch as I nearly slice into his spinal cord. His beautiful crimson blood spills over my hand and spurts on my cheek. I feel the brush of pain on my own neck, reminding me of our tied fates. I wince at the unbearable sear it sends through me.

"I'm sorry," he murmurs, so softly, so filled with despair. "I never... I never intended for any of this to happen." He softens his eyes on me.

I step back, shaking as I stare at the throat I've just cut. I know I had to do it, but it hurt me too. Cut so deeply into my foolish heart that still isn't ready to accept what he's done. My throat burns thickly with the pain I know he is feeling at this moment.

Arulius takes a step toward me and sets his hand on my cheek, red liquid pulsing from his wound. "Margo was never meant to be harmed. But you. I didn't know how precious you were. I was stupid—so, so stupid, love. I didn't think I'd... I never meant to hurt you afterwards." His voice cracks and he shuts his eyes. His dark lashes are brilliant against his shimmering skin.

"I hate you." I say it slowly, the admittance burning as it leaves my lips.

He jolts, looking back to me with pain in his eyes.

"I hate you!" I scream, pushing away from him and running towards Kastian. He stands close by and embraces me as I run to him. Margo brushes against my side too, standing firm and snarling at Arulius.

I wish our reunion was under different circumstances. I set my hand on her soft fur and take a deep breath to collect myself.

Arulius closes his eyes again, but this time it's more acceptance than anything. He raises his hand to his neck and wipes it like I inflicted nothing more than a paper cut. Underneath is but a scratch where I slashed him so deeply.

"You don't hate me, love," he says somberly. "You just hate the God of Wrath and Lies I've been made to be. I may be your villain. I may be the darkest night and the storm that caught you, even in death, but you don't hate me." He raises his hand to me as if expecting me to return to him. "We are one. We will always know what happens to the other. We are gods cut from the same thread, my love. Our blood is the same, and you can never deny it again. I could never deny yours... so please just come with me. Let me explain."

"There's nothing to explain," I spit. I can't believe he is trying to defend himself.

He frowns. "I was hoping it wouldn't come to this." He motions to his soldiers and they bring Moro and Wren forward, tossing them to their knees in front of him.

My heart stops. He wouldn't...

"Come with me, love. Come with me or I'll kill your friends. They will never see another day, and I'll take you with me anyway."

I can't let him win. I can't. "I'll save them like I did Kastian!" I retort, trying to keep my composure.

"Ah yes, that was rather a nuisance. Elodie, I am the God of Wrath. I have you now. You won't be reincarnating or saving anyone ever again."

"What?" is the only breathless response I have.

Moro's words trickle back into my mind. *She bound Talia's powers with the help of an Eostrix. Not just any—he was the God of Wrath. Once her powers were bound, she could no longer resurrect the Pine Hollows, the Cypresses, the Moss Sparrows, or any creature.*

He raises a dark brow at me. "Your choice, love." His golden blade stretches in front of Wren's throat. Kastian lets out a growl that rumbles deep in his throat. Margo echoes the growl with her own.

It's not a choice. It's a hand that I will never win because the lives of my friends are on the table.

I glance from Wren to Moro, their eyes filled with anger. Wren shakes his head but Arulius taps his head with the butt of his blade to stop him. I push off the ground and stand, unsteady much like the rest of me. I was so stupid. I was blinded by my suspicions of Wren, so much so that I ran into the arms of the real evil that plagued me.

I just saved Kastian, just reunited with Margo... I look them over once more. A soft goodbye.

But life isn't fair, is it?

I start trudging slowly towards Arulius. His gold-flaked body seems not as shimmery and gilded as it once was. His amethyst eyes are not as alluring. Since when did his armor reflect such evil... my hand reaches and brushes against my own neck brackets and ribcage armor. He made me his puppet without me even knowing it. His own personal Goddess of Life. To only use my gifts as he sees fit.

Kastian grabs my wrist. "Elodie, please... no." His grip shakes, giving away his emotions.

I meet his blue gaze and smile warmly, reaching my free hand to Margo's muzzle. "Please take care of her. Please, keep everyone safe... I'm so happy to have found you, *Borvon*. I hope we will find one another again, perhaps in another life." He flinches at that name, but now he knows that I know the truth of us. I may not have memories but I know our history at least a little.

Tears brim from both our eyes, nothing but love shining

from Kastian's oceans into mine. I can hear them saying back to me, *Always*.

He bends and places a kiss on my lips, solidifying our promise to reunite again someday. I wish I could have loved him better. I wish... I wish I could do it all over again. I blink the tears away and smile at him and Margo.

"Until another life."

Hate will burn and smolder deep in my heart for the remaining echoes of time. But for now, there has to be peace for my friends.

This is the cost I'm willing to pay.

I stop in front of Arulius, head down and eyes on his black boots. He waves his hands for his soldiers to take Wren and Moro back to Kastian. They drag them over to the death god, both still tied and gagged, and toss their bodies at his feet.

I seethe at the display but refuse to look at Arulius. I can feel his wicked grin, him waiting for me to look. But I don't. I keep my gaze on his boots.

"Arulius," Violet purrs. "Bring our little Elodie to my palace tomorrow. We have much to *discuss*." I can hear the tick in her voice that she intends to inflict pain upon me in her palace. Probably the same fate that Talia faced all those years ago.

Arulius brings an arm around my shoulders. "Of course, my lady." He dips his head. I widen my eyes. I've never known him to be so courteous.

Violet eyes my friends. Margo bares her teeth and growls.

341

"If you wish to leave while I'm still in a good mood, now would be the time." She waves her hands at them in dismissal.

Wren and Kastian gaze at me. I nod slowly. There's no other way for them to escape unscathed. We are sorely outnumbered, and with my healing ability being chained to Arulius... our options are only one. Retreat and pray that we would find another way to be together again someday.

Moro mounts Margo and my heart shatters that much more as she whimpers at me. I close my eyes and turn towards Arulius. I can't bear to watch them leave—to watch her leave.

Arulius looks down at me and brushes my hair from over my eyes. "I will take care of you, love. I will show you I'm not the evil god you think I am." I meet his amethyst gaze, his stupid brows so perfectly knit together with anguish.

"You've shown me that you are just that, Arulius. You've counted all your sins. Tell me. Why did you bond with me if our blood could never keep?"

His hand curls around my waist. "Our fate goes beyond our blood, love. Doesn't my heart get a choice too?"

His words tumble through me as I follow him into Nesbrim.

I hate him. I fucking hate him so much for the things he's done. And yet, my heart asks the same. *Do I get a choice?*

Acknowledgments

I would like to thank you, the reader. The support and interest I've received on this story is more than I ever could have hoped. I can't wait to have you along for the ride on the next book!

Thank you to my beta readers and editor. Your opinions and thoughts helped shape this story into the magical and painful one that it needed to be.

Thank you to my partner for all the endless nights of support, whether it be taking care of the animals while I write or help me think of the next steps my characters take. I couldn't have done this without your undying support.

About the Author

K. M. Moronova has always loved telling stories. She adores reading and writing dark fantasy with a hint of dread and romance. Often, she is found drying flowers and drinking coffee while relaxing in her garden. She loves spending her time with her husband exploring in the forest.

Made in the USA
Las Vegas, NV
13 August 2024

74e85a90-d81e-492f-a978-b631c419b7ceR01